Cadet
Willie McBride

'Operation Crocodile'

Colonel Rodney Dearing

**'Combat Power Wins Battles –
Diplomacy Wins Wars.'**

Visit us online at www.authorsonline.co.uk

An Authors OnLine Book

Text Copyright © Colonel Rodney Dearing 2009

Cover design by Siobhan Smith ©

Edited by Phenix

ISBN 978-07552-0455-7

Authors OnLine Ltd
19 The Cinques
Gamlingay, Sandy
Bedfordshire SG19 3NU
England

This book is also available in e-book format, details of which are available at www.authorsonline.co.uk

ACKNOWLEDGEMENTS

My grateful thanks are due to so many people who have supported me, knowingly or unknowingly, in the creation of this Cadet Willie McBride adventure story with their continuing encouragement and assistance. They include;

The members of the Rotary Club of North Harbour who listened ever so politely to my short stories during their meetings.

Graham Leay who gave me invaluable advice when he conducted my writing course at the Michael King Writers' Centre in Devonport, Auckland.

John Graham who provided me with a retailer's view of the commercial realities of bookselling.

Geoff Chamberlain who provided insights into the power of the internet.

Jill Marshall who slogged her way through my manuscripts and still managed to maintain her good humour while giving advice.

Major David Keay who provided unstinting encouragement over a number of years.

John Burgess who always gave patient and cheerful critical comment on my manuscripts.

The talented, professional team at Zeald.Com who put together my website www.coloneldearing.com.

The publishing team at Authors OnLine - Gaynor, Siobhan and Phil whose professional inputs have been invaluable in getting the book published; and,

My darling wife, Margy, who has always given me so much loyal support and kept my feet on the ground.

Colonel Rodney Dearing,
Auckland,
New Zealand,
March 2009

CONTENTS

1

MURDER ON LABUAN ISLAND

Colonel McBride's party never saw the sniper lying in wait.

He was hidden in the jungle about fifty yards away overlooking the entrance to the old coal mine and had a clear view of the Colonel's party, who were preparing to enter the tunnel entrance. His new SAS 7.62mm sniper's rifle was aimed directly at the Colonel's heart.

'Well, Hughie old lad. My information was correct. You and Sally have turned up on time after all,' the sniper murmured softly. He squinted through the Schmidt and Bender telescopic sights. 'Time to settle old scores, I think ... remove the competition. I've let you win too many times, Hughie ... even with the Sword of Honour all those years ago. But this time you've gone too far. The opportunity here at Labuan is too big for me to lose ... You'll both have to go.'

He shifted his rifle to aim at Sally, moving the crosshairs from her heart to her head. He lingered. His face and body softened. Then he quietly lowered the rifle. He rubbed a thin, red scar that ran from the corner of his mouth. It distorted his face so it appeared lopsided.

'Perhaps we should do this another way, Hughie. Perhaps I should give you and Sally a sporting chance. Just give you a damned big fright,' he whispered. 'Yes, that's what I'll do. Not be a Horrid Hannie.' He smiled grimly.

Colonel Hugh McBride and his wife Sally were standing with three other men, outside a tunnel entrance to the ruins of the old coal mine on the northern tip of the island. The entrance was surrounded by rough jungle littered with rusty equipment, empty iron buckets, and tangles of rusty steel wire, broken railway lines and dominated by a huge, empty brick chimney. It was a picture of neglect and potential disaster.

The Colonel and his party were dressed and equipped to explore the coal mine. They gathered around the Colonel as he began to give them a last-minute briefing on the job ahead.

'Now, I'll just go over a few important things again, so everybody is comfortable. You will remember that this coal mine used to be worked by Chinese convict labourers from Shanghai during the 1800s. Since its closure in 1911, following some fatal accidents, no-one has explored the mine, and it's become derelict. We'll be the first to really have a good look around. We don't want to be down in the mine for longer than a day. So, has everyone got sufficient tucker and water to last them for, say, two or three days, just to be on the safe side?' They all nodded.

'Good,' continued the Colonel. 'Now, from the entrance the tunnel slopes into the hillside for about 200 yards. It then leads to a vertical shaft which is about 100 feet deep. This shaft, in turn, gives access to three lower levels of horizontal tunnels. We'll make our way to the vertical shaft and secure our three sets of rope ladders at the top of the shaft. We'll then descend to the bottom and start our exploration in the lower tunnels leading off from there. The maps I've been able to get from the archives of the North Borneo Coal Mining Company are pretty poor. So for safety we'll keep ourselves roped together. We'll make a base camp at the bottom of the vertical shaft, and set up our lighting system down there as soon as we can. Any questions?' They shook their heads.

'Right you are then. Let's check our equipment and make sure everything's working well.'

The Colonel looked up. A tropical storm was approaching and the first squalls of rain were starting to fall from a blackening sky. He grinned. 'Looks like the weather's going to get very dirty. It'll be raining cats and dogs soon and the wind's starting to get up. We could be in the safest part of Labuan Island down in these tunnels.'

The exploration party completed their last checks, hoisted their packs and equipment onto their shoulders and followed the Colonel into the blackness of the tunnel.

A few minutes after they had disappeared into the tunnel the sniper emerged from his jungle hiding place and carefully moved to the base of the brick chimney. He was a tall man with stooping shoulders and a slight limp. The hood of his camouflage jacket completely hid his face. He carried a pack over the shoulders as well as the sniper's rifle and carried a large duffel bag in his hands.

He looked at his wrist watch, dumped his pack, rifle and duffel bag on the ground and sat down on a pile of broken bricks just inside the chimney. Lighting a cigarette, he waited, carefully watching the tunnel entrance.

As he watched and waited, the force and ferocity of the tropical storm increased. The wind grew savagely, driving the torrents of rain like brutal, destructive battering rams. Forked lightning crackled violently, and thunderclaps rumbled and reverberated, as if the heavens themselves were exploding apart.

But still he waited, getting up every now and again to stretch his legs. Finally, he appeared to come to a decision. He stubbed out his cigarette on the ground, and limped quickly to the bricked tunnel entrance. Here, he waited quietly for a few moments before drawing a 9mm Browning pistol from a shoulder holster. He sidled carefully along the walls and into the blackness of the tunnel. About 30 minutes later he returned to the entrance dragging three rope ladders. Dropping them just inside the tunnel entrance, he made his way over to the brick chimney to retrieve his pack and duffel bag, and returned to the tunnel. He rummaged around in the duffel bag and pulled out explosive equipment – sticks of plastic explosive, electric detonators, priming cord and tape.

He set to work positioning the plastic explosive and detonators into the tunnel's crumbling bricks and connecting them together with the priming cord. He worked unhurriedly with the precision of a highly trained expert. Finally, he picked up his pack and duffel bag and made his way to the safety of the brick chimney, paying out an electric wire behind him and connecting it to an electric detonating device. He was now ready to detonate the sticks of plastic explosives. They would bring down thousands of tons of rock to destroy the tunnel and brutally obliterate the Colonel's party trapped in the base of the vertical shaft.

He waited with his hand poised on the detonator's plunger. For what seemed an age, he stared intently at the tunnel.

Outside the brick chimney the tropical storm had strengthened to hurricane force. The wind shrieked like banshees, playing the chimney like a vast organ pipe. The rain was a solid deluge, which suddenly turned to a barrage of hail, the size of golf balls, smashing and flattening everything in its path. The noise was horrific and deafening. Forked lightning ripped the sky apart every few seconds. The thunderclaps reached an ear-splitting crescendo.

In the middle of this violent madness, the man slammed his hand down on the detonator's plunger. The hillside erupted and the tunnel disappeared in a colossal flash. Two hundred years of methane-soaked coal dust ignited. It took a full four or five minutes for the dust to settle and to form a coating of mud from the hail and rain. All that could be seen now was a gigantic scar in the hillside where the rock had subsided and filled the tunnel. The man gave a chuckle of satisfaction as he surveyed the result of his deadly work.

'Bye, bye, Hughie. *That* should give you something to think about for a long, long time. You let your guard down and the best man finally won. You might have been top dog once. But not any more. In the end, Horrid Hannie's got the real treasure to enjoy and a lot longer than you to enjoy it!'

He spat on the ground, picked up his rifle, pack and duffel bag and strode off into the storm.

***

Willie's Auntie Gwen was as soft as butter. She and her husband Peter had always lived in Oxford, where he was a plant pathologist, and she worked as a science teacher. They lived in a rather large, rambling detached house in Squitchey Lane, not far from where Willie and his parents lived in Woodstock Road. When Willie's parents were abroad, which they often were, he would stay with his Auntie Gwen and Uncle Peter. In this way he could continue to attend Marlborough School at Woodstock. Gwen and Peter didn't have any children. When Willie came to stay with them, they treated him like their own little prince. His Auntie Gwen doted on him and went to enormous trouble to cook him all his favourite meals. His Uncle Peter would take him out for long nature walks onto Port Meadow, where they would invariably end up in the Trout Inn for pork pies and lemonade.

'You two can stay away as long as you like, Hugh and Sally,' Auntie Gwen would say to her brother, Colonel McBride and her sister-in-law Sally. 'Peter and I will look after young Willie.'

His father and mother would smile, and say something like,

'We're so grateful, Gwen, that Willie's not too much trouble to you both. Next year we're planning to spend more time at home, so we'll have all the time in the world then to give him our full attention. He's just over fifteen years old now so it's about time we did our duty as good parents.'

No one seemed to know, or care, what Willie's parents actually did. As long as anyone could remember, both of them worked for some part of the Government. But which part, no one really knew. Something to do with overseas service, which meant they had to travel overseas quite frequently. Certainly, Willie's parents had never bothered to discuss it with him. Both of them had served in the military after they graduated from Surrenden Military School. But apart from a very few sketchy references to some distant service in the Special Air Service and Military Intelligence, their present lives seemed ordinary and unremarkable.

Willie just accepted his parents' way of life as routine. It never occurred to him to question them about their work, or where they went, or what they did. He was much more interested in doing the best he could in the school exams at Marlborough, in keeping his place as the No 8 forward in the School's 1st XV rugby side, mastering the computer programs in class, and completing his homework on time to avoid detentions. His objectives were immediate and short-term. He had given little thought to where he might be heading. His interests were more general than particular. It was only Uncle Peter who had brought up the subject of vocation.

'It's probably a good idea for you, Willie, to give some thought to what you want to do in life,' said Uncle Peter, as they were chatting over lemonade in the Trout. He added, laughing, 'Otherwise you'll just keep acquiring more interests, and be so rounded, that you won't be pointed anywhere! If you have a reasonably good idea of which direction you want to go, then you can give destiny a little shove to help you get there.'

Willie nodded, and mumbled the sort of agreement that suffices when the subject is of little interest and unimportant. His present life was a cosy routine of school, sports and holidays and there seemed little incentive for change. He was, therefore, completely stunned at the sudden turn of events that occurred, when he returned to Gwen and Peter's from school one day. Auntie Gwen was in tears, her eyes red and puffy from crying. Uncle Peter was ashen-faced and sombre. As soon as Willie came into the front hall, Auntie Gwen rushed over to him and hugged him tightly to her breast.

'Oh, my poor boy, my poor, poor boy,' she sobbed, stroking his hair.

'What's … what's the matter, Auntie Gwen?' Willie knew in his heart that something terrible must have happened.

'There's been a dreadful accident, Willie,' said Uncle Peter quietly, coming up and putting a comforting arm around his shoulders. 'Your father and mother have been involved in a dreadful accident in Borneo, and I'm very, very sorry to have to tell you that they are missing, presumed dead.'

It took a few seconds for him to come to grips with what his Uncle had said. The information whirled around in his mind again and again. Dreadful accident … Borneo … his Mum and Dad were both missing … presumed dead.

'Come into the lounge and sit down for a while,' said Uncle Peter. Willie and Auntie Gwen followed him into the lounge and sat down on the settee. Across the room, a man quietly stood up from his chair. He was also very serious and grave. He offered his hand and said, 'Please accept my condolences, Willie.'
Uncle Peter introduced the man. 'This is Sir Eyre Sanderson, Willie. He's from the Foreign Office in Whitehall. He brought the news of the accident.'

Sir Eyre resumed his seat as Auntie Gwen rose and went to the kitchen, saying softly, 'I'll just get Willie some tea and his favourite cake.'

Willie and Uncle Peter looked at Sir Eyre for a few moments before Willie asked, 'How did it happen?'

Sir Eyre looked a little uncomfortable, the pain of his duty showing, even with his formal appearance: tall, polished, with clipped moustache, immaculately dressed in a grey pin-stripe suit, blue striped tie, rimless glasses, and with wisps of silver in his light brown hair which indicated age and seniority. He took a deep breath.

'Well, Willie, from what we have been able to piece together, it seems it might have happened like this.' He paused, searching for words.

'Your father and mother started working for the Foreign Office almost as soon as they graduated from Surrenden Military School many years ago. During their service they undertook a variety of jobs on behalf of the Foreign Office, which generally required that they travel overseas, and work with our representatives abroad. Quite a lot of their work involved mining, and they both had special talents and unusual contacts which made them very valuable to the Foreign Office, and, in a broader sense, our country. Their last assignment was to explore some old, disused coal mines at Tanjong Kupong on Labuan Island, just off the coast of Borneo. It was during this last assignment that they simply disappeared. Old coal mines are very dangerous. Their weakened tunnel supports, pockets of methane gas and layers of coal dust can make them extremely hazardous. So it was with the coal mines at Tanjong Kupong, it seems. The whole mine seems to have simply collapsed in on itself. There was a massive hurricane at the time and there may have been a lightning strike which triggered an explosion of the methane gas. We sent out a search party to try to find your parents, and the three local men who were with them, but have found nothing. We can only presume that … er … in the circumstances, your parents were inside the coal mine when it collapsed.'

Sir Eyre paused to give Willie time to take in his account of his parents' deaths.

'They were both fine people and they'll be a sad loss to us all. I'm very sorry to have to be the bearer of such sad news for you.' Again Sir Eyre paused, and then his face brightened a little.

'However, you'll be well looked after. Because of the nature of their work, your parents always left instructions about the arrangements they wished for your future – just in case of accidents. I have been talking with your Auntie Gwen and Uncle Peter just now on how those arrangements can be carried out in your best interests. Your parents were particularly keen that you should attend Surrenden Military School to finish your secondary education there before going to university. Uncle Peter has suggested that you continue to stay here at Squitchey Lane with them for the next few days, and then start at Surrenden Military School next week at the start of the next term.'

Auntie Gwen appeared with a tray of tea and chocolate cake. She settled down beside Willie and hugged him tightly. 'It's a big shock, a big shock, darling. It's too much to take in straight away. But we'll take things slowly and we'll get through,' she whispered in his ear.

Willie looked up into her eyes, and felt a lump in his throat and the trickle of tears rolling down his cheek. Although his face was impassive, inside he was sobbing uncontrollably.

Sir Eyre rose from his chair, shook hands again with Willie and departed with promises to keep in touch with Auntie Gwen and Uncle Peter. Uncle Peter came and sat down beside him and put his arm around his shoulders.

'We've got a lot of things to sort out, but we'll make a start tomorrow. Let's have dinner now and make a plan for the next few days. We have a week before you start at Surrenden.'

That night as he lay in bed Willie felt the full impact of his loss. His mind flickered over the good memories he had of his parents. The way they looked at him with pride as he rode his first bicycle without assistance, and when he had scored a try in a school rugby match. He remembered his last birthday party they had arranged for him, when both his mother and father and six of his friends from school sang 'Happy Birthday' to him. He remembered their last holidays together in North Wales at the little seaside village of Cricceith. How his father taught him to swim in the sea, and the fun they had had fishing from a rented dinghy. He remembered how, when he was a little boy, his mother would sit on the bed and read him stories before he went to sleep. How his father had gently admonished him when he had told a fib and been found out. 'Don't do or say anything that you wouldn't be proud to tell Mum or me about.'

Now both of them had gone, presumably killed in a mining accident. He wondered briefly if they might still be alive somewhere. Lost in the jungles of Borneo, perhaps? There seemed to be considerable doubt about what *actually* happened to them. He suddenly felt determined to find out the full story and to set his mind at rest. He would take every opportunity he could to travel to the mine on Labuan Island in the future and see for himself.

Meantime, he should do his best to succeed at Surrenden Military School. That's what his parents would want him to do. Again, his mind flicked back to the faces of his parents. He could see both of them smiling encouragingly, wishing and willing him to succeed. He could feel their support and he knew that he would never be alone. But, at that moment, he did feel very much alone.

He turned his face into his pillow and sobbed before falling into a fitful sleep.

2

FIRST DAY AT SURRENDEN

Waterloo station was as busy as ever. Willie, Uncle Peter, and Auntie Gwen struggled through the morning surge of commuter crowds towards the Army Transport Office where Willie was to meet with transport to take him to Surrenden.

The Unit Joining Instructions referred to him as Cadet William McBride, and simply acknowledged that he was to enter Surrenden Military School on the fourth week of April at the beginning of Term 5. He was posted to Alamein Company, Victory College, and was to report to the Army Transport Office at Waterloo station. It was signed by Colonel Mortimer Dane, the Deputy Headmaster (Military).

The School Guide was a slim brochure designed for new entrants. It provided an outline of the school's organisation, a brief description of the activities available for cadets, an introductory welcoming letter from the Headmaster, Professor Rutherford, and a list of personal clothing and items that each new entrant should bring. Uncle Peter had been quite impressed with the Staff Listing in the School Guide.

'These are the people you will be rubbing shoulders with for the next four years, Willie,' he observed. Together they had examined the Staff Listing, with Willie privately wondering what sort of person he would find behind each of the names. The Staff Listing was broadly split into an Academic Wing and a Combat Wing. The Academic Wing comprised the normal departments of English, languages, mathematics, sciences, business studies and information sciences, all of which were headed by professors and doctors. But the Combat Wing was altogether quite different. It comprised the five separate centres, Communications and Intelligence, Firepower and Mobility, Education, Ceremonial, and Administration, mostly headed up by captains. Willie examined the Combat Wing Centres more closely and his interest sharpened. Battlefield surveillance, missiles and delivery systems, strategy and tactics, electronic control warfare, and armoured warfare. That would be much more exciting stuff to study than trigonometry or English grammar. Anyway, time would tell. He decided he would create a Reference Folder into which he would file things like the School Guide and Staff Listing for ready reference.

It was with mixed feelings, therefore, that he said farewell to his Uncle Peter and Auntie Gwen when they reached the Army Transport Office. Leaving those whom he knew and loved for the unknowns of a cold and unwelcoming world was sobering. He wondered whether those at Surrenden would understand his grief at the great loss of his parents. Or wouldn't they care a jot? Would they make him march up and down a parade-square until he dropped? Would he have to peel thousands of potatoes? He knew nothing of the military, except what he had seen in films.

He knew he had a lot to learn but he felt excited at being part of Surrenden Military School. He was already a Cadet, and he would be joining other Cadets, as part of Alamein Company, Victory College.

He entered the Army Transport Office and walked up to a highly polished counter just inside the entrance. Behind the counter was a grizzled looking older soldier in green camouflage uniform who regarded him with faint amusement. On his sleeves he wore the three stripes of a Sergeant and on his shirt he had a nameplate proclaiming 'Handley'.

'Can I help you, young fella?' asked Sergeant Handley with kindly indulgence.

'Yes please, sir,' said Willie. 'I'm going to Surrenden Military School and I was told to report here for transport.'

'Surrenden Military School, eh?' Sergeant Handley's manner changed sharply to that of considerable interest. 'Have you got your Joining Instructions there?'

'Yes sir,' said Willie, handing over the instructions.

'McBride … William McBride … hmmm,' muttered Sergeant Handley as he studied the instructions. He glanced up suddenly, leant forward over the counter, and looked closely at Willie. 'You wouldn't be Colonel Hugh McBride's little nipper, would you?'

'Er … yes, sir. He was my father.'

'What do you mean 'was' your father? Where's he nowadays? He and I served together when we were much younger. I heard he was now with the Foreign Office or something like that. And don't call me "sir". "Sir" is only for officers. You call me Sergeant Handley.' He pointed to the stripes on his sleeve and to the nameplate on his shirt.

'He and my mother died in a mining accident earlier this month, sir. ... I mean ... Sergeant Handley,' replied Willie.

'Oh no. I'm so sorry to hear that,' said Sergeant Handley. His attitude quickly softened and he looked at Willie with sympathy. 'That's a terrible thing to have happened.' He heaved a great sigh and shook his head. 'Not many of our old unit left now. Ah well, it's only to be expected, I suppose. We're all getting on in years.' He looked at Willie with new respect and said briskly, 'However, we mustn't dwell on the past must we, sir? Your transport to Surrenden School will be along shortly. Now you just go into the Waiting Room through there and make yourself comfortable. Help yourself to some hot coffee and biscuits on the stand. There are two other cadets for Surrenden School already waiting. I'll call you when your transport arrives, sir.'

Willie went into the Waiting Room, pulling his suitcase behind him. There was a girl and a boy in the room, both of whom were about his age, with their suitcases beside them.

'Are both of you waiting for transport to Surrenden Military School?' he asked.

'Yes, that's right,' said the girl. 'Are you going there too?'

'Yes, and I'm very pleased I'm not the only one,' replied Willie, grinning and with obvious relief in his voice. 'I'm William. William McBride. But most people call me Willie.'

'I'm Penelope Pendragon,' said the girl, now smiling broadly, and heaving a great sigh of relief. 'Me too. I was dead scared I was going to be by myself.'

'I'm Gareth Jones,' said the boy, introducing himself. He laughed out loud. 'And I'm bloomin' pleased to meet you guys. I hate being alone too.' He shook hands with both Penelope and Willie before shifting an aluminium toolbox and suitcase with a pair of cricket boots attached to one side to make space for Willie's suitcase. He moved to the coffee stand.

'Anyone else for coffee and biscuits?' he asked, grinning. He took a handful of biscuits. 'I can recommend these Cheddars.'

'Yep, I'd like some,' said Willie and Penelope in unison.

They settled themselves in their seats, sipping their coffees, and began to chat, while taking guarded glances at each other, but not so as to give offence. Gareth was sturdy, rather stocky, with straight flaxen hair and green eyes. Penelope was a tall, slender girl with long golden hair, blue eyes and a well-formed face. They quickly established that all three were going to join Alamein Company, and that, one way or another, all had lost one, or both, of their parents, who had been serving in the military.

'My Dad was a Sergeant in the Royal Engineers,' said Gareth. 'His group of engineers were building a bridge to open an important supply route in Afghanistan, but they were hit by an enemy ambush.' There was a moment of quiet reflection. 'I'm staying with my Aunt Dinnie in Llanelli now, 'cos Mum died three years ago of cancer.' He shot a quick glance at Willie and Penelope before lowering his eyes and saying softly, 'and I haven't any brothers or sisters, before you ask.'

Again there was a moment's silence as Willie and Penelope mentally compared their situations with that of Gareth's.

'I'm very sorry for you,' said Penelope. 'I lost my Dad in the Middle East too. He was an officer in the Wessex Guards and was helping train policemen in Iraq. My Mum and I live in Jersey now. Mum has a glasshouse business growing tomatoes, and I help her as much as possible.' She suddenly grinned. 'I hate tomatoes now. I've had 'em boiled, baked and fried, sliced, diced and strained. You name it and I've had it. I don't want to see another tomato as long as I live.'

They all chuckled. Gareth and Penelope looked expectantly at Willie to hear his story.

'Well, I lost both my Mum and Dad in a mine accident in Borneo. They were working for the Foreign Office at the time,' he said. He shook his head slowly. 'I don't have any brothers or sisters either, so I suppose I'm pretty much on my own too. Except, that is, for my Auntie Gwen and Uncle Peter.'

'We all seem to have a lot in common then. Three miserable gits facing a cold world,' remarked Gareth lightly. 'We'd better stick together.' His infectious grin and quirky sense of humour appealed greatly. His manner was straightforward, bouncy and perky, like a Jack Russell terrier.

'That's not a bad idea,' said Penelope. 'It would be great to have some real live friends. I mean, our family moved about *sooo* much – because of Dad's postings – so I had to find friends on the internet. You know – with e-mail, YouTube, and Facebook. I never really became close friends with anyone live.' She was well spoken and her manner was direct, but slightly reserved and refined. Despite her apparent elegance, there seemed to be an inner toughness about her.

'I love computers and the internet,' said Gareth, his eyes lighting up. 'Dad and I actually built a small computer from parts we got from an electronic shop. I've got it here in my toolbox.' He tapped the aluminium box on the floor and smiled. 'Along with heaps of other great tools and test equipment. Haven't met a problem yet that I haven't been able to fix, or put on a temporary band-aid!' he exclaimed triumphantly.

Willie found it difficult to describe his interests, finally falling back on Uncle Peter's description of being so rounded that he wasn't pointed anywhere. 'I don't know very much about computers either,' he said, feeling a little bit inadequate. 'But I used to go down to the library with my Uncle Peter. He'd show me how to find out which books were available, and – y'know - how to get onto the internet and that sort of stuff. But he'd look up things like BBC and chess games.' He suddenly brightened up. 'But we used to get out DVDs to watch at home. Mostly sci-tech sort of things – *Matrix*, *Aliens* and *Star Wars*. Actually, I like films, James Bond and that sort of stuff.'

'*Aliens*? Yuk!' exclaimed Penelope 'I was so scared. I couldn't sleep for weeks. Nope. I like animal films, like *Black Beauty* and *Black Stallion*.'

'I like James Bond films too,' said Gareth. 'But my favourite films are the Indiana Jones ones. *Indiana Jones and the Last Crusade*. Now that was a great movie. Museums, military and magic.'

'And the name Jones,' said Penelope slyly. They all laughed.

They continued to chat frankly and openly about themselves, their background and their likes and dislikes, which came from the sure knowledge that they each shared a common tragic loss, and would understand their feelings.

Sergeant Handley suddenly popped his head through the door. 'Right, you Surrenden mob. Your transport's arrived, so pick up your luggage and make your way through the double doors there.

Don't leave any of your stuff behind.' He looked at Willie and smiled. 'You take care of yourself, Mr McBride sir, and good luck!'

'Thanks, Sergeant Handley.'

Outside in the transport terminus a soldier dressed in a dark green camouflage uniform with two stripes on his sleeves was waiting. 'Are you Cadets McBride, Pendragon and Jones?' enquired the soldier.

'Yes, we are,' they replied in chorus.

'That's good. I'm Corporal Jenkins from Surrenden Military School. I've got your transport here. Follow me, please.' He turned to Penelope. 'Here, Miss, let me help you with your luggage.'

They followed Corporal Jenkins to a camouflaged long-wheel-base Army Land Rover and loaded their luggage into the back of the vehicle, and themselves into the front seats.

'Surrenden is only about fifty miles from Waterloo,' said Corporal Jenkins. 'So we'll be there shortly. It's just past Pluckley Village.'

'I heard that Pluckley is the most haunted village in England,' said Penelope.

'Yes, that's right,' said Corporal Jenkins with a grin. 'You don't want to be out at night by yourself!' Then his attitude became quite thoughtful and serious. 'Although, I must say, funny things do sometimes happen at Pluckley and Surrenden. The district's steeped in history. It all goes back to the days of William the Conqueror.'

They settled back in their seats and dozed off as Corporal Jenkins drove out of the London traffic and down into the quiet Kentish countryside with its quaint villages. As they approached Pluckley they found themselves driving into a late morning fog which shrouded the road, buildings and woods.

Corporal Jenkins pointed through a gap in the fog at a large granite church on the hill, surrounded by gravestones. 'That's the Parish Church of St Nicholas over there. It's over 900 years old. And there's the Black Horse Inn with the U-shaped Surrenden windows. Apparently, the local gentry, who lived in the original Surrenden Manor house, escaped from Cromwell's men through those funny shaped windows. Now all the buildings in the village have them.'

He paused for a moment as he turned into a pillared, arched entranceway, with a guardroom, and huge, double wrought-iron gates. Centrally placed on the archway was the Surrenden Military

School's coat-of-arms: a red shield placed on top of a wreath of oak leaves. At the centre of the shield was the rearing black Surrenden stallion, flanked on either side by two unusual signs of science and technology. One was a blue and green coloured double helix of DNA, and the other a gold atom around which orbited three golden electrons.

'Here we are, now. Surrenden Military School,' announced Corporal Jenkins. 'Even more historical and magical than Pluckley. It's said that this used to be the site of a Celtic township in the pre-Roman days. People have often said they have seen groups of Druids at night at their rituals over in those oak forests over there. But they've been too terrified to investigate. They even say that the School's museum is especially magical and it's a gateway to other worlds. But it all sounds like piffle to me.' He laughed derisively.

The school sat on higher ground than the fog-bound village in the valley below. Here, the air was clear and crisp. The three new cadets eagerly peered out of the Land Rover windows to get their first view of their new home. It was impressively large. A long line of red-brick, dormitory buildings were centred on a very large administrative office building, from which rose a steepled clock-tower. Several bulky, brick buildings behind the clock-tower housed central facilities, such as the school hall, kitchens, mess-halls, gymnasiums, indoor swimming pool, classrooms and science laboratories. In front of the clock-tower was an asphalt parade ground. Surrounding the buildings were rugby and hockey playing fields, tennis courts, and an obstacle confidence course.

'I'll drop you off at the Alamein Company Common-room,' said Corporal Jenkins. 'The Company duty students will look after you from then on.'

They drove up to a two-storied brick building with large Surrenden windows, a central porch with a tiled floor, and dark wooden double doors.

'Here we are,' exclaimed Corporal Jenkins, and, seeing an older boy and girl fling open the Common-room's double doors, added, 'There's your welcoming committee!'

The two Alamein Company duty students, Junior Under Officer Sarah Metcalfe and Junior Under Officer James Murphy, were senior students in their last year at Surrenden. They were dressed in camouflage uniforms, dark blue dress caps, and both wore a broad red sash from their right shoulders to the left side of their waists to indicate they were the duty students for the day. They shook hands with Willie, Penelope and Gareth and welcomed them to Alamein Company.

'Grab your bags and we'll show you your rooms,' said James with a smile. 'Then we'll go to see SAS at the Quartermaster's Store, and get you set up with your initial issue of uniforms and things. Oh, by the way, SAS is the nickname we give the School's Storeman, Staff Sergeant Samuel Acorn Squirrelle. Not sure if he ever served in the SAS. He's so old it's more likely that he served in the Long Range Desert Group during the Second World War.'

Their rooms were all in the same block, with the girls on the top floor and the boys on the ground. The rooms were rather small with just enough space for a bed with built-in drawers underneath, a built-in wardrobe and drawers, a study table with book-shelves on the wall, a small chest of drawers, and a hand-basin with a mirror above it. There was an oil heater on the wall under a double-glazed window, which looked out onto shrubs and landscaped gardens. The floor covering was thick vinyl, coloured army brown, over which a thick red rug had been thrown.

'They're cosy little cells,' joked Sarah, as she showed Penelope her room. 'But there really is enough space, if you're not a magpie and keep bringing things home.' Willie's and Gareth's rooms were adjacent.

'Actually, you're very lucky to get these rooms,' said James. 'They've just been modernised. Had hot water installed. Previously, we had to get a jug of hot water from down in the shower and toilet area at the end of the block!'

After the three had stowed their luggage into their rooms, James and Sarah took them down into the main area behind the clock-tower building to the Quartermaster's Store, pointing out the various facilities of the school on the way. James pointed to a large block of classrooms with huge glass windows and sprouting fume-exhaust chimneys. Inside, cupboards of coloured chemicals, prisms, and laboratory equipment overlooking laboratory benches, stainless steel sinks and plumbing lined the walls.

'That's the "Rutherford Science and Technology Laboratory Block". It's just been opened last year, and is named after the present Headmaster, Professor Savant Rutherford. We call it the "Savvy Science Centre", after the Head. Just about all the staff have nicknames like Savvy.' Sarah pointed to a huge, two-storied red-brick building with Surrenden windows and a bow front.

'That's the School's Museum. It's actually the old Surrenden Manor House that's been added to, and modernised, goodness only knows how many times. And those buildings down the driveway near to us are the classrooms. Those further away are the New College and Old College company accommodation and the Combat Wing.' James pointed to another large red-brick building attached to the rear of the office block with the soaring clock-tower.

'This is the Administration Block, which houses Security, the Education Centre and the Quartermaster's Store. So here we are. Let's go in and introduce you to SAS.'

Staff Sergeant Samuel Squirrelle was an old soldier who had seen a lot of service. He had been posted to Surrenden Military School many years ago, but, despite his age, it was believed he could remember almost every cadet who had attended Surrenden. He was a trim little man, about the size of a jockey, with a lined face, bright eyes and a ready smile. His movements were quick, like that of a squirrel, as he went from shelf to shelf to gather the items to be issued.

'McBride ... hmmm ... McBride,' he pondered, his face wrinkled in thought, as he was introduced to Willie, and then he added softly, 'Ah yes. I remember him. Did very well in his senior year. Was our top cadet in that year, I think.' When Willie told him of his parents' death, he said sympathetically, 'I'm very sad to hear that he has passed on, sir.' He paused for a moment, and then smiled at Willie. 'But I'm pleased that you've come to join us at Surrenden, Mr McBride, and hope that you will be as successful as your father.' He pointed at three enormous piles of clothing and equipment, which he had assembled on the Issues bench in front of him.

'Now this is the initial issue for each of you. Just check each item against this list, and when you're satisfied you've got everything put your signature on the bottom.' He handed them two sheets of paper, each closely printed on both sides.

Willie looked at his list. It was written in typical Army style:

Pants, Camouflaged, Size 12	Sets 6
Shirts, Camouflaged, Size 12	Sets 6
Boots, Infantry, Rubber-soled, Black	Pairs 3

Underpants, Green, Size 12	Sets 6
Vests, Green, Size 12	Sets 6
Headdress, Caps peaked, Blue	Quantity 1

There were 127 separate items, including a field compass, binoculars, a laptop computer, a Geographical Positioning System instrument, a transistor radio, a field torch, Dress clothing including a Surrenden blazer, Surrenden tie, grey longs, white shirts, a khaki Burberry coat, field pack, webbing and all their school books and reference materials. Two sets of regulation summer- and winter-weight Surrenden pyjamas completed the issue.

'This is just your initial issue,' SAS explained. 'When you go out into the field for exercises, you'll be given special issues. All weapons are stored in the Armoury, and are only issued for exercises or range-work.' Gareth examined the laptop computer.

'This is a pretty grunty notebook,' he said excitedly. 'Look, it's got a 2.2 GHz processor, 120 Gig hard drive and a 2 Gig random access memory.' He looked up at Sarah. 'Are we on the internet?'

'Absolutely,' replied Sarah. 'We're not allowed to use mobile phones while at school, so everybody uses e-mail on their computer. The school has its own website, www.surrenden.co.uk and its own local area network, so everyone has their own e-mail address. Yours, for example, will be gareth.jones@surrenden.co.uk. Willie's will be william.mcbride@surrenden.co.uk and Penelope will be penelope.pendragon@surrenden.co.uk.' Each laptop is fitted with a wireless connection which means we can keep in contact with the school while we are at home or away and vice versa. I know it sounds exciting, but when you have to submit your study assignments using the computer and you're late, you can't use the excuse it got lost in the mail.'

'I'll never be able to fit all this stuff into my room,' said Penelope, shaking her head mournfully, and looking at the huge pile.

'Oh yes you will,' said Sarah brightly and reassuringly. 'It will all pack away quite nicely, you'll see. Come on. I'll help you carry it all back to the company lines.'

They staggered back to their rooms, and over the next couple of hours packed the items away into the wardrobes and drawers. Remarkably, they did manage to find places to put everything. When they had finished they re-assembled downstairs in the

Company Common-room to join the other students, who had gathered briefly for the routine daily Co-ordination Meeting before dinner. The senior cadet for Alamein Company was Senior Under Officer Giles Hanbury. He was in his last year at Surrenden, and was hoping to be selected to enter the Royal Military Academy Sandhurst next year. He welcomed Willie, Penelope and Gareth to Alamein Company, gave out some sports notices and drew everyone's attention to the Old Pupils Spring Visit, or 'Blast from the Past', as it was irreverently called, due to take place in four weeks time at the end of May.

'We'll follow the traditional programme for this year's "Blast from the Past",' said Giles. 'We'll play the old pupils at cricket, do some small-bore shooting, and have a riding competition during the Saturday. Then we put on a theatrical performance for them on the Saturday evening. As you know, it'll be *Pirates of Penzance* this year, and some of you have already auditioned for parts. Then we'll finish off with a Church Service on Sunday morning.' He turned to the new trio.

'All three of you will be expected to take part in the *Pirates*, but you can take your choice of which sport you'd like to join.'

'I'll take the riding,' said Penelope quickly.

Willie remembered the cricket boots tied to Gareth's luggage. He looked at him. 'If you want to play cricket I'll do the small-bore shooting.'

Gareth looked pleased. 'Yes, that'll be great.'

'OK,' said Giles. 'Put your names down on the Notice Board for those events. Now, there's also a new Duties Roster pinned up on the Notice Board, so make sure you know what duties you're slotted for.' He looked at his three new cadets. 'You guys should be aware of the Lucifer-Mortlock Trophy, or the "Devil's Mug" as it's called. It's awarded annually to the best new cadet. A cadet from Alamein Company has never won the "Devil's Mug", although it's been going for about 20 years now. So it would be a real breakthrough if one of you three won it.' He didn't sound at all hopeful. 'By the way, you three are to report to Professor Lusty tomorrow morning at 0800 hours. She's the Deputy Head and her office is in the Admin Block.'

When he'd finished, and most of the Company had left the Common Room for the Mess Hall down the corridor, Willie, Penelope and Gareth gathered to examine the Duties Roster, to see if they had been included. The Duties Roster was for the duration of the school term, and included such tasks as Common Room cleaning, Mail sorting and delivery, Corridor cleaning, Shower and toilet area cleaning, Museum assistant curators (cleaning and polishing), kitchen duties and Mess hall cleaning. All three of them were rostered as Museum assistant curators (cleaning and polishing), and were to report to the Museum's Curator, Lieutenant Shrewdfellow, after the 'Blast from the Past'.

That night, as Willie lay in his bed, memories of his first day at Surrenden flooded through his mind. It had been a great day. He had started off being very apprehensive and uneasy, but now he felt comfortable and not at all homesick. He'd met two terrific new friends in Gareth and Penelope. He was part of Alamein Company now and he had a programme of new and exciting things to do, starting first thing tomorrow morning. He was astonished how many people he'd met that day who had known his parents. All of them seemed to think his parents had been really super people. He felt, somehow, that those people would also like to know what had happened to them and were encouraging him to find out.

The small-bore shooting sounded fun, but he wasn't too sure about taking part in the *Pirates*. He felt very uncomfortable speaking in public. Perhaps he would be given a role with the backstage crew. He hoped so. Meantime, however, there were more pressing things to attend to – like getting up on time.

He set his alarm clock on the bedside table for 5.30 am the next morning, and, to his surprise, fell asleep within seconds.

3

BLAST FROM THE PAST

Willie slept like a log and woke bleary-eyed at the shattering clatter of the alarm clock. The new day was just dawning and the first calls of the birds' morning chorus had begun. He dashed down to the showers and hurried back to get dressed in his camouflage uniform for the first time. His long trousers, long-sleeved shirt, brown shoes, black beret and blue Surrenden stable belt all seemed to fit him reasonably well; but his beret was a real embarrassment. It stuck upright on top of his head like a sinister circular spacecraft.

There was a knock on his door. 'Are you up yet?' It was Gareth.

'Yes. I've been up for ages,' replied Willie, stretching the truth a bit. He opened the door to find Gareth also dressed in his uniform and grinning like a monkey under his black beret.

'Looks like you're wearing a black cow-pat,' said Willie.

'Take a look in the mirror,' countered Gareth. 'You don't look too cool yourself. You look like a real hayseed.'

They both pulled the side of their berets down hard, but to no avail. They just sprang back. 'Ah well,' said Willie. 'Perhaps it needs a bit of time for gravity to take effect. Come on. We'll go down and grab some breakfast.'

'I hope it's something good,' said Gareth. 'My Auntie Dinnie reckons that breakfast's the most important meal of the day. She *always* has porridge, fried bread, toast and marmalade and really, really strong black Irish tea. Trouble is, she often leaves everything cooking too long and it all gets burnt. Burnt porridge and fried bread is yuk!'

The Surrenden breakfast *was* good. It was laid out in buffet style for the cadets to help themselves, just as one would expect in a hotel dining room. After a couple of helpings of fruit juice, stewed fruit, poached eggs on toast, bacon and tomatoes, Gareth leant back.

'Y'know, I could really get to love this place,' he said with great satisfaction.

They made their way back to their rooms, tidied themselves up and found their way to the Administration Block and the office of the Deputy Headmistress, Professor Lusty. Penelope was already there in the hallway waiting for them. She laughed when she saw them.

'Lovely berets you're wearing, you guys. Off to Ascot Races for the "Best Hat" competition?' Both boys blushed self-consciously. 'Don't worry,' said Penelope reassuringly. 'I'm sure they'll fall into place in a day or two. Or you could steam iron them, like I've done with mine.' They both made a mental note to follow her advice.

Professor Winifred Lusty welcomed them into her office with a flourish. She was a large lady with *presence*. She was very business-like, and hugely energetic. She wore thick horn-rimmed glasses and lots of make-up that drew attention to her face and wide, toothy smile. Her dark grey hair was drawn up in a bun, and kept in place by a large tortoiseshell comb. Her academic gown heaved and swirled as she sailed from the door to her desk.

'Come in, come in, my dears. We're so pleased to welcome you to Surrenden Military School. Sit yourselves down and make yourselves comfortable.' She seated herself behind her desk and took three files from her in-tray. 'Now, I've got the academic record here for each of you from your previous schools, and … hmmm … I must say from what I see here each of you is going to have to work very hard to reach our Surrenden standards.' Her smile faded and she looked severely at them over her glasses. The trio suddenly felt very small and wished they were somewhere else.

'You will, of course, continue with the core subjects of English, mathematics and the three sciences of chemistry, physics and biology. I think the three of you should also complete our courses in history and computing/information technology. You may also make a choice of one of Business Studies, geography, or a foreign language. We teach Chinese here as well as French and German. We will expect you to take an active interest in Music.' Her toothy smile suddenly returned. 'So you can see, you've got a full academic programme ahead of you, my dears. You will only succeed if you work hard, and for that reason I suggest you plan on two hours study a night.' She handed them a Study Timetable. 'Here's your study programme and class allocation. I'll be keeping a close eye on your progress, and I expect to see some good results. All three of you can excel if you put your minds to it. Best of luck.'

With another swirl of her academic gown, she ushered them out of her office into the panelled hallway. Shell-shocked, they stood in silence looking at one another, their mouths open like guppies. They had all those subjects to study, and some were really, really hard subjects too. Then there were two hours of study at night.

Gareth groaned. 'There go my chances to improve my batting. I was hoping to get in heaps of practice down in the nets this season.'

Penelope studied the timetable given them by Professor Lusty. 'This is just so unfair. Old "Crocodile Teeth" in there has left me with only Saturday afternoons and Sunday. How am I to get to know my pony at the Pony Club in time for the Blast from the Past competition?'

'Well, what about me?' said Willie. 'At least you two know about computers and stuff. It's all Greek to me.' He studied his timetable more closely, and brightened up. 'Well, there's English, biology and history. I'm OK with those three. Business Studies and Chinese sound pretty interesting.'

'Ugh, I can't stand English and history,' said Gareth. 'English has too many punctuation marks and tenses. My spelling's ... um ... not too good. My history's terrible. There are too many dates, kings and battles for me to remember.'

Willie had an idea. 'Tell you what, Gareth. How about I help you with your English and history, and you help me with computers and physics?'

'Good idea.'

'Oh, it's all very well for you two to help each other,' said Penelope a little crossly. 'Who's going to help me? My maths is terrible. I wouldn't know an isosceles triangle if I fell over one.'

William and Gareth looked at each other and grinned.

'My maths isn't too flash either,' said Willie. 'Why don't the three of us have a maths study session together once or twice a week in the Company Common Room? Nobody else seems to use it in the evening.'

'That would be great,' said Penelope with relief. 'With a bit of help I might even be able to find time to get over to the Pony Club.'

Over the next few weeks they managed to find time to squeeze in their other activities, while developing a good study routine. Willie and Gareth practised and played cricket for the Second XI, and Penelope started riding in the Intermediate Class at the Surrenden Pony Club, in the nearby village of Little Chart.

The three of them took up small-bore shooting under the keen eye of Captain Sheldrake from the Combat Wing's Firepower and Mobility Centre. He was in the Missile Corps, and taught Missiles and Delivery Systems. He would laugh when anybody thought it strange that he taught about large battlefield missiles, but was also responsible for the School's Small-bore Rifle Club's range. 'Look,' he would say. 'A missile's a missile whatever its size and shape. A paper dart's a missile. So are pebbles, pellets and rocket projectiles. They all follow the same rules of aerodynamics, and all need to be handled safely and with respect.'

The Surrenden Small-bore Rifle Club was actually more than just a rifle club. It included Gallery Rifle shooting with .22 rifles, Olympic Pentathlon shooting with .177 air pistols and air rifles, and Olympic archery shooting. The trio quickly learnt the safety rules for each discipline, and which one they preferred. Gareth was accomplished at archery, and spent some time making a new sighting mechanism which he could attach to the bow to increase his accuracy. Penelope was quite adept with the .22 rifle, while Willie, who had a strong steady grip, found he was quite a sharpshooter at both the Gallery Rifle and the Olympic Pentathlon shooting.

Their participation in the *Pirates of Penzance* operetta was another matter altogether. Penelope was given the role of a young lady in the Chorus of Girls, where she positively glowed. She loved the costumes, the music and the singing. She simply adored theatre and eagerly looked forward to the rehearsals.

'You're naturally so good at acting, Penelope,' observed Gareth. 'I can't believe that you actually have to work at acting a part. You're just a natural drama star, I reckon.'

Gareth had been given a role as a pirate in the Chorus of Pirates, which he'd really liked. But his voice was a bit flat and raspy for the songs, so he was given a dagger to clench between his teeth and instructed to hum the tune, and look ferocious during the pirate songs. 'I'm musically challenged,' he would joke. 'The only Welsh boy in the world unable to join a choir. I think they just include me to help make up the numbers. It doesn't matter though, 'cos I'm enjoying being part of the action.'

Willie, however, did have a reasonable singing voice. He was given a part as a policeman in the Chorus of Police and wore a policeman's uniform, complete with a helmet and chinstrap, lamplight and truncheon. He enjoyed the part hugely and particularly liked the two songs, 'When a felon's not engaged in his employment' and 'With cat-like tread, upon our prey we steal'.

'Playing a policeman is the perfect role for you,' teased Penelope. 'Always doing your duty and taking care not to break the rules.'

'That's right, Penelope,' added Gareth, rubbing his head ruefully, 'as well as bashing innocent pirates over the head with his truncheon.'

The whole theatrical production was being supervised by Bridget Nottles, the wife of the School's Bandmaster, Captain Nottles, who was arranging the music and conducting the School's small orchestra. The cast included Giles Hanbury as Major-General Stanley, Sarah Metcalfe as Mabel, and James Murphy as the Sergeant of Police.

Bridget Nottles was a dynamo of a person, with a sharp eye for detail. She demanded almost impossibly high standards of performance, knew everyone by their first name and every word in the operetta. Rehearsals were fun, fast and furious.

'Articulate, Giles, articulate,' she would say when Giles came to sing the famous Major-General's song. 'The audience has to hear each word. Don't sing gibberish.' No-one was spared her critical appraisal.

'Your eye make-up is too little and is smudged again, Penelope. Accentuate those big eyes of yours so the audience can *see* the emotion.'

'Don't hang back in the chorus line, Willie. Move forward so the stage lights can light up your face. Let the audience see your tonsils and hear that great voice of yours.'

This routine of concentrated study, sports and rehearsals continued unabated until, in no time at all it seemed, the Old Pupils Spring Visit was upon them. The Old Pupils, accompanied by their wives, husbands and partners, arrived during the Saturday morning. They met with the cadets in the Alamein Company Common Room at midday, before moving to the Mess Hall for lunch. They were a happy group of people, laughing and joking with one another, and taking a keen interest in meeting the present Alamein Company cadets. Giles Hanbury stood on a stool so all could see him, and welcomed them back to Surrenden, amid much hand clapping and well-intentioned interjections.

'Ladies and gentlemen, it's my very great pleasure to welcome our Old Pupils back to Surrenden Military School on the occasion of this annual Spring Visit. We cadets look forward to this event as an opportunity to learn from our betters' ... much laughter and calls of 'Hear, hear' ... 'and to listen with open mouths at your stories of derring-do.' ... more laughter and calls of 'Did I ever tell you about the time I ...' 'But I should warn you that my fellow cadets and I have trained hard over these past few weeks, so expect no mercy on the cricket pitch, on the shooting range, and in the equestrian events.' ... more laughter ... 'We will then entertain you this evening with a magnificent performance of that wonderful Gilbert and Sullivan operetta, *The Pirates of Penzance*. Ladies and gentlemen, welcome back to Surrenden, and I now invite you to join us for lunch.'

Willie, Gareth and Penelope mingled with the Old Pupils, introducing themselves and making sure their guests had ample supplies of beer and wine. To the trio the Old Pupils seemed to be *so* old, with their wrinkled faces, thinning hair and well-nourished, plump bodies; but they quickly came to realise that the Old Pupils had something that could only be acquired over time – life experience. This was a golden occasion for the present cadets to learn from this experience, so as to recognise opportunities when they were presented, and avoid any pitfalls as they, in turn, moved through their lives.

After lunch everyone dispersed into their respective groups for the competitions, and Willie reported to Giles Hanbury at the Small-bore Rifle Range, as part of the Alamein Company team. He checked out the Old Pupils team. There were three women and two men and they seemed pretty relaxed about things. Their Team Leader was Muriel Fancourt, who had a reputation for being an excellent shot and very, very competitive. After the team members had been introduced to each other they paired off to commence the .22 rifle Gallery Shoot.

Willie was paired off to shoot against Muriel Fancourt, and he quickly appreciated Muriel's competitive spirit as they settled down to fire the first of 20 rounds at the targets 25 yards away.

'You did say that your name was Willie McBride, didn't you?'

Muriel propped up her rifle with her elbows and glanced through the scope.

'Er ... hmm ... yes,' replied Willie, briefly distracted. 'Yes. Willie McBride.'

There was a few seconds silence as they adopted their shooting positions.

'Were your parents Colonel Hugh and Sally McBride, who disappeared in Borneo recently?'

Willie's body froze as his mind flashed back on painful memories. He took a long breath and rested his rifle, looking across to Muriel, who had just fired her first round. He could see at once that her question was not one of concern, but rather one of casual curiosity.

'Yes.' He felt vaguely annoyed that his private memories had been needlessly invaded. 'Did you know them?'

'I'll say,' responded Muriel, turning her head to face him. She was smiling in a secretive way. 'We were all great mates when we were here, but after graduation we all went our separate ways. I'm very sorry. Please accept my condolences.' She turned back to her shooting and squeezed off another round. Her voice lacked warmth and real concern, exposing her remarks of sympathy to be hollow and meaningless.

Willie felt rattled and suddenly became aware that he had not yet fired his first round. He settled back into his firing position and sighted the target through his scope.

'Yes, those were the days. Your parents, Hannibal and I used to have great fun together.'

Willie lost his focus and his first round went wide. He rested his rifle again. 'Hannibal who?' he asked, trying to finish the conversation off quickly.

'Hannibal Lucifer-Mortlock,' replied Muriel. 'He's a knight now, you know. He's such a dear man, but he's extremely competitive. He simply doesn't like to lose. He presented the School with the Lucifer-Mortlock Trophy.'

'Oh yes, of course,' replied Willie, vaguely remembering Giles Hanbury mentioning something about a 'Devil's Mug' when he, Penelope and Gareth first arrived at Surrenden. He adopted his firing position again and fired off two rounds. His aim was a little better this time, but he was unsettled and failed to score a bull's eye. His mind wandered, imagining his parents, Muriel and this unknown man Hannibal together. He could hear Muriel firing steadily away and making self-congratulatory comments to herself.

'*Yes*. You nailed *that* one, girl.'

'*Another* bull's eye. You're really in top form this afternoon, Muriel.'

He started to think that his rate of fire was too slow, so he fired off three rounds quickly and was surprised to see that they all scored inners.

'Of course, Hannibal rather fancied your mother, Sally. Did she ever mention that?' There was more than just a hint of malice in her voice.

Willie was too stunned to reply and rested his rifle. He turned his head to face Muriel, who was continuing to fire at a steady controlled rate.

'No,' he replied flatly. 'She never mentioned anything about that.' He could feel anger and curiosity rising at the same time. Anger that this woman knew something about his parents that he didn't, and perhaps should, and curiosity to know more, which meant he had to be nice to Muriel to find out.

'Ah … no … perhaps I shouldn't. I really shouldn't have mentioned it. It's all in the past. It's best forgotten. Even that terrible fight between Hannibal and your father just before graduation.' There was triumph in her voice now. She had aroused Willie's curiosity deliberately and was now denying him satisfaction, the unanswered question to linger and fester. It did. As he settled back to continue firing, his mind was in a whirl. His hands were quivering and his mind couldn't focus on the job at hand. His remaining shots scattered around the bull's eye, while next to him he could hear Muriel keeping up a continual barrage of self-applauding comments.

He felt utterly despondent when his targets were collected by the scorer and taken to Giles, his Team Captain. Giles wasn't a bit fazed about Willie's score.

'Ah, I see Muriel "sledged" you and got under your skin,' he said and laughed. 'I should have warned you she'd try that on you. You're a far better shot than she'll ever be. Put it down to experience, Willie. Just let sneaky, underhand comments slide off you like water off a duck's back. They're just made to put you off your game, or make you so angry you won't make good decisions. Anyway, your score's pretty good and much better than the others.'

Willie was grateful to Giles for his encouragement, and vowed he would be more alert and resilient in future. The afternoon competitions finished with the Old Pupils losing the shooting, winning the cricket, and drawing the equestrian events at the Pony Club. The trio met in the Company Common Room to swap experiences. Penelope, in her jodhpurs, riding boots and shirt, was still flushed with her successes.

'It was brilliant,' she enthused. 'This was my first real riding competition and before it started I was all churned up. Y'know, like my tummy was a washing machine. But my pony, Quirky, was great. She got over all the jumps, without even one fault, and looked really, really good in the grooming event.' She tossed her head and bragged: 'I came second equal in the overall points score.' The boys congratulated her.

'We knew you'd do well if Quirky didn't fail in the jumping,' said Gareth. He was still dressed in his cricket flannels and jersey. 'Our team did pretty well in the cricket too, but we weren't good enough. The score finished up 236 for the Old Pupils and 156 for us.' He shook his head in wonderment. 'They were crafty devils, y' know. They bowled their spinners first before we had a chance to get our eye in, then they hit us with their fast bowlers. Boy, were their fast bowlers fast. Poor James Murphy, our best batsman, had a bit of bad luck. He broke his ankle when he was trying to avoid being run out. Anyway, I did OK. I took two catches and scored 26 runs, including three fours.'

'Wow, that was more than OK,' said Willie. 'That's what you'd call fantastic. Our shooting team won, but I didn't shoot my best. I was badly put off by the Old Pupils' team leader, Muriel Fancourt. Giles said I was "sledged". Muriel kept chattering on about how well she was shooting. That was all right. But then she said she used to hang out with my mum and dad when they were all at Surrenden, and that threw me a bit.'

After an early dinner they all went to the School Hall, which had been set up for the presentation of the *Pirates*. Bridget was there at her bossy best, supervising, directing and ordering everyone about, as if the performance was to be filmed by international television. The school's orchestra was already in place and tuning up their instruments, flicking through their music sheets on the stands, and looking very smart in their dress uniforms. The stage crew were in panic mode, touching up the scenery props here and there with paint, testing the lighting and sound systems, and the hoisting gear for the stage backdrops. The dressing rooms were scenes of chaos as the performers, half-dressed in their costumes, clustered around the mirrors to do their make-up, practised their lines and tuned their voices.

Bridget ran in, cast her eye over the singing and acting talent in the Chorus of the Police, and pelted over to Willie.

'Willie,' she cooed, 'James is in hospital with a broken ankle and we need a replacement to do the part of the Sergeant. I think you're our best man to do the job, and I'd like you to give it a go. Do you think you can do it?'

Willie was gobsmacked. While he enjoyed being a leader, he hated being in the front under the full glare of the lights and the centre of attention. He was not naturally flamboyant, swashbuckling or theatrical. He was much more comfortable taking a leading role behind the scenes, where efficiency and organising ability really counted. His natural inclination was to shrink away from Bridget's invitation, but then his sense of duty came to the fore.

'Of course I can do it, Bridget,' he replied brightly. 'I wouldn't refuse promotion to Sergeant.'

Bridget gave a huge sigh of relief. 'I know you can too, Willie,' said Bridget with a smile. 'I'll get the Wardrobe Mistress to quickly tack on the Sergeant's stripes onto your uniform. It's a bit like a field promotion, isn't it? Here's the script for the part of the Sergeant. You'd better have a quick look at it before the curtain goes up.' She darted away to save impending disasters from occurring elsewhere.

Willie gulped, a sense of panic rising in his stomach. What had he let himself in for? The Wardrobe Mistress hurried over with the Sergeant's stripes, as Gareth appeared at his elbow in his pirate's costume, grinning with amusement.

'Blimmin' heck. It's Sergeant McBride already, eh, boyo? If you keep getting promotion this quickly, you'll be a Field Marshal before Christmas.' He slapped him on the back and said encouragingly, 'You'll do fine. You already know the songs and your singing is almost as good as a Welsh choir.'

Willie had just under an hour to get himself ready for his new role, as the Sergeant and his Police chorus didn't come onto the stage until Act 2. Nevertheless, he found it very difficult to concentrate. The Opening Overture and the songs of Act 1 seemed to pass by so quickly. Judging from the audience's increasingly noisy applause, they were enjoying themselves. He suddenly felt a burden of responsibility not to let the rest of the cast down. Just before Act 2, Bridget came backstage to ensure all was well with the preparations. She was bubbling over with excitement and full of smiles and encouragement.

'You look so professional, Willie,' she said. 'Go out there and give it everything you've got. Remember, when you're singing, you're in charge and the music and words will live through your expression. Give them life. Give them meaning.'

He was suddenly aware that Gareth and Penelope were by his side. Both were flushed with the excitement of their performances during Act 1.

'The audience is great,' said Penelope.

'They're mighty,' agreed Gareth. 'Even if I went out there and sung a solo I'd get a standing ovation.' He grinned at Willie. This little quip from his closest friend finally dispelled his fears. He straightened up, lifted his head and threw back his shoulders. He felt his confidence return. Of course he could be the Sergeant of Police – and an outstanding one at that.

When his turn came to sing his first song, 'When the foeman bares his steel!', he felt his confidence increase. He strutted on the stage, felt the warmth of the stage lights on his face, and gave his words every atom of life and meaning. His connection with his audience was immediate and strong. They loved it and when he had finished their applause was deafening. Furthermore, as he went on stage to sing his remaining songs, the audience greeted him with applause even before he had started to sing.

Bridget was beside herself with delight. The production had been a phenomenal success, and at least one stage star had been born. After two curtain calls, the whole cast were equally delighted that their efforts had been so much appreciated, and Willie joined Giles and Sarah for the third call to receive a tumultuous reception. Willie felt almost intoxicated with this totally unexpected public appreciation. He briefly thought of taking up acting as a career. He would join the Royal Shakespeare Theatre Company and tour the world! But these dreams gradually subsided as he reluctantly came to accept the realities of life. His mind flashed back to the deaths of his parents and the sudden, unexpected importance of Hannibal Lucifer-Mortlock.

That night he cast his mind back over the day's events. It had been an unforgettable day, marred only by his encounter with Muriel Fancourt and her remarks about his parents. He decided to look up Hannibal Lucifer-Mortlock on the internet. He was surprised to find so many references, but found the most useful to be the following article from Wikipedia:

Hannibal Lucifer-Mortlock

Sir Hannibal Lucifer-Mortlock (born 10 September 1953, Kuching, Sarawak, Borneo) is a billionaire British oligarch. He was knighted in 2000 for services to the British mining industry. According to Forbes magazine, the Borneo-born oligarch is Britain's 5th richest man, with a fortune estimated at US$ 6.3 billion and the world's 135th richest person. He has accrued his wealth from mining, shipping and investments. Lucifer-Mortlock is married to the Swiss Olympic skiing coach, Corinne Haltameyer. He is a graduate of Surrenden Military School, Royal Military Academy Sandhurst and Cambridge University. He is the majority shareholder of Global Metals International, an Asian conglomerate, and is known in business circles as 'the hard man of Asia'. He spent three years in jail in Borneo's Batu Lintang prison in 1983 for various crimes including fraud, bribery and extortion, but these convictions were overturned in 1986 by the Supreme Court, which ruled that the case had been 'fabricated'.

Business Profile

His business interests include stakes in precious metals, iron ore, steel, natural gas and media companies. He is the sole owner of the Singapore-registered company Gilligan Holdings, described as a global conglomerate with major investments in mining, shipping technology, media and pharmaceuticals. He is the majority shareholder in Tutong Oil Plc, which owns oilfields in Borneo.

Other Activities

He is a major shareholder in Manchester United Football Club. On 5 September 2005, Lucifer-Mortlock paid more than US$52 million for an art collection owned by the late Sir Edward Elgar. He announced his intention to give all of the artwork to the British Government. However, there are reports that Lucifer-Mortlock has no intention of giving the collection to the

State and is instead keeping the collection for himself. He was the victim of an unsuccessful assassination attempt in 1998, which left him with a badly injured leg and a permanent limp. He now owns the Battle Abbey estate, near Sedlescombe, a Tudor mansion set in extensive grounds, a substantial part of which has been converted to a private zoo.

References
1. The Global Billionaires (6th Edition. Published 2007).
2. 'Hard man of Asia who made his fortune through mining', *Singaporean Guardian*, 11 November 2006.

Willie read the article three times in order to take it all in. Despite Muriel Fancourt's description of Lucifer-Mortlock being 'such a dear man', he could find no indication of it. In fact, the article pointed otherwise, and gave the distinct impression that Lucifer-Mortlock was a bully, fraudster, liar, extortionist, and a cheat, even if he was extremely wealthy and a Knight of the Realm. The title 'Sir Hannibal Lucifer-Mortlock' sounded far too grand for such a skunk, and it was a mouthful anyway. A name like 'The Lag' would be much more fitting.

In a way he was relieved to come to these conclusions. In the deepest recesses of his mind he had been comparing his father with The Lag, trying to understand why his mother had chosen his father. Perhaps she had seen The Lag's real character, a rather nasty character which Muriel Fancourt had not seen, or more likely, refused to acknowledge. Perhaps Muriel had even fancied The Lag herself! He wondered what his father and he had quarrelled over, and hoped that his father had given him a thrashing. Ah well, it was all in the past and probably didn't matter now.

Then again perhaps it did. Perhaps it was too early to make such an important decision.

4

BRITTANICA

Lieutenant Reginald Artefact Shrewdfellow was a very old boy of Surrenden, and had experienced a dismal military career. He had graduated into the Ordnance Corps and had been consistently overlooked for promotion. With apparently little ambition, he had drifted back to Surrenden as a Military History master, where, for no apparent reason, he appeared happy and content. As far as anyone could remember, he'd always been in charge of the School Museum, the Old Relics Park as it was known, and, not unnaturally, he had been given the nickname of 'Reggie the Relic' by some wag years ago.

Reggie was a tall, spare man with a long, thin face to match. He always appeared to be upright and severe, with crisply pressed uniforms, sparkling brown officer's shoes and a brown officer's cap, which looked as if it had just been starched and issued from the Quartermaster's store. He always wore a black and gold ring, on which a strange and ancient design had been inscribed. A little trifle he'd picked up at a local auction, he would explain light-heartedly, when it was being admired.

He was waiting in the hallway for Willie, Penelope and Gareth, outside the huge set of rooms that was the School's Museum.

'Come on now, you lot,' he greeted them warmly. 'Don't hang back. We've all got quite a bit of work to do, and I want you to have a good look round first. This Museum is a very important part of the school, and it's brimful of interesting odds and ends.' He led them into a huge reception room, dimly lit, enclosed with richly wood-panelled walls and extraordinarily high, white vaulted ceilings. Doorways punctured the reception room walls and led to side galleries. The walls were lined with enormous glass cabinets, filled with military memorabilia, photographs, weapons of all kinds, flags and ensigns, Army equipment, models of uniformed soldiers, horses and warships. The huge Surrenden windows at the far end of the exhibition gallery were partially obscured by an enormous, sand-coloured Crusader tank, and by three massive field guns – a howitzer, a mortar and a large-calibre artillery piece. Suspended from the ceiling were four fighter aircraft – a Sopwith Camel, a Spitfire, a Vampire jet and a Fleet Air Arm 'Stringbag'. Half the fuselage of a Douglas DC3 had been attached high up on one wall, its silver wing protruding over the display cabinets on the floor.

At the very end of the gallery, directly under the Surrenden windows, was a memorial statue, surrounded by a fan of flags, Regimental Colours and ensigns, their embroidered drapes held upright in polished brass floor stands. The memorial comprised a huge bronze globe of the world, over which the Greek Goddess of Peace, Ireni, had been floated, her arms outstretched protectively, and her hands holding out olive branches, so as to embrace all of Earth. Huge paintings and photographs of war heroes, and leaders, hung from the walls and window frames, and looked down at the memorial in silent homage.

Reggie led them to a dark wooden side-door, on which a notice had been painted in gold lettering:

CURATORS' WORKROOM AND STORE
MUSEUM WORKERS ONLY

'Here we are,' he said cheerfully. 'We'll start in the engine-room of the establishment. Come in and make yourself at home, and we might as well have a cup of tea, while I explain what your duties will be. By the way, in the Museum, you will henceforth be known as Assistant Curators, and will have full responsibility for helping me to run the place.'

The Curators' Workroom and Store were, in fact, two adjoining rooms. The first was more of a staff room than a workroom, with a heavy oaken, dining table set in the centre surrounded by six oak carver chairs. Against the walls were soft, comfy lounge chairs and two large settees. Three small cupboards were strategically placed beside the settees. A telephone sat on one. At the far end of the room was the door which led to the storeroom. A bright little blue and white kitchen with benches, cupboards, sink and electric water boiler had been installed on one side of the door, while six dark green, metal upright cupboards stood on the other. Beside the metal cupboards were five wooden shelves fixed to the wall, on which were stacked electrical control equipment for the Museum's lights, videos and sound systems for the main exhibition gallery, and four side galleries.

They all helped themselves to a cup of tea and a slice of Madeira cake which Reggie took out from the kitchen cupboard and settled themselves at the table.

'Now,' said Reggie. 'Do any of you know much about how museums operate?' They all shook their heads.

'Mmmm … I thought that might be the case,' he continued cheerfully. 'So I'd better start by telling you a bit about 'em. First of all, you should know that there are literally hundreds of types of museums in the world, from traditional mixed-community museums to specialised museums dealing with pretty much every subject on earth. Why, there's even a "Museum of Barbed Wire" and a "Museum of Washing Machines"! There are Regimental Museums and Science Centres, Natural History Museums, Aviation Museums, Marine Centres and Military Museums, to name just a few. I shouldn't be surprised if there was a "Museum of Shoelaces" or a "Museum of Rugby".' He paused and grinned at the thought of a 'Museum of Shoelaces'.

'Our Museum here at Surrenden, is a *Military Museum*, and covers all military history from Roman times to the Jet Age of today. Of course, we can't collect and exhibit everything. We've had to be selective. So we've specialised a bit towards Military Leaders, and the impact of Science and Technology. So here, you'll see an example of the first high-powered artillery, or an early aircraft, or some early protective armour.

We treat the Military Leaders section quite a bit differently, with photographs, models, paintings, uniforms, personal memorabilia and letters. We have a display case full of their officer swagger sticks and even have a Field Marshal's baton. We hold most of their uniforms in the store-room next door. I know that some people don't particularly like museums and find them boring, but that's not really the case at all. They are places of magic, knowledge and truth. They provide visible bench-marks in our human progress, and linkages to other worlds. Each exhibit in a museum has a story to tell, and if you just take the time to really, really study them, their story will burst out and talk to you, almost as if they are alive.'

Here, Reggie halted momentarily and looked at each one of them keenly, to see what effect his words were having. All three of his listeners were hanging on his every word. The telephone on the cupboard suddenly jangled.

'Drat,' exclaimed Reggie as he reached over to answer its call. He listened and spoke briefly to the caller, and, nodding his head, hung up the receiver. 'Look,' he said, 'I have to leave you for a few minutes, to discuss a matter with Captain Mastermynd. While I'm away, have a good look around and check out the exhibits and the uniforms. When I get back, we'll continue with your introduction and get a start on some cleaning and polishing.' He strode out of the Museum and shut the door behind him. The three Assistant Curators looked at each other for a few moments and then burst out laughing.

'Hello, Assistant Curator Jones, have you got enough cleaning rags?' enquired Penelope with mock politeness.

'Yes, thank you, Assistant Curator Pendragon,' replied Gareth politely, and with exaggerated severity. 'But I see you've missed a smear on that cabinet you were cleaning. You really will have to do a better job if you want to get paid.'

'Ah well,' said Willie in a disappointed voice. He was a bit down-hearted with the thought of the very mundane and trivial duties of a Museum Curator. 'I s'pose what we miss out on money we'll probably make up for in experience. Come on, let's have a look around.'

They ambled on down the walkway between the large glass display cabinets, until they came to a huge cabinet, with three sliding glass doors, containing long shelves holding dozens of officers' swagger sticks. Each stick lay on a lining of red velvet, and behind each stick was a photo or a small painting of the owner, with some biographical notes written below. Each swagger stick was different. There were long, thin ones; short, fat ones; ones with highly decorated knobs and ones with silver tips. Some were made from wood, and some were made from metal. There were carved ones and smooth ones. Some were very plain, and others were inset with precious stones, or richly decorated with silver and gold.

One stick, however, stood out from all the others. It was the Field Marshal's baton. It was in the centre of the highest shelf, and nestled in a heavily decorated silver cylinder, on a protective bed of royal blue silk.

Willie stood back and surveyed the entire glass cabinet of swagger sticks. As his eyes travelled along the line, he was astonished to feel faint vibrations emanating from the sticks as if each was seeking to capture his attention with subtle pulses and tremors. None seemed stronger, or more appealing, than the other. But when his eyes alighted on the Field Marshal's baton he was struck with a powerful attraction, which resonated to the very core of his soul. He examined the biographical notes below the photograph of the Field Marshal. It read:

FIELD MARSHAL WILLIAM JAMES SILK
1st VISCOUNT SILK OF SURRENDEN
KG, GCB, GCMG, CBE, DSO, MC
(6 September 1895 – 14 December 1968)
Commands: Fifteenth Army
Chief of the Imperial General Staff
Battles/Wars: World War 2
China Campaign, Middle East Campaign, Burma Campaign, Battle of Kuching
Malayan Campaign

Willie slid open the middle glass door of the display cabinet, and picked up the baton from its silver cylinder. It was made from solid silver, covered in red velvet with inserts of black onyx motifs, depicting the rearing, black Surrenden horse. One end was crowned with the Royal emblem of a golden lion and a white platinum unicorn. The other end was in the shape of the base of a Corinthian column, banded in gold and black onyx.

Then, in his mind, a clear image of the Field Marshal appeared. He was a tough-looking man in formal uniform, resplendent in gold lanyards, medals, red and gold sashes and stars. He was clean shaven, except for a tawny coloured moustache. He had dark brown eyes, and his face was tanned from the tropical sun. His khaki officer's hat was encircled with the red band of the General Staff, and its brim was heavily embroidered with gold. He seemed to be smiling and encouraging. Immediately Willie felt a strong bond with him. Here was a man of his word. One who could be trusted.

In the absence of his father, it would be good to have such a father-figure. Someone you could trust. Even if he was just a thought-image. He could be a sort of mentor; a point of reference one could go to for guidance when the going got tough.

He replaced the baton in its silver cylinder and noticed a gold ring nestled in the protective bed of blue silk. As if his hand was guided by an unseen force, he picked it up. It was almost as if it were meant to be. It was a very unusual ring. Heavy, chunky gold and obviously very old. Perhaps from Roman times or even Celtic. It was inlaid with a rearing black horse. A Surrenden horse.

Without thinking, he slipped the ring into the inside pocket of his school blazer, where it would be safe. It just seemed the right thing to do. He just hoped that it would not be missed from the display case, particularly by Reggie the Relic.

He looked about to see how the others were getting on. Both Penelope and Gareth were busy handling other swagger sticks. From the incredulous expressions on their faces, they were also experiencing thought-images.

'Hey, you two,' called out Gareth. 'This is really scary. I picked up this brass bullet case and an image of a Major-General suddenly appeared in my mind.' He flourished a brass shell case which had a silver badge of the Corps of Engineers fixed to its base. The tone of his voice became tinged with pride. 'His name is Major-General Archie Halliwell and he used to be the Engineer-in-Chief. Y'know … like … it would be great to have a mentor.' His face was flushed with eager pleasure. 'I've never had someone I could really share my thoughts with.'

'Me too,' said Penelope, her face glowing with excitement. 'I've got a mentor to share my thoughts with too. Her name's Amelia Smith and she used to be the Principal Army Matron. Her image just popped into my mind when I picked up this Nursing Corps badge. It's great, isn't it? Now I'll never really be alone again.' She put the Nursing Corps badge in her pocket and turned to William. 'Have you got a mentor, Willie?'

He nodded. 'Yes. I've got a Field Marshal Silk.' He fished the Surrenden ring from his pocket and held it up so the others could see. 'This is my link with him.'

'Wow, this is just the coolest place,' said Gareth as he slipped the Engineer-in-Chief's shell case into his pocket. He grinned. 'Don't think anyone's going to miss a tiny little bullet case, do you?'

'Or a Nursing Corps badge,' added Penelope.

'Or a small ring,' said Willie. 'Actually, we're not really "taking" them. We're just "borrowing" them for a short time.' They all laughed in agreement.

'Well, come on,' said Willie. 'We had better go and have a look through the Storeroom before Reggie gets back.'

They returned to the Workroom and opened the door to the Storeroom and were unprepared for what they found awaiting them. Immediately in front of them, and facing the door, were up to fifty fully clothed, but unarmed, models, exhibiting the battle dress and uniforms of their period. The models were fixed in various postures, as if snap-frozen in time. There were models of Roman Legionnaires, Cavaliers and Roundheads, World War 1 soldiers in gas-masks, soldiers in jungle uniform, in desert uniform, and white winter uniform. There were tank crews, naval gun crews and bomber crews, Hussars, bandsmen, and Highlanders in kilts. Hanging high up on one wall was a row of paratrooper models, their heads on their chests, and their limbs hanging limply like washed-out dolls.

Lining the walls behind the models were rows of military uniforms, each carefully hung on cushioned hangers, and covered in a clear plastic sheath. At the far end of the Storeroom was another door, painted in Sherwood Forest green and with a brass door handle. The air in the room was chilly and a little draughty, as if there was an open outside door somewhere, and a smell of pungent mothballs and disinfectant permeated the room.

'Crikey, its blimmin' cold in here,' said Gareth. 'Feels as if the central heating system's broken down.'

'You're right, it's absolutely freezing,' agreed Penelope, shivering a little and closing the door to the Workroom behind her.

'Oh, come on you two. It's like a refrigerator in here,' said Willie. He shivered. 'I've got goose-bumps. Let's leave this lot and see what's behind this other green door.'

'OK, OK, we're coming,' replied Gareth, grinning as both he and Penelope started to swing their arms, and march towards the door in time with one another. Willie grasped the brass door handle and swung the green door open. It moved effortlessly, as if it was simply a coloured sheet of light, without any substance or weight.

'Squad, halt!' ordered Penelope, and both she and Gareth came up to the door.

All three peered ahead into the space that the open green door now revealed. It was more of a tunnel than a room; a light, airy tunnel, with a white floor, and white walls, that formed an archway at the roof. At the far end of the tunnel, they could see another green door, also with a brass handle, and a black stallion motif. The three stepped forward into the tunnel and Penelope closed the door behind them. They walked slowly towards the door with the stallion motif. Their footfalls and movements made absolutely no sound. They suddenly felt a sense of weightlessness, as if they were in a vacuum. It was as if they were travelling inside a white thread in space without the force of gravity. They reached the other door. Gingerly, and very slowly, Willie reached up to grasp, and turn, the door handle. He carefully pushed the door open, and saw, to his relief, a good sized room, with dark wood panelling, and an old-fashioned light-bulb glowing from the ceiling. They all entered the room and closed the green door behind them.

'Wow, that was a strange tunnel,' said Penelope. 'It almost felt as if we were suspended in space for a while.'

'Well, this looks like a cleaner's room. So we must have come down to earth,' said Gareth, looking about the room, with its wooden table and chairs, and a row of buckets and mops lining one wall, alongside a large china sink. On the other wall was a wooden bench-top, with some cupboards and drawers built-in underneath. The room was spotlessly clean, with a highly polished wooden floor and a white, pressed tablecloth spread over one end of the table. In the centre of the tablecloth was a glass vase and a copy of a newspaper entitled *The Brittanican Times*.

Suddenly, the heavy wooden door to the room opened, and in walked the cleaning lady. She wore a crisp, long, black and white striped dress, with a matching cotton blouse with long sleeves, black shiny boots, and a bright red maid's hat. In her hands she carried a blue feather duster and a dustpan. She was happily singing a tune to herself as she came in, but she stopped short when she saw them.

'Hello, so there are three of you now,' she exclaimed. 'But you're not the normal two. You must be new here.' She paused and smiled at the three astonished visitors. 'My name is Gladys. How do you do, Miss?' she beamed, extending her hand to Penelope. 'Welcome to Brittanica. I'm the Head of the Cleaning Staff here at the Foreign Office, Whitehall.'

'Thank you, thank you very much,' gasped Penelope, scarcely

able to comprehend this strange turn of events. 'These are my two friends, Willie and Gareth,' she continued, gesturing towards the boys. 'My name is Penelope.'

'Ah, lovely name, Penelope. Don't often hear that name these days. More's the pity. And as for Willie and Gareth, well, they must be two of my most favourite names. Good solid Brittanican names, they be. How do you do, sirs?'

'Er … hem, fine thank you, Gladys,' replied Willie, rather hesitantly, his mind still numb from surprise. Gareth remained silent and open-mouthed in disbelief, but shook hands with Gladys.

Penelope, who had recovered a little of her composure, enquired, 'You said you were Head of the Cleaning Staff here, Gladys. Do you have a big staff?'

'Not as big as we need, Miss. Whitehall is quite a large place to keep clean, with all its offices and coal heaters. It's a real struggle to get the staff to keep things to a high standard. They always want to cut corners and are happy with second best. And the secretaries don't help much, either. They're such an untidy lot, with all their papers. That is, of course, all except Mr Woodhouse. He's so organised and tidy.' Here she paused.

'Oh … of course. How silly of me. You're new here, so you haven't met Mr Woodhouse yet. The other two always went to see him after they arrived. Follow me and I'll take you down to his office.'

She turned to walk down the corridor. The three started to follow her, but just before he left the room, Willie quickly flipped open *The Brittanican Times* newspaper on the table. It was dated 31 March 1902.

'No way,' he muttered to himself, before hurrying to catch up with the others. They proceeded down a dimly lit, painted and panelled corridor, from which office doors led to other rooms. Gladys gave a running commentary pointing to this door and that as they progressed.

'This office is used by the Deputy Assistant Secretaries. They're such an untidy lot. This room is used by the Mail Sorting staff. You'd never believe the mess they make. And here's the kitchen and Secretaries' Dining Room. This office is used by the Deputy Assistant Secretary for African Affairs. He has spears on his wall instead of pictures, and you've never seen so many drums all over his floor. Here's the typing pool. They've got the latest Remington machines from Americana. This office is used by the Deputy

Assistant Secretary for Far Eastern Affairs. He's such a nice person, you know, but he's still trying to use chopsticks when he eats his lunch in the Staff Room. His floor is just covered in Ming vases, and they're so hard to keep clean. Now here's the office of the Deputy Assistant Secretary for Oceania. Lord only knows where Oceania is, but he has painted masks, coconut shields and sharks' tooth necklaces hanging on his walls. Ah, here we are. This is Mr Woodhouse's office.'

She pointed to a richly polished wooden office door, on which was painted in gold lettering:

Sir Cecil Primrose Woodhouse
Assistant Foreign Secretary

Gladys knocked on the door, and a male voice said 'Enter.' They all followed Gladys into the office.

'Some visitors for you, Mr Woodhouse. They're from my Cleaning Room.'

The trio stared in disbelief. The very epitome of what one would imagine a senior public servant of the Foreign Office to be, Woodhouse was extremely well groomed, dapper in his dark grey wool morning coat, grey silk waistcoat, white stand collar, blue striped tie and grey striped trousers. He was rather tall and elegant. Distinguished and precise, he still had an air of individuality with his bright blue eyes, rimless glasses and long stemmed meerschaum pipe. A top hat and furled umbrella hung from the hat-stand beside the door. He reminded Willie of Sir Eyre.

'Well, well,' he said, smiling and extending his hand. 'This is a very pleasant surprise indeed. My name is Woodhouse, Cecil Woodhouse.'

'Very pleased to meet you,' said Willie, 'I'm McBride, Willie McBride, and these are my two friends, Penelope Pendragon and Gareth Jones. We've been exploring and somehow seem to have found our way here.'

'I'm very pleased you did,' replied Sir Cecil. He turned to Gladys and said, 'Could you ask my secretary to bring in some tea and cakes, please, Gladys?'

'Of course, Mr Woodhouse,' replied Gladys, and she left the room, closing the door behind her.

Sir Cecil then turned back to the three, and gestured towards some beautiful chairs, upholstered in dark green, buttoned-down leather. They settled themselves down as Sir Cecil continued. 'You said that you were exploring. Whereabouts were you?'

Penelope had now gained her confidence, and was dealing far better than the boys with the strange circumstances they now found themselves in. 'We were in the Surrenden Military School Museum, where we're Assistant Curators. We noticed a green door at the end of the Storeroom, which led to a white corridor, which in turn led to another green door to your place here.'

'Ah yes, of course. Surrenden Military School. I have heard quite a lot about it, but have never been able to visit. I understand it's a very good school. Very strong on Science and Technology, I believe.' Sir Cecil looked over his glasses at Willie.

'You mentioned that your name was Willie McBride,' he said. 'You wouldn't happen to know a Colonel Hugh and Mrs Sally McBride, would you?'

Willie gasped in astonishment. This was bizarre! He was stunned. How in God's name could Sir Cecil know of his father and mother? He quickly gathered his wits about him. 'Yes, of course. They're my parents,' he answered. 'How do you know of them?'

Sir Cecil ignored his question. 'We haven't seen them for some time now. How are they?'

Willie looked directly at Sir Cecil, and in a level voice said, 'They're missing, presumed dead. They were on a mission for our Foreign and Commonwealth Office on Labuan Island. They were exploring an old coal mine there, when apparently lightning from an electrical storm ignited methane gas in the mine, and caused an enormous explosion. Their bodies were never found, but it's not thought that they survived.'

Sir Cecil was visibly moved and shaken at Willie's reply.

'Oh, my poor boy. What a dreadful thing to happen.' He placed his hand on Willie's arm. 'That's appalling news. Simply appalling. This has just confirmed our worst fears. They will be greatly missed.'

'How do you know of them?' repeated Willie.

Sir Cecil paused for a moment, as he pondered the implications of Willie's news. 'Your parents were such fine people. They have been our close friends for many, many years, ever since they were attending Surrenden Military School. They too, were closely connected to the School's Museum and frequently came to visit us through the Time Thread tunnel. Over the years we grew to trust one another. Although they came from a different world than ours – a more advanced world, I believe – they were kind and tolerant of us. As I understand it, our way of life and present stage of development was not too dissimilar to your own world and experience. In so many ways, our worlds seemed to be twin images of one another.'

There was a knock on the door, and a young clerk entered holding a silver tray, on which there were china cups and saucers, teapot, and a large plate of Chelsea buns and tea cakes. She placed the tray on the table saying, 'There you are, sir. I've just made the tea.'

'Ah, thank you, Doris,' said Sir Cecil, as she withdrew from the room. Then, turning to the three, he gestured invitingly, 'Please help yourselves. By the way, please call me Woody. Most other folk do.'

'Thank you very much,' the three chorused and tucked into the tea and cakes.

Woody continued with his explanation of the relationship Brittanica had with Willie's parents. 'Your father and mother seemed to understand our problems, and were often instrumental in helping us to find solutions. They were particularly good at assisting us to progress our developments in science and technology. They undertook a variety of missions, often quite dangerous missions on our behalf.' Woody paused for a moment, and looking very keenly at Willie said quietly, 'In fact, they were the best secret agents Brittanica ever had.'

Secret agents for Brittanica! Willie could scarcely believe his ears. Penelope and Gareth gasped as they too struggled to comprehend the close nature of Willie's parents with this parallel world. Woody saw their confusion and smiled.

'You're finding all this a little hard to believe, aren't you? Let me tell you, so did we at first. And to be perfectly honest we're still not sure how it all happens. When your parents tumbled in on us through the back wall of the cleaner's room we were astonished. After making their acquaintance they returned to their world the way they came. Through the back wall of the cleaner's room. Your parents continued to visit us fairly regularly and together we began to form a theory of what was happening. It seems that our Edwardian World is a twin world to your Modern World. However, our Edwardian World is some years behind yours. The two worlds are connected by a Time Thread tunnel, which permits Modern World humans to travel through it, but, alas, not we inhabitants of our Edwardian World. Nevertheless, our two worlds are, apparently, extremely similar in almost all respects.'

'Wow,' exclaimed Gareth, 'that's unreal! That's why we felt so funny when we went through that tunnel!'

'Yes, it is unreal,' nodded Woody, 'but the arrangement certainly gave Brittanica a huge advantage as Willie's parents brought us guidance in our science and technology developments.' He turned to face the three of them. 'We Brittanicans share the sad loss of your parents, Willie. But I would like to think that the affection and generosity shown by them to us would be continued by yourself and your two friends. Would the three of you give favourable consideration to following Willie's parents' footsteps and becoming secret agents for Brittanica?'

The three were stunned at the invitation, and they stared at each other while they came to grips with the situation. Penelope and Gareth looked towards Willie for some sign of what they should do. After all, it was **his** parents who were previously involved, and, therefore it was primarily his decision to make. Willie's mind was in a whirl as he struggled to create order in a chaos of conflicting thoughts and emotions.

There was the strong possibility that if he did become a secret agent for Brittanica he might tumble on a clue as to what actually happened to his parents. Perhaps they might be somewhere safe in this twin Edwardian World!

He looked at Penelope and Gareth, and sensed that they were waiting for a decision from him. Their eyes asked the question and he acknowledged with a smile and a nod. Both Penelope and Gareth nodded their heads in reply and started to grin broadly. Willie turned to Woody.

'Yes, Woody,' he replied. 'We'd like to become secret agents for Brittanica but it would have to be with two conditions. The first is that we are given full briefings, and support for each mission. The second is that we only undertake missions as a team.'

'Agreed!' responded Woody. He moved quickly to a mahogany cabinet behind his desk and brought out a bottle of Perrier and four crystal glasses. As he poured the mineral water into the glasses he said, 'I'm so pleased that you are willing to follow your parents' footsteps. Together with Penelope and Gareth, you will make a very formidable team I'm sure. Let's drink a toast to our successful future.'

He raised his glass, 'To the success of Surrenden and Brittanica!' They raised their glasses and drank to the toast.

'Now,' exclaimed Woody, 'I'd better issue you with your codebooks, so we can keep in touch without prying eyes discovering our plans.' He rummaged around in a steel safe in the wall to bring out a grey coloured, cardboard-covered codebook containing twenty sheets of paper.

'Here's one for your group,' he said. 'We use the One Time Pad code in the Foreign Office. It's very simple to use, but here is a sheet of paper with directions of how to operate the system. Simply put, I have a master copy here, and I have given you an exact copy of my master. Each sheet within the pad is separately lettered, and can only be used once. After it is used it must be destroyed. When I want to contact you, I'll write a letter in code and post it through the letter box opening in the green door at the back of Gladys's cleaner's room. You do the same when you wish to contact me.'

'This code looks pretty simple, but I can see why it would be almost impossible to crack,' mused Gareth, scanning through the codebook.

'Well, we'll have lots of time to study it up later,' said Willie, suddenly mindful at the mention of the green doors of the time that they had been away from the museum. 'Thank you, Woody, for your explanation of things. But I think that the three of us had better return to Surrenden now and come back to see you at a later date.'

'Yes, of course,' agreed Woody. 'Follow me and I will show you back to our Gladys's room.' He guided them back through the corridors to the cleaner's room, ushered them in, and said his goodbyes. 'I have to leave the room now,' he said, 'otherwise the green door won't open.' With that, he gave them a cheerful wave a slight bow and closed the door.

The three looked at each other and around the room, their minds still reluctant to comprehend the magic of the moment. 'Ah well, we'd better get back to the museum as quickly as we can,' Willie said a little urgently, 'before Reggie discovers that his Assistant Curators are AWOL!' They quickly opened the green door, scampered through the Time Thread into the Curators' Workroom, closed the door and sat down at the table. Their cups of tea were still warm.

'It's almost as if we didn't leave,' gasped Penelope, as she closed the green door.

'Unbelievable,' muttered Gareth, shaking his head. Suddenly the door to the main museum gallery opened and in strode Reggie the Relic.

'Sorry about that,' he said cheerfully, 'but it was a matter that couldn't wait. Now, I hope you have made good use of the last few minutes and had at least a bit of a look around. This is a pretty big museum, you know, and there's a great deal to see.' As he said this, Reggie looked at Willie with studied casualness.

'Yes, sir,' replied Willie, choosing his words carefully. 'We were able to see a few things we hadn't seen before in the Storeroom.'

Reggie looked intently at Willie and smiled broadly. He nodded contentedly at Willie's answer as if a huge burden had been lifted from his shoulders.

'That's fine, then. You'll all have a better appreciation of what this Museum has to offer. Perhaps I should mention here, Mr McBride, how sorry I was to hear of your parents' deaths. They were frequent visitors to the Museum and highly respected by all who knew them. I think they were two wonderful people who were able to make the most out of their visits to the Museum.' He does know something, thought Willie. In fact, he probably knows everything.

'Thank you, sir,' he replied, again choosing his words with great care. 'I'm sure that we, too, will be able to make good use of the Museum, and grow to love it as my parents obviously did.' Reggie continued to smile and nodded his head as if to signify that he understood the real meaning of Willie's reply.

'Excellent, excellent,' exclaimed Reggie. He looked at his watch. 'Good Heavens, is that the time? Well, we haven't got time for me to continue with your briefing. But, I'll issue a Museum key to each of you now so that you can come up here in your spare time and continue to look around. Perhaps you could also start dusting the display cabinets! Let's meet again next week and we will finish our briefing then.'

The three returned to the Company Common Room. They were exhilarated with their experiences, and filled with anticipation as to what missions they may be asked to undertake on behalf of Brittanica.

But it was Penelope who said what was uppermost in their minds at that time.

'OK, you two brain-boxes. If we accept that we have just visited a twin world, how is it that we can travel to it? We know we have the green door in the Storeroom which opens to the Time Thread, and that leads to Gladys's room in Whitehall. But is that the only connection?'

'Wormholes,' exclaimed Gareth with conviction. 'Wormholes are the only way it can happen. My science teacher used to study time travel and he'd talk for hours about "warped space-time", or some stuff like that. It's pretty heavy duty maths. Anyway, he'd talk about wormholes being like hollow tunnels between different worlds.'

'Doesn't sound very scientific,' said Penelope dubiously.

'Let's look it up on the internet then,' suggested Willie. He scooted up to his room and returned with his laptop. He felt confident that there would be some reference on wormholes. Anyway, he was convinced that they had just visited a twin world and he wasn't about to let his conviction perish in a deluge of doubts about wormholes.

But there *were* references to wormholes. In fact, there were even references to different types of wormholes. They quickly scanned the wording, not really understanding the science or the meaning of the words used, but simply looking for confirmation that the idea of wormholes was generally accepted by the scientific community.

'Look there,' said Willie, pointing to the wording. 'See. It says – *"Wormholes are believed to be part of space-time foam. There are two main types of wormholes: Lorentzian wormholes and Euclidean wormholes. Lorentzian wormholes are mainly studied in general relativity and semi-classical gravity, while Euclidean wormholes are studied in particle physics. Transversable wormholes are a special kind of Lorentzian wormhole which would allow a human to travel from one side of the wormhole to the other."* So it seems they do exist. Well … at least in theory. But who knows how many there are connecting our twin worlds? Doesn't seem right that there would only be one, does it?'

'Nah. There must be many more than one,' affirmed Gareth. 'I reckon there must be hundreds, even thousands, p'raps. All you've got to do is find the door.'

But Penelope was not going to be convinced so easily.

'So where can you find these doors?' she asked. 'We've only come across one in the Museum and that's well hidden.'

Both boys looked blankly at one another.

'I dunno,' said Gareth finally. 'P'raps the wormholes run along fractures in the time-space warp and the doorways just appear in things like caves and basements … and stuff.' His voice tailed off lamely. Then his face brightened up suddenly. 'Course there's no reason that the wormholes could stay like they are for ever and ever. They could change with a new fracture and the doors could appear somewhere else, couldn't they?' He paused and grinned at the other two.

'You could be right,' agreed Willie. 'I also reckon that when a wormhole door's discovered it becomes a really important discovery and people mark them with things like temples. Do you remember Corporal Jenkins telling us about the Druids and the legend that the Museum's a gateway to other worlds?'

The other two nodded. For the time being, and in the absence of any other explanation, they accepted that they had travelled through a space-time wormhole to Brittanica.

'OK then. But we will have to keep our mouths shut about being secret agents,' cautioned Penelope.

'And about everything else,' Gareth chipped in. 'Otherwise people will think we've gone barmy!'

'That's right,' agreed Willie. 'But we'd better keep a sharp eye out for any messages from Woody, and check our mailbox very regularly. One of us will have to go to the Museum curator's storeroom each day to check it out for letters.' They made out a duty roster starting that very day, for one of them to visit the storeroom.

Willie returned to his room and turned his attention to his next week's school programme and timetable. He was surprised to find that the full week had been given over to military training at the Combat Wing. It was probably just more foot drill, kit inspections and fitness training on the obstacle course, he thought.

But nothing could be further from the truth and he was unprepared for the unusual training that lay in store.

5

SURVIVAL BULLRING

Major Seymour Spartacus De Roche was the ideal man to head up the School's Combat Wing. Hard, tough and uncompromising, he had served with the Wessex Parachute Division in several hot spots around the world. It was not for nothing that his nickname was 'Rocky'. He revelled in physical challenges and was a recognised triathlon champion. He was a graduate of the Royal Military Academy Sandhurst, and it was common knowledge that he was hoping to gain selection for the Joint Services Staff College, Camberley, to continue his hitherto brilliant military career.

He stood in front of the class of new entrants, his arms folded over his chest and his face stern, as he surveyed the 21 pale and anxious faces of the students, including those of Willie, Penelope, and Gareth. He was tall and athletic. His bronzed face was topped with a Number 1 haircut. Dressed in his camouflage field uniform he looked as formidable as a cobra.

'This world's a tough place,' stated Rocky flatly. 'Nobody owes you a living. But everybody wants results. Good results. It's my job to make sure you deliver those results, and are successful. No matter how many difficulties you have to beat, or obstacles you have to hurdle. However, success isn't handed to you on a plate. You have to work hard for it and while you're under my direction you WILL work hard. No "Ifs" or "Buts". The main elements of success are 1% inspiration and 99% perspiration. I'll leave others to tell you about the secrets of "inspiration". I'll just concentrate on the "perspiration" part. Tonight you will be deployed on a survival exercise, "Exercise Chicken Feed", so if you want to survive you'd better pay attention to today's activities.' If he didn't have his students' attention when he started, Rocky certainly had it now.

Willie felt his heart beat faster in anticipation, with the sudden realisation that he knew nothing about surviving in the countryside. Not only that, but he had no idea about how to light a fire. He couldn't cook, let alone catch any food to eat. Except for spending a night in a tent on Uncle Peter's back lawn, he had never spent a night outdoors. He couldn't read a map, and his knowledge of First Aid extended only to putting a sticking plaster on a cut finger.

He quickly glanced around at the faces of the other students. Except for Gareth, he could see at once that they, also, were in shock at Rocky's announcement. Gareth seemed to be fairly relaxed at the prospect of the exercise, and Willie began to realise just how lucky he was to have a friend with so many practical skills. Penelope also didn't seem to be overly fussed. Perhaps, he thought, she might have already discovered how to survive off the land from the internet.

Rocky continued. 'Whatever you do in life, you should remember the Six Ps. The Six Ps stand for *"Prior Preparations Prevent Pathetically Poor Performance"*. And so, to prevent pathetically poor performance, you are going to spend the rest of today making your preparations for "Exercise Chicken Feed".'

He gestured to the back of the classroom, where some staff members were waiting. 'You'll spend an hour of training at each of seven stands, set out in a Bullring circle. There will be a staff member at each stand to instruct you in selected aspects of survival skills, as follows:

Stand 1 – Simple Map-reading. Lieutenant La Dolce.

Stand 2 – Survival Shelters Made Easy. Company Sergeant-Major Larkin.

Stand 3 – First Aid Without Pain. Matron Sweetingham.

Stand 4 – Trapping and Fishing for Food. Company Sergeant-Major Truscott.

Stand 5 – Fires and Field Cooking for Dummies. Warrant Officer Class 2 Rangitira.

Stand 6 – Keeping Fit and WarmStaff. Sergeant Hardman.

Stand 7 – Clever Orienteering to Arrive Safely. Company Sergeant-Major Brain.

As soon as your group has finished your hour's tuition at one stand, you will move clockwise to the next stand within the Bullring, until you have completed all seven stands.'

He split the class into seven groups and Willie found himself forming Group 6 with Gareth and Penelope. They started the day's training at Stand 6 with Staff Sergeant Skippy Hardman, the Physical Training Instructor. Staff Sergeant Hardman, nicknamed 'Ozzie', was on secondment from the Tasmanian Regiment of the Australian Army. He was small, gingery, and freckled like a bouncy ball with chicken pox.

He greeted Willie's group with a cheerful grin. 'G'day, Group 6,' he said, his Australian nasal accent sounding like a buzz saw.

'Let's start with 20 press-ups to get your blood moving and your brain focused.'

Obediently, Willie, Penelope and Gareth completed their 20 press-ups, and, panting from their exertions, sat on the ground and listened to Ozzie. He explained to them about the importance of keeping fit at all times, how it was vital to keep warm to survive, to wear warm clothing, comfortable footwear, and a woollen hat to retain heat and a good blood flow to the head. He showed them how to use a light, reflective survival blanket, and how important it was to shelter from chilling winds, which could lower their body temperatures to dangerous levels. He finished off by demonstrating the techniques involved in a Fireman's Lift.

'You could carry an elephant for miles using the Fireman's Lift,' claimed Ozzie, juggling Willie across his shoulders. 'I'm not hurting you, am I, Mr McBride?'

'No Staff, not at all,' replied Willie, gritting his teeth as Ozzie's sharp shoulder dug into his groin.

'There you are then,' smiled Ozzie, looking at Gareth and Penelope. 'It's as easy as pie, and very comfortable for the person being carried. This is important, if the person you're carrying is wounded.' After a few minutes of practising carrying each other using a Fireman's Lift, Ozzie pointed to a high ridge running just behind the school to Stand 7 being run by Company Sergeant-Major Zacharias Brain.

'Make your way as best you can to the next stand up there,' he said, grinning. 'Stand 7 is about 200 yards away up that steep, rocky slope.'

They could see Sergeant-Major Brain in the distance and moved directly towards him, slipping and sliding on the loose rocks as they pulled themselves, puffing and panting, up the difficult slope. The Sergeant-Major watched with amusement. He was a tall, thin man, who stood well over six foot five inches in his socks. 'Stretch' was a good-humoured career soldier, who had seen action in Bosnia and the Middle East.

'Welcome to Group 6,' he boomed, as they neared his Stand. 'You must be the 'Direct Action Group!'

'Why ... gasp ... do you say that ... gasp ... Sergeant-Major?' panted Willie, as they arrived at the Stand, struggling for breath from their exertions.

'Well, look about you,' replied Stretch, motioning with his arm. 'There's a gentle path over here that leads down the ridge, through that copse and around to the back of Stand 6. You could have got here in half the time, and with half the effort, if you'd taken a few moments to study the ground.' They looked around while recovering their breath. Stretch was right. There WAS a well-formed, gentle track which led from the back of Stand 6.

'You see,' continued Stretch, 'most people are inherently lazy. They always like to take the easy way if they can. So it is with moving around the countryside. Look at the countryside as if you were a road-builder. You'd avoid difficult areas such as rivers, streams, marshes and rocky slopes if you could. You'd come up on the high ground to get long, easy stretches. This often means NOT going directly from point to point, but taking a longer route to avoid obstacles.'

Stretch then talked to them about route planning, gauging the slope of hills, estimating distances in different light, how to cross streams and rivers safely, and direction finding using the sun and a watch, as well as a prismatic compass. 'Take a bearing on Classroom 3 down there, just to the right of the trees,' ordered Stretch, pointing to the brick building. 'What reading do you get and how far do you think it is from our present position?' They all pointed their compasses at the classroom and estimated its distance.

'I make it on a bearing of 278 degrees and the distance about 300 yards, Sergeant-Major,' volunteered Gareth.

'Yes,' affirmed Stretch. 'That's pretty close. So now I want you to keep your eyes on your compass, and walk on the bearing of 278 degrees counting the number of paces you take. You'll then have a good idea of how the intervening ground affects your direction and the length of your pace. When you get to the classroom, you'll find Lieutenant La Dolce there. She'll show you how to navigate around

the county with great precision using mainly signs and symbols.'
He smiled encouragingly. 'Best of luck for tonight's survival
exercise!' They set off as Stretch instructed and were surprised to
find how easy it was to drift off course and how many paces they
had to walk to reach the classroom.

'I seem to have a left-hand bias,' exclaimed Penelope. 'And my
paces are as small as granny-steps.'

'Just as well you don't play golf then,' commented Gareth,
chuckling. 'Otherwise you'd be in the rough. My Auntie Dinnie
plays golf, and she hooks the golf ball to the left all the time. She
spends a lot of time in the "shrubbery". I tried to design a microchip
for her golf ball once, which sent out a radio wave when she
switched on a homing device. It worked all right, but her new golf
ball was the size of a melon!'

Lieutenant Cynthia Enigma La Dolce, or 'Squiggles' as the
students called her, was waiting for them in Classroom 3.

'Good morning, Group 6,' welcomed Squiggles, adding slyly.
'You've already found your way here so I presume you already
know how to read a map.'

'Not really, Miss La Dolce,' admitted Penelope. 'I generally get
lost when I try to use a map.'

'Ah,' said Squiggles, wagging her finger in mock reproof.
'Never admit to being lost otherwise your team will lose
confidence in you. You're never "lost". Just "misplaced". Then
you can seek "confirmation of your position" from others. Be
inclusive. Make adjustments to your positioning and INCREASE
their confidence in you!' She pointed to five aerial photos spread
out on some tables.

'These are five air photos of our School taken at different
heights and at different times of the day. Have a look at them and
see if you can point out the clock-tower building to me.'

They gathered around the air photos and examined them closely.
One photo must have been taken from just a few hundred feet
above the School, because even the roof guttering was clearly
visible. The others were taken from greater heights and included
increasing areas of the surrounding countryside.

'Has everybody identified the clock-tower building?'

They nodded and pointed out the building on each air photo.

'OK, now show me the road from the School to Pluckley Village
and Pluckley Station, the railway line from London, the nearby

town of Ashford, the M20 motorway between Ashford and Folkestone on the coast, and along the coast to the nearest large town of Dover.'

Again they nodded and quickly pointed out the various features on the air photographs. They were gaining confidence now and could pick out other recognisable features on the Kentish landscape.

'Right. Well done, team,' said Squiggles. She then pointed to five maps which were spread out on tables on the other side of the room.

'Let's do exactly the same with these maps. There's one map there where you can see the outline of the clock-tower building. See if you can find it.' They gathered round the maps and examined the sign detail, and the Symbols Key at the bottom left-hand corner.

'It's just like a code,' exclaimed Gareth, with considerable satisfaction. 'Look, Penelope. There's the clock-tower building in these other maps.'

'Oh, yes,' replied Penelope. 'Then it merges with the other School buildings on the other maps, until, on this last one, it just shows as a written note, "Surrenden Military School".'

'Well done, Penelope. You've got it,' applauded Squiggles. 'Now, let's see what other information we can extract.' She then told them about contour lines and spot heights. She showed them how to visualise the shape of the landscape; how the waterways started high up on the hills, and merged into rivers, eventually flowing out to sea. Where they were most likely to find marshy ground, bridges, towns, ports and railways. Finally, she showed them how to refer to the location of features using grid-lines and grid references.

'I'm going to give you a grid reference now,' said Squiggles, 'which is the location of your next stand on Survival Shelters. See if you can find it on the map and then you can move out to it. Good luck on your exercise tonight and try not to get misplaced!' They examined the map. The grid reference worked out that the next stand was in an adjacent wood about 350 yards away.

Company Sergeant-Major Lawrence Larkin, who was taking Stand 2, was waiting for them, reading a book, and stretched out on a thick mattress of shrub branches and bunches of grass. About three feet above his body was a thick mantle of tree branches and leaves, tied together with reeds, to form a substantial roof. Sergeant-Major Larkin, or 'Larry' as he was nicknamed, had seen active service in the Malaysian jungles, where he had been on long-range reconnaissance patrols, and working with the fierce pygmy people in the mountains. Although Larry would never talk about it, it was rumoured that he had become a 'blood brother' to a pygmy tribe who were head hunters. Whatever his relationship was with these barbarous warriors, Larry still had his head on his shoulders. However, he had adopted a number of their habits. He would sometimes 'hunker down' on the side of the parade-ground, or pick his teeth with a twig, much to the annoyance of Regimental Sergeant-Major Lord. When on field exercises, Larry would sometimes carry a Ghurka 'kukri' knife. A present, he said, from a Ghurka soldier whose life he had saved.

Larry was not a 'parade-ground' soldier. He was happiest when he was out in the field. He always moved carefully and silently like a cat, his eyes and ears tuned to the slightest hint of danger. As the trio arrived at the Stand he sat them down in the shelter and showed them how it was made.

Keep yourself off the ground, he advised. If possible, make up a rough hammock for sleeping, suspending it between a couple of trees. 'Keep your roof low, and use a plastic sheet if you have one. Always build your cooking fire away from your shelter, otherwise you can land up like a smoked fish. Make sure you have a nice clear area for your shelter and try to get shelter from the chill night winds.'

Finally, he pointed to a thin branch he had placed across a path through the woods from which he had suspended a couple of empty baked bean cans. 'Try to get a little bit of early warning on the approach of a possible enemy,' he cautioned. 'Put a little booby trap, like those rattle-cans, on the most likely approaches to give yourself a few vital seconds to react.' A ghost of a grim smile flittered across his face. 'Who knows? It might just save your scalp in the future! You can move to the next Stand now over in the School Hospital, but watch out for booby traps!'

Matron Sweetingham was expecting them when they arrived in the School Hospital. She greeted them with a cheery smile. Although she wore the traditional starched white nursing uniform, cap and red cape of a Hospital Matron, she was not at all stern and bossy. She had seen service in a Field Hospital in the Falklands and later in a Field Hospital in Kuwait. She was a gentle, kind and compassionate woman who was much loved by everyone who knew her. Her tender nature was matched by her nickname, 'Sweetie'. Not only was she good at surgery, but she also had a comprehensive knowledge of First Aid in the field.

As the trio entered the Hospital she pointed to a male soldier in a ripped camouflage uniform lying on the floor, seemingly unconscious. Blood seeped from his arm and leg, and his face was chalky white.

'Do what you can for him, will you,' she said, 'while I get some dressings.' And with that she walked out of the room. The injured soldier groaned in pain. They all stared at each other in alarm but it was Penelope who moved instinctively to the casualty.

'Let's see what we've got here,' she said with some authority, dropping to her knees to examine the casualty. As she started her examination, she grinned. She recognised the patient as Junior Under Officer James Murphy. He moved his head slightly and winked at her.

'The first procedure we should remember is ABC – Airways, Breathing and Circulation. Hmm … Airways seem clear. His breathing's shallow and he's obviously in shock. He's got two bad gunshot wounds to his right arm and leg which are bleeding badly. His arm is possibly broken. Best thing we can do now is to put a field dressing on his wounds, immobilise his broken arm, keep him warm and get him to a Dressing Station.' She got to her feet and reached for the First Aid kit as Sweetie re-entered the room. Willie and Gareth were both astonished at Penelope's swift and purposeful actions.

'How d'yer know all of that?' Willie asked.

'Learnt it as a St John Ambulance cadet in Jersey,' chuckled Penelope. 'I joined up with a friend as an after-school activity. I never thought I'd have an opportunity to put my training to the test like this though.'

'Congratulations, Miss Pendragon. You did very well indeed,' said Sweetie. She pointed to some medical charts and diagrams hanging on the wall, and some First Aid equipment laid out on a table. 'We haven't got much time to cover such a large subject as First Aid. But we'll cover some main areas now and you'll complete your First Aid Certificate before the end of this term.' She then instructed them about the body's blood circulation and the locations of 'pressure points', where the blood supply could be effectively cut off to permit treatment of wounds.

'I bet that's what Lofty Bloomfield used when he was wrestling,' volunteered Gareth.

'What do you mean?' asked Sweetie.

'Well,' explained Gareth, 'the Welsh heavyweight wrestling champion, Lofty Bloomfield, used to win a lot of his matches by applying what he called a "Sleepy Hold". Lofty used to say the hold was a normal head-lock, but I bet it was actually on one of his opponent's pressure points like that carotid pressure point that stops the blood flow to the brain.'

'More likely on his opponent's windpipe, Mr Jones,' replied Sweetie, a little icily. 'Probably a head-lock that slipped into a neck-lock, I'd say. Anyway, we're talking about helping people now, not disabling them.' Willie and Gareth looked quickly at each other and grinned. Sweetie pointed to the First Aid equipment on the table.

'You can also save lives with these Army wound dressings. These are non-adherent wound dressings which have been sterilised by gamma radiation. They should be put straight onto the wound after it has been washed with this sodium chloride solution.' After they had opened some wound dressings, and practised applying them to imaginary wounds to their arms and legs, Sweetie pointed out of the Hospital window to a wooded area on Surrenden Stream about 400 yards away.

'Your next stand on "Trapping and Fishing for Food" is over there. You can go over there now, but don't go putting a "Sleepy Hold" on Sergeant-Major Truscott, Mr Jones!' They all laughed, and the trio set off to the next stand.

'Trusty' Truscott was a tough, weather-beaten Irish countryman, who had spent his early years in the back-blocks of Australia, as a Government hunter in pest eradication programmes fighting plagues of rabbits and possums.

'They're nasty little blighters,' he would say about possums. 'They might look nice and cuddly, but I've seen 'em rip a dog to shreds with their sharp claws.'

Trusty loved dogs, and adored his brindle brown Staffordshire terrier called 'Nipper'. Nipper loyally followed his master whenever, and wherever, he could. He tolerated the students and their playful antics with him, as would a household dog with children. He even tolerated those students who used him like a bowling ball, to bowl him along the length of the highly polished vinyl corridor floors on his chubby backside.

Nipper welcomed them with a low growl and a wagging of his

tail. He seemed to be quite fond of Willie, who reached into his pocket and slipped him some choc drops, while giving him a knowing pat on the head.

'Ah, I wondered why Nipper was looking so well fed,' exclaimed Trusty, smiling broadly as he emerged from the wood. 'He seems to like you, Mr McBride.'

'Yes, we've met before. We get on pretty well, Sergeant-Major,' replied Willie. 'But I'm still not sure if it's me or my choc drops.'

'We'll probably only know when you run out of chocolate,' said Trusty. 'And that's probably the time you're starting to wonder where the next meal is coming from anyway. So follow me, Group 6, down to the stream and let's see what we can find to eat.'

They followed Trusty down a barely discernible path which threaded its way through the low bushes and trees to the reedy banks of Surrenden Stream. Trusty held up his hand for silence and then whispered, 'Shhhh … Come up quietly to the stream's edge. See if you can see any fish in the water.'

They did as he instructed and peered into the stream. It was about 10 yards across and varied in depth from ankle deep to mid-thigh. The sun, filtered through the leaves of overhanging trees, created dapples of bright light, and the stream gurgled and burbled its way over the pebbly bottom. They could see nothing. 'Look into the deepest parts near the banks,' instructed Trusty. 'Look for dark shapes near the bottom.' Still they could see nothing. They waited patiently for two or three minutes. Then, suddenly, Gareth pointed to a shadowy dark shape close to the bank near the reeds.

'There,' he whispered hoarsely. Sure enough, lurking close to the reeds and at the deepest part of the stream, they could make out the sinuous outlines of a fish.

'Excellent,' breathed Trusty. 'A nice fat, succulent eel just waiting to be caught for dinner. Come on. We'll move upstream and put in our trap.'

They followed Trusty upstream for a few yards to where he had positioned a basket-like eel trap on the grass beside the stream. 'I spent a few minutes this morning weaving some thin saplings and reed grasses together to make this very basic eel trap,' he explained. 'You can see that it has a central funnel inside a larger framework, which has a little door in it which gives me access to the inside of the trap. I found a dead hedgehog in the woods this morning and I've slipped it into the trap as bait for the eel. I've tied some twine to the trap so I can secure it to the bank, and stop it being washed away by the stream.' He turned to Willie.

'Mr McBride. If you'd just put the trap into the water now, upstream from the eel that Mr Jones just spotted, and we'll see what happens.'

Slowly, and very carefully, Willie lowered the trap into the stream. It wasn't long before an eel appeared from the reeds downstream to examine the trap. It swam around, looking for a way to get at the flesh of the dead hedgehog. Then another eel appeared, drawn by the scent of hedgehog's blood. The two eels were joined by a third, and soon it became apparent that they were in competition for the hedgehog's remains. Their movements became bolder, and it was not long before there were two fat eels thrashing around inside the trap, attacking the hedgehog's body like piranhas.

'There you are,' Trusty exclaimed triumphantly. 'Looks like you've been quite successful. Miss Pendragon, would you please lift the trap out onto the bank?'

'Does it have to be me, Sergeant-Major?' asked Penelope, who had been watching proceedings with increasing alarm. 'We're going to have to kill them after I lift them onto the bank, right?'

Trusty looked up at her and understood her compassion. He nodded. 'Yes, Miss Pendragon, we will. But we humans have to kill animals for our food. It's no different if it's a sheep, a pig or a cow. If we don't get food to eat, we'll die. Try to think of it in that way. If we don't use these eels for food we won't survive.'

Penelope gulped and summoned up her courage. She didn't like it, but she understood what Trusty had said was brutally true. Carefully she gathered in the trap and flipped it onto the bank. The two eels in the trap now realised their predicament, left the hedgehog's remains, and started searching desperately for an escape route. But there was none.

'Right, Mr Jones,' instructed Trusty, 'slip a forked branch through the trap's access door. Pin down the heads of the eels, so they can't move, and finish them off with your penknife.'

Gareth did as Trusty instructed, and pulled the two dead eels from the trap. Nipper, who until now had been quietly watching events from some nearby bushes, suddenly took a much increased interest in things, and rushed over to Gareth, wagging his tail and sniffing the eels.

'Nothing doing, Nipper,' laughed Gareth. 'You stick to your choc drops from Willie!'

'Well done, Group 6,' said Trusty. 'You're shaping up to be great survivors. You've caught your next meal. Take them with you and make your way downstream for about 200 yards to your next stand, "Fires and Field Cooking for Dummies", run by Warrant Officer Rangitira.'

Before he joined the Military Security Corps some years ago, Warrant Officer Kiwi Rangitira had grown up in New Zealand with his Maori family in North Auckland. He was a huge man with heavily tattooed arms, a ready smile and an infectious chuckle. He was very keen on rugby, and now coached the forwards for Surrenden School's First XV. Kiwi loved his food, especially pork and fish. His eyes lit up when he saw their eels.

'Hee heee hee,' Kiwi chortled with glee. 'A great catch you've got there, Group 6. A really tasty dinner. Now, the first thing you've got to do is skin 'em. Then you gut 'em. Then you frizzle 'em 'til they just melt in your mouth. Got that? Skin, gut and frizzle.'

Under Kiwi's directions, Penelope pulled the eels' skins off like stockings off a leg. Willie slit them up their middle, and removed all their guts, and Gareth skewered the meat onto a sharpened sapling before placing the skewer over some fire embers for the eel meat to roast. It took only half an hour of preparation and cooking, before Kiwi carefully removed the spluttering, browned eel meat and shared it out between the trio.

'There you are,' exclaimed Kiwi triumphantly. 'A well-deserved feast for you. Well, this is the last stand for your group today, so you can now move back to your Company rooms and get ready for tonight's exercise. Report back to the Combat Wing with the other cadets at 1800 hours tonight for your exercise briefing.' The trio started back to the Company Common-room.

'Ugh,' grimaced Penelope, struggling with a mouthful of eel. 'That's horrible! It's like a spongy rubber ball. It's so oily. It's got to be worse than tripe, which means it's the pits.' She spat the eel meat out onto the grass, wiped her mouth with her sleeve, and shuddered.

'Eel-meat is very nutritious,' teased Gareth. 'My Aunt Dinnie eats jellied eel, and she's a member of our local Tripe and Onions Club. SHE says they're delicious!'

'Well, I'm not your Aunt Dinnie,' responded Penelope, a little crossly. 'You can take MY share of any eel-meat back to her.'

'It's not very likely that there'll be any eel-meat, OR tripe and onions, on tonight's exercise,' said Willie, laughing. 'What do you think we should do to prepare ourselves?' They discussed what sort of equipment they should take, what food they could pack away in their pockets, and what clothing they should wear. They had been told by the more senior cadets that the survival exercise was pretty tough. When pressed for more details, the senior cadets would just grin and shake their heads. 'You'll just have to find out for yourselves,' was all that they would say.

Instinctively, the trio knew that the day's training was important to each of them. It was important for them not only to learn very basic survival skills, but also helping them to develop their sense of resourcefulness and self-reliance: that vital 'can-do factor'.

Willie felt particularly relieved and pleased that they'd completed the training. He felt much more confident now, even though he knew he had so much more to learn. It was at least the first step on the ladder and, who knows, the skills might come in very handy on his quest to find out what had happened to his parents.

And so it was with considerable anticipation that they went to their rooms to prepare for a severe test of their life skills and endurance.

6

EXERCISE 'CHICKEN FEED'

It was quite dark when the class assembled back in the Combat Wing at 1800 hours as instructed, for their briefing.

Rocky was waiting for them in the brightly lit interior of the Combat Wing classroom. He was not alone. Beside him were seven very tough-looking regular soldiers in camouflage field uniform, each carrying a light machine gun, a pack, a radio and wearing dark green webbing. In the darkness outside the buildings were seven Land Rovers and their drivers.

'OK, let's get started,' said Rocky in a very business-like tone. 'You've all had the luxury of a whole day to train yourselves for this exercise, so you should be well prepared. I should remind you too that the marks you score for this exercise will go towards your marks for the Lucifer-Mortlock Trophy. Firstly, I want you to empty the contents of your pockets and packs on the tables in front of you and step back with your rifles. I want to see how well you've learnt today's survival lessons.'

Reluctantly, all the cadets obeyed Rocky's instructions, unsure of what might be the next step, and a little embarrassed to have all their personal belongings on display. Rocky and the seven soldiers listed each item the cadets put on the table.

'Ah, Mr McBride. What have you got here? Normal warm clothing, spare socks, first aid items, Swiss Army knife, torch, spare batteries, transistor radio, water purification tablets, gas lighter, knife, fork and spoon, aluminium mess tins, enamel mug, map of Surrenden area, prismatic compass, soap, small towel, plastic sheet, spool of nylon line, three fish hooks, sleeping bag, can-opener, camouflage cream, shaving soap and safety razors. Hmmm …

That's pretty good. Well done. You can pack these items away in your pack. But what's this stuff here? Two tins of sardines, tea bags, a tube of condensed milk, six blocks of chocolate, doggy choc drops, a packet of glucose, two packets of chocolate biscuits, spearmint chewing gum, a large packet of rice, a packet of curry powder, some iodised salt, a packet of raisins and three packets of Trail Mix nuts and dried fruit. That's also pretty good. Well done again. But you won't require this food. I'll just scoop it into this plastic bag, tie it up and label it with your name.'

Rocky proceeded on down the line, examining and listing the items heaped on the tables by the cadets. He was less than complimentary about some of the items he discovered.

'You can't eat laptop computers, hair-cream, after-shave lotion, sun glasses, calculators, spanner sets or shoe polish. And yogurt, Camembert cheese, milk, lettuce, cucumbers and salad dressing won't help boost your energy levels,' he rasped.

'Now, I want to brief you now on tonight's exercise.' He gestured towards a wall map of East Anglia, which had been overprinted with the word 'Eastland'. 'We are at war with Eastland, as shown on this map. You are all soldiers of the elite Surrenden Airborne Assault Squadron, whose job it is to escort these demolition experts across country to attack selected high-value targets.' Here he waved his arm in the direction of the seven tough-looking soldiers.

'You will parachute into Eastland tonight using Land Rover aircraft. Each of you will carry a brick of explosives, and, to save weight on equipment, you will be issued with special lightweight rations. When you land in Eastland you will have to avoid Eastland military forces, and ensure that your demolition expert successfully destroys his target by midnight tomorrow night. For security reasons, only the demolition expert knows the location of his target, but he will divulge this information to you when you land in Eastland. Your demolition expert will also carry a radio to maintain communications with us here at base. When your group has successfully destroyed your target, you will be evacuated back to base by helicopter. You are to pick up a map of Eastland, ten blank rounds of ammunition, and your brick of explosives as you leave the briefing room. Are there any questions?'

There was a shocked silence from the cadets as they struggled to understand the implications of Rocky's short briefing. Up until now, many of the cadets had never been required to move out of their comfort zone. Now the boundaries of that comfort zone were about to be widened considerably. Rocky looked around the room and smiled encouragingly. 'No questions. That can only mean that everybody is happy.' He paused, then added, 'OK, I now want you to meet your demolition expert and for your group to board your Land Rover aircraft.'

The demolition expert allocated to Group 6 was Sergeant 'Buddy' Routledge, an SAS veteran of several hotspots in the Balkans and Middle East. His face was lined and already painted with camouflage cream. He looked fit, alert and thoroughly competent. He had been in some very uncomfortably tight situations before and had triumphed. His blue eyes twinkled and he smiled broadly as he introduced himself to the trio.

'Mr McBride, Miss Pendragon, and Mr Jones. How are you? I'm Sergeant Routledge, your demolition expert. Which one of you is the Group Leader?'

They introduced themselves and Penelope and Gareth pointed to Willie. 'He is.'

'That's fine,' responded Sergeant Routledge. He turned towards Willie. 'You just treat me as you would any other member of your team, Mr McBride.'

'Thank you, Sergeant Routledge,' acknowledged Willie, then said jokingly, 'but you'd better know that I run a tight ship here. Any nonsense and you'll have to walk the plank and be fed to the sharks!'

They all laughed, as Sergeant Routledge raised his hands in mock horror and said. 'Yes, Sir. Yes, Sir. I'll try to behave.'

'Seriously though, Sergeant,' continued Willie. 'This is our first exercise. We've never done anything like this before. We'd all appreciate your advice at any time.'

Sergeant Routledge looked at Willie with new respect, and he nodded. 'Yes, of course, Mr Mc Bride. You sound just like your father.'

Willie looked up sharply at Sergeant Routledge. 'Did you know my father?' he asked.

'Yes, I did,' replied Sergeant Routledge quietly. 'He was an excellent officer, and I was very sorry to hear that he had gone missing recently. Perhaps he may re-appear one of these days.'

There was a moment of awkward silence, before Penelope spoke up.

'We'd better get moving, hadn't we? We've got quite a big job in front of us.' They all busied themselves, packing their brick of explosives, folding their maps and adjusting their equipment.

'Where are these lightweight rations Major de Roche said we were to be issued with?' asked Gareth.

Sergeant Routledge chuckled and replied, 'I think they're already in the back of the Land Rover.' Gareth opened up the back cover of the Land Rover and peered into the blackness of the baggage area and felt for the rations with his hands.

Cluck, cluck, claar, cluck, cluck!

'Crikey,' exploded Gareth, jumping back in alarm. 'There're some blimmin' birds in here!' He shone his torch into the baggage area. 'There are three live chickens lying in here with their legs all trussed up.'

'Oh, my God,' breathed Penelope. 'Surely they don't expect us to eat LIVE chickens?'

'No,' replied Willie. 'We're expected to kill them and THEN eat them, funnily enough. Ah well, we'd better put them in our packs to begin with. We'll decide later what we'll do with them.'

They stuffed the live chickens into the tops of their packs as best they could, so the birds had their heads poking out and could continue breathing. Then they loaded themselves into the back of the Land Rover, and settled down for their 'flight' through the blackness of the night to Eastland. It took about an hour of driving down side roads and byways before the driver pulled up beside a forested area, and announced, 'This is the de-bussing point for your Group.'

They eased themselves with their packs out of the back of the Land Rover and onto the side of the road. As soon as they were clear, the driver accelerated away up the road, and the vehicle disappeared into the darkness of the night. They stood for a minute, taking stock of their situation. The road seemed to run roughly north-west, with forested high ground to the north and open pasture dropping away to the south. They could see a scattering of lights of some farm houses in the open ground to the south. Apart from that, there was little else to be seen.

'I think we should move up into the woods and make camp until daybreak,' said Willie. 'We need to see more features on the ground before we can work out where we are. By the way, Sergeant Routledge, what's our target?'

'It's a suspected munitions factory at Pivington Mill,' replied the Sergeant.

'Oh, I know where Pivington Mill is,' volunteered Penelope. "That's just north of Pluckley on the road to Egerton. We pass it when we exercise our ponies from the Surrenden Riding School at Little Chart.'

'If we went up into the woods for about 20 to 30 yards we should be safe enough, don't you think?' suggested Gareth, pointing into the blackness of the roadside woods.

'Yes, good idea,' replied Willie. 'We should get off this road now and into some cover. We won't light a fire in case the reflection of the flames on the trees gives away our location. And I think we should have one of us on sentry watch throughout the night.' They moved up into the shelter of the wood, found a small clearing and made camp. They had only just got into their sleeping bags when they all heard the high-pitched whine of an armoured vehicle's engine. It was an armoured car of the Eastland forces. It seemed as if the crew were searching for them.

'Not now,' muttered Willie to himself. 'Don't let us be caught when we've only just started.'

The armoured car drove slowly up to their drop-off point and stopped. Its searchlight flickered across the trees above them, then crossed the road, and swept along the low hedgerows criss-crossing the open pasture.

'No, nothing here,' said a voice, and the armoured car proceeded slowly up the road, stopped for a minute or two on a small crest about 100 yards from their campsite, and then continued on up the road and out of sight.

'Whew,' said Gareth, as the armoured car disappeared. 'That was a close call. Just as well we'd moved off the road.'

They settled down to sleep, with each taking a two-hour turn at sentry duty. Willie took the last two hours before dawn. As he sat quietly and listened to the little rustlings and stirrings in the darkened wood, his thoughts turned to his parents and how they must have felt in the darkness of the mines and tunnels they would have explored. He pictured himself with them in the coal mine in Labuan with the huge storm and its lightning outside. It occurred to him that the possibility of a lightning strike at the mine's pithead must be extremely unlikely. It was far more likely to have been ... explosives. Yes, explosives! That would have been far more likely. He became excited. This was a real breakthrough in his thinking. He would ask Sergeant Routledge, as an explosives expert, what he thought.

As the first blush of light appeared in the sky, he gently roused the others. Sergeant Routledge was already awake and sitting quietly on his pack, listening carefully to the first stirrings of life about them. Willie went across to him.

'Could you give me some advice, Sergeant Routledge?'

'Sure. Of course. What's the problem?'

'Well it's not really a problem. It's just a technical matter about explosives.' Willie outlined the situation as he knew it about his parents' deaths. 'If you were going to blow up a mine, how would you go about it?'

Sergeant Routledge stroked his chin. 'Hmmm ... I see your drift. Well ... it's actually very easy to blow up the opening of a mine. You just have to blow away the supporting sides and let the weight of the rock above collapse down into the opening. But if you really wanted to seal the mine and its tunnels to make any rescue attempts unworkable, you'd put some explosives further down the mine on the roof of the tunnel. That way the force of the explosion would be directed up into the rock to break it up and collapse it down under its own weight. If I were doing the job, I'd use quite a bit of plastic explosive, detonating cord and electric detonators. Connect them all together and set them off from a safe distance outside. Pick up any left-over materials and no-one would be the wiser.' He paused and looked sympathetically at Willie. 'Is that what you think might have happened?' he asked softly.

'I don't know. It was just an idea that came into my head last night.'

'One thing's for sure,' said Sergeant Routledge. 'If that did happen then the person responsible would have had to have had explosives training ... military or mines explosives training ... and be pretty cold-blooded.'

'Thanks,' said Willie gratefully. The only person he had heard of who might fit that description was Lucifer-Mortlock, but that seemed far-fetched. It was much more likely to have been a miner who had a grudge against his parents. He sighed. It was not going to be easy to track down the truth. He turned his mind to the matters at hand. The chickens looked bleary eyed and made a couple of croaky clucks, as if to clear their throats and announce to the world that they were still alive.

'Do you think we've got time to get a fire going and roast one of these chickens?' asked Gareth. 'I'm as hungry as a horse, and a roast chicken leg sounds really great.' Penelope was shocked.

'You're not thinking of actually killing one of these poor little birds are you, Gareth? Just look at them. They're terrified.' She turned to Willie. 'Why don't we just let them go right now? This exercise will finish by midnight tonight, and we won't starve in the meantime.'

'I know how you feel, Penelope. But no, I don't think that we should let 'em go. We may decide not to eat them but they have been given to us as part of this exercise. I think we should continue to carry them. Who knows? This exercise might just be extended for a further couple of days. Then we'll have to look at chicken soup. I think we should give them some water to keep them going. Hopefully we may not need them.' He gestured towards the road, and changed the subject. 'Come on. Let's see if we can find our position.'

They moved carefully to the edge of the wood and peered out. Over the road they could now plainly see across the open pasture to the east and south. About half a mile away was a row of electricity transmission lines running south-west to north-east, and about a mile away was a railway line running almost north-south. It was Penelope who drew their attention to what looked like low barges moving up and down a wide canal, running almost parallel to the electricity lines.

'Look,' she said, jabbing her finger on her map. 'I reckon we must be in the Great Heron Wood on the road to Kenardington. That canal over there must be the Royal Military Canal. You can see the electricity lines; the canal and the railway line meet just below the village of Warehorne, which you can see on the hillside over there about two miles away.' They all examined their own maps carefully and compared the features on the ground.

'Yeah, I reckon you're right,' agreed Gareth.

'So do I,' said Willie. 'Good on you, Penelope! For someone who tends to get "misplaced", that's pretty smart map-reading.'

'By my reckoning, we've got about 12 miles as the crow flies to Pivington Mill,' said Gareth, pondering. 'The time is 0600 hours now, so we've got about twelve hours of daylight to cover, say, 15 miles cross country.'

'That's right,' agreed Willie, carefully scrutinising his map.

'There are a good number of woods and walkways we could use, which will allow us to keep well away from the urban areas. The only real area of danger would be the open area around Pluckley Station, on the London to Ashford railway. We could split the route up into, say, six sections, and allocate about two hours for each section. That way, we would know we would be making good progress, and not run out of time. What do you think, Sergeant Routledge?'

'Sounds like a good, workable plan to me, Mr McBride,' agreed the Sergeant, who was standing nearby.

'OK. How about this as a possible route for us to take?' asked Penelope. 'The first section would be from Great Heron Wood to Hunt's Wood. The second section would be Hunt's Wood to Henghurst, then Henghurst to Plurenden Wood. The fourth section would be Plurenden Wood to Honeyfield Wood, and the fifth would get us to the forest just south of Pluckley Station. We'd cross over the railway by the disused Brickworks, then move via Frith Wood to Pivington Mill.' The others followed her suggested route on their maps, checking for alternatives, and noting the walk-ways, and possible areas where Eastland forces might have observation posts.

'I like it,' said Gareth with enthusiasm.

'So do I,' said Wilie. 'The only real problem I can see is the railway line. It will be a barrier for us. You can bet your bottom dollar it will be well covered by the Eastland forces. We'll just have to take our chances when we get there.'

They started off in single file, with Gareth as lead scout, followed by Willie, then came Sergeant Routledge with Penelope as the 'Tail-end Charlie'. They had no trouble following their planned route, moving quickly and silently through the woods, and briskly on the walk-ways across the open fields. Other than seeing some cars moving along the roads between the villages, and some farm labourers on tractors working the fields, they saw no-one. There was no sign of Eastland forces.

As the day progressed and they neared their target, their spirits rose, and they put aside their growing pangs of hunger. The chickens, still with their heads poking up out of the top of the packs, looked very much the worse for wear. With rheumy eyes, droopy combs, half-opened beaks and ruffled feathers, they appeared to be barely alive. Even Gareth started to feel sorry for them!

It was mid-afternoon when they reached the forest to the south of the railway line. All seemed peaceful and quiet. They moved slowly along a mossy path which led to Pluckley Station. The sun was at their back, and a ghost of a breeze gently rustled the leaves in the trees and shrubs about them. But it was all TOO peaceful and quiet. It was as if life in the forest was holding its breath, and waiting for something to happen. Sergeant Routledge looked uncomfortable. All was not well. He signalled to get the others' attention, and waved them to retrace their steps back to a position some 100 yards to the rear.

'Shhhh,' he whispered. 'Something's not right here. I think that there's an Eastland ambush on the path up ahead. We can't cross the railway at Pluckley Station. We'll have to move off to one side.'

'Phew, thanks for that Sergeant,' breathed Willie. The others nodded that they understood. Willie studied his map and then said very quietly, 'We'll turn off to the west, and go parallel to the railway for a while.'

They started off again in single file with Penelope leading, and headed along a faint track which led into thicker scrub and brambles. They were progressing well when suddenly Penelope stopped, and signalled for them to close up to her. She pointed to the ground in front of her. Running across the path, coming from the main-line railway, was a set of very derelict, rusty, narrow-gauge railway tracks. Again, Willie examined his map. There was certainly no sign of another railway track, branching off from the main-line. Where on earth could this old railway track come from? Then he remembered the disused Brickworks on the other side of the main line.

'This is probably an industrial railway for the old Brickworks,' he whispered to the others. 'They might have used it to bring in supplies of clay to make the bricks.'

'In that case it must go UNDER the main railway line,' said Penelope.

'That's right,' agreed Gareth with enthusiasm. 'If there's an underpass tunnel, we just might be able to cross the main railway line right under the noses of the Eastland forces without them knowing.' Willie and Sergeant Routledge both nodded and grinned at each other.

'OK,' whispered Willie, 'we'll follow these rails. But go slowly and extra quietly. This is pretty thick scrub and could be a bit noisy.'

Penelope led the way, but after only about 200 yards, she suddenly stopped, sank to her knees and raised her rifle to her shoulder. Willie inched softly forward to join her. Ahead they could see through the underpass tunnel to some bushes beyond. But off to the right of the underpass entrance, half-hidden in the scrubby bushes, was a small Eastland forces Section base camp. Hunched over a radio, with his back to them, was a radio operator. He appeared to be all alone. Sergeant Routledge and Gareth came up from behind to join Penelope and Willie.

'Looks like the base camp of a small patrol,' breathed Sergeant Routledge, carefully surveying the scene in front of them. 'Probably the base for a section deployed forward in the ambush position on the path to Pluckley Station. Looks to me as if there's only one man.' He turned to Willie. 'What do you think we should do?'

Willie thought furiously, his eyes searching the underpass surroundings. His group's mission was to escort Sergeant Routledge to his target at Pivington Mill. To get through this situation they would need surprise, a firm base and overwhelming firepower. The surprise bit shouldn't be too difficult, as he could see that the Eastland soldier had carelessly left his weapon leaning up against a tree. Penelope and Sergeant Routledge could provide a firm base and then both Gareth and he could overpower the Eastland soldier. He motioned for the others to come closer, so that he could lower his voice to a very soft whisper.

'Right,' he said. 'Here's what we'll do. Gareth and I will overwhelm the radio operator, while you, Penelope, and Sergeant Routledge give us covering fire if required. As soon as Gareth and I have taken the radio operator prisoner, Penelope and Sergeant Routledge move quickly through the underpass, and secure the area on the other side of the main railway line. Try not to make any noise as we don't want to stir up a hornet's nest.'

Penelope and Sergeant Routledge nodded their agreement and leopard-crawled over to the left flank to take up their covering-fire positions. When they were in position they waved. Willie and Gareth began their careful approach towards the unsuspecting radio operator, their footfalls muffled by the leafy debris on the forest floor. Slowly, step by careful step, they neared the Eastland soldier, who still suspected nothing and was busy listening to the voice traffic on the radio. They were almost upon him when the live chicken in Willie's pack gave a despairing croak, to alert people that he was STILL alive and needed water.

'Claughk, caughk, claughk,' cackled the chicken, his calls echoing in the woods.

The startled Eastland soldier jumped to his feet, and wheeled around to see what had made the noise, only to find himself staring down the barrel of Willie's rifle.

'Be quiet. Lie face down on the ground,' ordered Willie, in a harsh and authoritative voice. Surprised and stunned by his unexpected situation, the Eastland soldier quickly obeyed the order.

'Put your hands behind your back,' instructed Willie, again mustering as much authority as he could. The frightened and numbed Eastland soldier quickly obeyed. Gareth, grinning from ear to ear, took out a roll of tape from his pack, taped up the soldier's hands and legs, and carefully taped around his head and across his mouth so that he could breathe, but not cry out.

'That should keep you trussed up and quiet for a while,' said Gareth. 'Now, don't be a naughty boy and try to run away!'

Willie picked up the Eastland radio and stuffed it into his pack beside the live chicken, which complained miserably with some half-hearted croaks.

'OK,' he said to the Eastland soldier. 'We're going to leave now. But I shall put through a radio message to Exercise Control to alert them that you're here and have to be freed before dark. Do you understand?' The Eastland soldier nodded as best he could.

While Willie and Gareth had been dealing with the radio operator, Penelope and Sergeant Routledge had moved quickly through the railway underpass and safely secured a position on the other side.

'Nice work, Mr McBride, and Mr Jones,' complimented Sergeant Routledge, chuckling quietly when Willie and Gareth joined him and Penelope.

Willie grinned and nodded towards Gareth. 'We did all right, didn't we? But we'll have to get a move on. As soon as that radio operator's section finds out what's happened they'll be after us as quick as a shot. Anyway, Sergeant Routledge, could you put a radio message through to our base station to let them know what we've done.'

'I've already done that, Mr McBride,' confirmed Sergeant Routledge. 'They were a bit shocked at first and even called Major de Roche to the radio. Apparently, it's the first time that a cadet group has ever successfully attacked a unit of the Regular Army, and got away with it!'

He pointed back to the underpass railway tunnel. 'By the way, do you remember what I told you earlier about blowing up the mine? Well, this is where I'd put the explosives.' He pointed inside to the tunnel's roof and then to the outside brick supports holding up the archway. 'Just two or three sticks of plastic explosive would do the trick and collapse the whole tunnel here.'

Willie looked back at the underpass and nodded. He could readily envisage how easy it would be to completely destroy the mine. 'What about the coal dust? Would that be ignited?' he asked.

'Unlikely,' replied Sergeant Routledge. 'The coal dust would have to be tinder dry and suspended in the air. But, in the case of the coal mine on Labuan island, tropical rain over scores of years would have consolidated any coal dust into a pretty solid cake. No, I think it would be very unlikely that a lightning strike had anything to do with the explosion. Look how the rain has entered into this tunnel here and made the entrance quite wet.'

Willie could see at once the wet areas on the tunnel floor and nodded. All the expert opinion he'd heard so far seemed to point to a man-made explosion. He would have to follow up this possibility with Sir Eyre at a later date.

They moved quickly away from the Pluckley Station area up into the welcoming cover of Frith Wood. It was now late afternoon and the shadows were lengthening. They were all feeling the pangs of hunger and were tired from the effects of the day's physical exertion and their excitement.

'This is just the time NOT to relax or take short cuts,' warned Sergeant Routledge. 'We're within a whisker of successfully completing the mission. All we have to do now is get our explosives stacked up against the wall of Pivington Mill.'

They struck out from the edge of Frith Wood, following a walkway which led through a field of cabbages, to a copse overlooking a road leading to the Mill. The gloom of evening covered their movements and they felt increasingly secure. But their feeling of safety was rudely shattered when an illuminating shell was fired up into the sky from an armoured vehicle parked beside the copse ahead.

'Hit the ground and keep your eyes shut,' said Willie in a hoarse whisper. He dived forward and lay still. The illuminating shell burst up in the sky, lighting up the countryside with a brilliant glare as its magnesium powder burned and spluttered under its parachute. They lay as still as statues for what seemed an eternity, as the parachute drifted slowly to the ground. As it hit the ground its light extinguished. The countryside was plunged back into darkness. They scrambled to their feet, and adjusted their direction towards the other side of the copse from where the armoured car was parked.

They had almost reached it when another illuminating shell was fired. Again they dived for cover in among the cabbages.

'Feel like a cabbage, smell like a cabbage, I AM a cabbage!' whispered Penelope, and they all giggled.

'We've just discovered a brand new English perfume,' whispered Gareth. 'Eau de Greens. It will be a best seller!'

Again they all chuckled. As the illumination shell extinguished, they covered the remaining few yards to reach the copse. They could hear the crew of the armoured car about 100 yards away, noisily chatting among themselves, and finishing off an evening meal of fried chicken, rice, vegetables and strong tea. The cooking smells drifted through the copse.

'Blimmin' hell,' cursed Gareth, licking his lips. 'I just love fried chicken. I'm sure we would have had time this morning to fix ourselves a really nice breakfast from these vultures we've been carrying around all day.'

'Well, maybe,' replied Willie. 'If this exercise is extended for another day then we might have to revisit our earlier decision. Then it might just be "vulture" legs for breakfast. Meantime, let's see if we can get this explosive into the Mill.'

They all lay hidden on the ground on the edge of the copse and studied the ground in front of them. They could clearly see the black shape of the Mill about 200 yards away, sitting at the end of a tree-lined driveway. Apart from the Eastland armoured car at the other end of the copse, there was no sign of any other enemy forces.

'What if we approached the Mill using the cover of the trees, but down on the side of the fields?' suggested Gareth.

'Not many other options really,' observed Penelope. 'It would take us forever to go around the flank, and make our approach from the rear of the Mill.'

'Yes, I think you're right,' agreed Willie. 'We'll keep low and make a dash across the road. Then we'll keep the tree line between ourselves and the Eastland armoured car.' One at a time they sprinted across the road, and regrouped in the cover of the trees. They were none too soon. The crew in the armoured car switched on their searchlight, and started sweeping the open fields and probing the hedgerows and woods with its brilliant finger of light.

'Phew, that was close,' whispered Gareth.

'Sure was. Let's get cracking and get down to the Mill, and put these explosives into position.'

They ducked down low and froze as the searchlight beam came near. It lit up the trees above them and swept out into the open fields. They hurried down to the Mill, unpacked their bricks of explosive and gave them to Sergeant Routledge, who, in turn, stacked them against the wall of the Mill.

They had done it! They had succeeded in their mission!

They all felt an overwhelming sense of relief, and clustered in a group to quietly congratulate one another. It was then that the searchlight found them. Blinded by the brilliant light, they were transfixed, not knowing which way to turn. They were trapped like a pack of possums in a car's headlights, fearing the worst and shielding their eyes from the glare. Then a high-pitched whistle sounded and the searchlight was doused.

A voice from behind a nearby shed said, 'Well done, Group 6. You succeeded in your mission. The exercise is over for you.' It was Major De Roche. He emerged from the gloom, and said with a smile, 'I see you've still got your survival rations. You're probably not hungry then. You won't need the hot meat pies, sausage rolls, ice cream and hot tea over there in the support truck.' He pointed to a camouflaged three-ton truck parked under some nearby trees, with an empty wire cage beside it. He paused for a moment. 'Only joking! Untie the chickens and pop them into the cage. There's food and water for them in there. Then help yourself to as much food as you like. Your transport back to the School will be here in 30 minutes.'

They lost no time in carrying out Rocky's instructions. SAS was in the back of the support truck, helping to serve out the food.

'Ah, Mr McBride,' he said. 'I hear that your Group did very well. Actually captured one of the enemy. That's never been done before.'

'Thanks, Staff,' replied Willie. 'It was a good team effort.'

'Yes, Mr McBride, it *was* a good team effort,' added Sergeant Routledge quietly. 'You're a chip off the old block. You'll do well, I'm sure. I have to go now as my transport is waiting for me, but I'm sure our paths will cross again in the future, and I look forward to that. Best of luck for the future, sir.' He shook hands with Willie, got into a waiting camouflaged SAS vehicle, and disappeared into the darkness.

The transport back to School duly arrived around midnight. They clambered up into the back of the truck, and slumped gratefully into the seats. They were absolutely exhausted from the events of the day.

'Can't wait to get a shower,' said Penelope. 'I still smell like a cabbage.'

'Those pies were pretty good,' said Gareth. 'But I could still go a roast chicken leg.'

But there was no comment from Willie. He was already fast asleep.

7

GLOBAL UNDERGROUND

It was Penelope's turn to check the Curators' Storeroom when the first letter from Brittanica arrived. It was a plain white banker's envelope, addressed in Woody's copperplate handwriting, to:

> Messrs McBride, Pendragon and Jones,
> Assistant Curators,
> The Museum,
> Surrenden Military School.

She put it carefully in her uniform pocket and went to the Company Common Room to meet Willie and Gareth.

'It's come,' she said breathlessly, in great excitement. 'Our first letter from Woody.'

'Open it up then,' urged Gareth. 'I bet it's in code. I've been going through the directions sheet that Woody gave us with our codebooks and getting in a bit of practice coding and decoding. Let me have a go at decoding this letter.'

Gareth took the letter up to his room where he had hidden the codebook. After about half an hour he returned, his face flushed with triumph. He had a brown manilla file in his hand.

'I've done it. All I had to do was look up the right sheet in the codebook and then transpose each letter in the alphabet in Woody's letter with the correct one in the codebook. Simple really,' he announced gleefully. They settled around a table in the corner of the room and Gareth spread out the letter and some sheets of paper. Woody's letter, which comprised a single sheet of paper, had a group of letters in the top left-hand corner, followed by eight lines

of letters. Each line had six groups of letters, with each group containing just five plain text letters.
FECIRF
   xfyhogtklm depib hgrxbfliha lvcte
   lpdyb ofduwncdzpofrgp mlspt esnzl
   frimc qloyc lmisc eyaln lmysbwknui

Decoded, Woody's message read:
HAVE URGENT JOB FOR YOU stop PLEASE MEET ME TOMORROW AFTERNOON FOR BRIEFING stop JOB COULD TAKE THREE DAYS stop
WOODY

'That's brilliant,' exclaimed Willie. 'Tomorrow is a Saturday, so we could all go straight after morning sports and lunch.' They could hardly wait for Saturday afternoon to arrive. Immediately after lunch they hurried up to the Museum only to find Reggie the Relic in the Curators' Workroom.

'Oh, this is a nice surprise,' said Reggie, looking up from the worktable and smiling broadly. 'Have you come to do a bit of housekeeping?'

Before anyone else could reply, Willie quickly responded. 'Well, yes sir, we've come to tidy up one or two things in the Storeroom.'

'Ah ha,' replied Reggie, nodding his head knowingly, and climbing to his feet. He looked at his watch. 'Good heavens, is that the time? If I don't get down to the Mess, I'll miss lunch.' He turned to look at the three and said quietly, 'Make sure you've got all the equipment you need and leave things as they should be. I'll still see you next week to finish off our briefing about Museums.'

'Yes, sir,' responded Willie. 'We'll be careful with everything.'

Reggie looked Willie straight in the eye, 'That's fine. Just let me know if there's anything you need,' he said in a concerned and helpful way. He left the Workroom closing the door behind him.

As soon as he had left, Willie faced Penelope and Gareth and put his finger to his lips. 'Shhh,' he mouthed. They all waited quietly until they heard Reggie the Relic close the Museum's main door as he left.

'What's the matter?' whispered Penelope.

'Nothing's the matter,' replied Willie. 'It's just that I think

Reggie knows more about Brittanica and the Time Thread than he's letting on to us. But at the same time I think he knows that we are involved with those things and he's approving.'

'Why do you think that?' questioned Gareth.

'It's just the way that he speaks. Everything he says has a double meaning, particularly when he looks so directly at me.'

'Oh, don't be silly, Willie,' said Gareth impatiently. 'You'll soon be thinking the whole School staff knows about Brittanica.'

'No. Not at all. I think it's a very closely guarded secret, with just Reggie the Relic, ourselves, my parents obviously, but, perhaps, even our Foreign and Commonwealth Office.'

'Now you've *got* to be dreaming,' said Gareth. 'Why don't you include the Americans, the French and even the Chinese while you're about it?'

'Hmm, don't laugh,' replied Willie. 'What we're seeing could be just the tip of the iceberg. Stranger things have happened.'

'Well, icebergs or ice-blocks, British or international. It doesn't really matter at the moment,' interrupted Penelope. 'We've an appointment with Woody and we'd better get cracking.'

'You're right,' said Willie, turning his mind to the matter at hand. 'Let's go and visit Gladys!'

They went through to the Storeroom, closed the door and entered the Time Thread tunnel. They emerged into the empty Cleaners' Room. They waited quietly and it was not long before Gladys entered.

'Ah, there you are. How are you? I've been waiting for you. Woody said you might come to visit us today,' she beamed. 'Come on and follow me. I'll take you to his office.'

They followed Gladys to Woody's office, to find Woody deep in conversation with another man, whose conservative dress identified him as also on the Foreign Office staff. They stopped talking as soon as the three entered the room. Woody came towards them, his hand outstretched in welcome and his face beaming warmly.

'How wonderful it is to see the three of you again,' he said, shaking the hands of each of them. 'This is indeed a great honour for us to welcome you back to Brittanica.' He gestured to the other man. 'May I introduce our Deputy Assistant Secretary for Oceania, the Honourable Nathaniel Thomas.'

'How do you do, sir,' said Willie, as he shook hands.

The Honourable Thomas was a little embarrassed by the

formality of the greetings. 'Oh, please call me "Nugget". Everybody else does. The nickname comes from my rather lengthy legal name of Nathaniel Urquhart Gerald Evelyn Thomas.'

He shook hands with Penelope and Gareth. Nugget's dark grey suit fitted snugly over his chubby frame. He had a couple of extra wobbly chins, a shiny bald head, and rimless spectacles perched rather low on his nose. His trousers were held in place over his well-fed tummy by a thick black belt and red braces. He wore grey spats over his black shiny shoes. His eyes were dark brown, and he dipped his nose when he was talking, so that he could peer over his glasses. His rounded, shiny appearance reminded everyone of an elderly, black billiard ball.

Woody continued. 'I've asked Nugget to come and meet you, and help me brief you about a small, but important mission I'd like you to undertake for us.' He indicated the dark green, button-down chairs. As they sat down, Woody filled his meerschaum pipe with a fresh plug of tobacco, lit it, and took a few puffs.

'You will recall that the last time you were here, I spoke about how important science and technology was to Brittanica. Simply put, it is highly desirable for us to recognise the opportunities science and technology present. Not only to keep us ahead of our competitors, but also to bring the benefits to our citizens. One of the responsibilities of our Consuls and Governors posted abroad is for them to keep us informed of any interesting science and technology developments in their patch. Yesterday, Nugget advised me of the possibility of an important development in Oceania. I thought that it was so important that you should hear it from Nugget as well.' Nugget rose to his feet, and cleared his throat.

'Ahem,' he started. 'Well, this report came from our Governor in New Zealand, The Honourable Orme Ranfurly. New Zealand, by the way, is at the other end of the globe. It has been a colony under our jurisdiction for the best part of 100 years.' He pointed to three small islands on a wall map hanging behind Woody's desk.

'It's had its fair share of development problems over the years, what with immigrants flocking there from Brittanica, and other parts of the world. But it has three major towns: Auckland and Wellington in the northern island, and Christchurch here, in the middle island, called the South Island. The whole economy is based on agriculture and farming. Ranfurly reported that a farmer, called Rudyard Percival, living near Christchurch, has developed a flying machine driven by a motor. Ranfurly has seen the machine and claims that it incorporates many advanced features. He thinks that it might have possibilities for travel and the carriage of goods by air. If that was the case, it would give us significant advantages over having to use road vehicles, trains and ships. Do you think such an invention would be useful?'

'Absolutely,' responded Willie. 'It's revolutionised travel in our world, and I'm sure it would in yours, too.' He turned to Woody, and asked quietly, 'What would you like us to do, Woody?' Woody took another puff of his pipe.

'We would very much like you to go to New Zealand, examine this new invention, and, if you think it worthwhile, bring it back to Whitehall,' he replied, looking directly at Willie. 'If you agree to undertake this mission you'd travel to New Zealand by our diplomatic tomotram, be based in our Consulate in Christchurch with Ranfurly, and return to Whitehall by tomotram.' He paused, and then looked at each of them in turn. 'Would you like to undertake this mission for us?'

Willie looked at Penelope and Gareth, and from the look in their eyes could see their eagerness and agreement. He was also excited about the prospect of going on a mission to New Zealand, but he suddenly had a great idea.

'Yes, Woody, I know I could say that all three of us would very much like to accept this mission to New Zealand. However, I have a favour to ask of you. Would it be possible for us to make a detour so that I can visit Labuan Island and visit the coal mines there?'

'Yes, of course that can be arranged,' replied Woody. 'How silly and thoughtless of me not to have considered it earlier.' He turned to Nugget. 'Who's our man at Jesselton in North Borneo now? Is it still Cavendish Beaufort?

'That's right,' said Nugget. 'He's been there for years and loves the place, apparently. He gets on famously with the locals, and he's building a railway.' He turned to Willie. 'The nearest tomotram tunnel to Labuan is the town of Jesselton, the capital of North Borneo. You have to take a ferry from there to the port town of Victoria on Labuan. Actually, the island is being run now on our behalf by the Brittanic North Borneo Company and is administered on a daily basis by their mine manager. Cavendish will give you a good briefing when you get to Jesselton. I'll let him know to expect you.'

'After you've had a look around Labuan you can move on south to New Zealand,' said Woody, pointing to the wall map. 'I'm sure you will enjoy a visit there. Ranfurly has been our Governor in New Zealand for the last five years. He's particularly fond of farming, fishing and rugby. In fact, he loves rugby so much that we call him Scrummage, after one of the important facets of the game. Follow me now and I'll show you our Tomotram Depot and introduce you to the General Manager of our TomoTravel Company.' Woody led them along the corridor, to the door and stairs leading down to the Tomotram Barn. They descended ten flights of well-worn, stone steps to emerge into a vast underground cavern the size of a football field.

The barn was arranged like an arena, with a central flat area filled with trams of all kinds, including military, repair and recovery. The central area of parked trams was ringed on three sides, with four levels of office blocks and workshops, while the fourth side had ten black tunnel entrances. Traffic control lights stood on posts at each tunnel entrance. The nearest office block looked much grander than the others, with white concrete walls, beautiful wooden sash windows, dark green shutters, and an imposing, carved, entrance door.

Woody knocked on the large oak door. A security shutter opened and an eye inspected them briefly, before the door was flung open by an elderly man. He was of medium height, and dressed in a navy blue jacket and trousers with silver piping. He wore a peaked red cap on which was stitched an emblem of a golden crown placed on top of the letters 'GTC'. His face was cheery, and his cheeks were rosy red; but his face was mostly hidden by a thick, grey beard, bushy moustache and eyebrows. Around his waist he wore a broad brown leather belt from which hung a bunch of keys and a large fob watch.

'How do you do, Sir Woodhouse? It's nice to see you again. Please come in, sirs, and young lady,' he said with a warm welcoming smile. 'The Chairman and the Directors are waiting for you upstairs in the Board Room.' He gestured towards a wide curving staircase, with richly carved mahogany banisters and plush red carpet.

'Thank you, Bruno,' replied Woody, and led the way up the stairs to a pair of huge oaken doors, on which were two brass plates, inscribed with the words:

Board Room

They had just reached the doors when they were swung open by another bearded man, who also greeted them cheerfully.

'How are you, Woody? How good to see you. Are these your three friends you spoke of? Do come on in, all of you, and let me introduce you to my directors.' He turned to the trio and shook hands with each of them, smiling broadly and looking them straight in the eye. He introduced himself.

'I'm Alfredo Alessandro,' said the tall, elegant man in the navy suit. 'I'm the Chairman of Global TomoTravel Corporation, which operates the tomotrams on behalf of Brittanica, and these are my brothers, and fellow company directors.' He swung his arm towards a group of similarly dressed and bearded men in the room, seated around a massive rectangular, mahogany boardroom table.

'Thank you, Alfredo,' replied Woody, who obviously knew Alfredo and his brothers well. He turned towards the others, and announced, 'Gentlemen, I would like to introduce three very dear friends of mine, Mr Willie McBride, Miss Penelope Pendragon and Mr Gareth Jones. Willie is the son of Colonel and Mrs McBride, who, you will recall, disappeared recently. I would like you to give every support to Willie and his friends, as you did for his parents.'

There were cries of 'How do you do?', 'Pleased to meet you' and 'Sorry to hear of your loss,' from the assembled group. They warmly welcomed their four visitors into the room, sat them down in huge, comfy leather chairs, and offered them steaming hot mugs of tea, and platefuls of chocolate biscuits. Alfredo turned towards the three.

'Woody has asked me to tell you a bit about ourselves, the company and the global tomotunnel system.' He paused, as if gathering his thoughts, and then, indicating the other directors around the table, he began.

'I think I should start by saying that Global Tomotravel Corporation is a family company, belonging to the Allessandro family, many of whom are present here. Our prime activity is global travel using specially modified electric trams, travelling through a global labyrinth of volcanic tunnels, known as "tomos". For the past 150 years, the company has been contracted by the Foreign Office of Brittanica to provide global transport for their diplomatic mail, personnel and activities.

The company had very humble beginnings. It was started by my forebears, a family of miners, about 300 years ago. They lived and worked mainly in the Middle East. It was while working in an area known as Arcadia that they discovered the burial chamber of a king who had ruled thousands of years before. His name was Sardin, and in his burial chamber were hundreds of clay cylinders. These cylinders, or scrolls, as they were called, had inscriptions and maps drawn on them. The scrolls, now known as the "Sardin Scrolls", detailed a vast world-wide complex of inter-connected volcanic tunnels. Of course, my family were overjoyed at this discovery, stopped being miners, and became global transport operators, offering transport services to different governments. However, they soon realised that they could not serve all governments, as some were engaged in unlawful activities, and some didn't pay their bills. So the family moved here to Brittanica and contracted their services to Brittanica's Foreign Office, who did pay their bills!'

Alfredo paused, and gestured towards the glowing green, red and blue lines of the electric wall diagram of the global tomotunnel system.

'Fortunately, we still had the Sardin Scrolls safely in our possession, and are able to reach all the Brittanican diplomatic posts around the world using the tomotunnels. These tomotunnels have unique electro-magnetic properties, which permit very fast electric tram travel, by a form of magnetic levitation. Over the years, we have established the different magnetic properties for most parts of the world, and are able, therefore, to set the tomotram controls with the desired location settings before a journey is started. Our tomotrams have specially modified electric motors which give us excellent speed and direction control.' Alfredo paused and had a quick sip of tea before continuing.

'Of course there are thousands of miles of tomotunnels. There are far, far too many for us to look after by ourselves. So we have contracted out the maintenance of them to the Helvetians. Well … to World Wormholes Corporation, to be precise, who employ gangs of Helvetians to keep the tomotunnels clear, maintain the signalling system, and service the fresh air ventilation machinery.' Alfredo grinned and chuckled to himself.

'Generally, the Helvetian gangs have been pretty good, although they do like to play little practical jokes on us every now and again.' The other directors around the table also chuckled knowingly, and reminded one another of certain Helvetian pranks that they, themselves, had experienced. Alfredo moved towards the Board Room door and said, smiling, 'Let me show you around our tomotram depot and its workshops, so that you get a better idea of our transport capabilities.'

They all followed him downstairs and into the first barn. It housed ten very modern-looking, streamlined trams. Not at all like the rather primitive, early open trams, as they'd expected. These were sleek and efficient vehicles, sheathed in sheet metal, each about 70 feet long, with articulated centres and rounded ends, large shuttered windows, retractable steel bogey wheels, and double folding doors at each end, just behind the driver's compartment.

'Wow,' gasped Gareth in admiration, 'these are top machines.'

Alfredo glanced at Gareth with a smile. He was very pleased indeed to get such an obviously sincere compliment from one of his visitors.

'Well, we have put a lot of research and development into them over these many years,' replied Alfredo. 'I think we've probably got a performance edge over tomotrams being operated by other countries. We use the steel bogey wheels for parking, and the articulated centres give us better cornering in the tomos. Each tomotram has four electro-magnetic engines, which interact with the magnetic forces in the tomos, to give the tram levitation and speed. Speeds are very variable, but in some straight tomo tunnels we have reached 700 miles an hour. Stabilisers are fitted to even out magnetic 'bumps' to give a smooth ride and permit a 'hover' capability.'

'How much can the trams carry?' Willie asked.

'About five tons in the "normal" mode,' responded Alfredo. 'But because our journeys are generally long, and quite some distance from recovery and maintenance support, each tram has been fitted out to be largely self-sufficient. Each has a small kitchen and toilet, workshop space, and sleeping accommodation for six persons, as well as seating for a further ten, and space for further stores and equipment. We generally carry a crew of two, a driver and a diplomatic post man. Because of the nature of Foreign Office business, the crew is normally supplied through Woody's Department.'

'The tomotrams all look so well cared for,' exclaimed Penelope, running her hands over the glossy dark blue and gold paintwork of the nearest tomotram. 'And they are painted in such pretty colours with matching curtains. You must have a big job to keep them looking so magnificent, Alfredo.' Alfredo positively glowed with pride at Penelope's remarks, while Gareth simply lifted his eyes skyward and mouthed to himself: 'And they look so pretty and colour-co-ordinated too, Alfredo!'

'Thank you so much for those compliments, Miss Pendragon,' exclaimed Alfredo. 'They are much appreciated. Now I do want to show you another important area over here.' He led them over to a small office and storeroom, marked 'Despatch Office'. The two uniformed men in the office stood smartly to attention when they saw Woody.

'Ah, I'd like to introduce two members of my staff to you.' said Woody. He motioned towards the chubby one. 'This is our driver, Mr Arthur Bottomley, and this,' he said, indicating the other, military looking man, 'is Sergeant James Braddock, our Diplomatic Postman.' He then gestured towards the trio and said to the two men, 'These are three important new personnel who have joined our staff in the same capacity as Colonel and Mrs McBride. In fact, Mr William McBride here is the son of Colonel and Mrs McBride. His two associates are Miss Penelope Pendragon and Mr Gareth Jones. I would like you to act as their driver and postman just as you did for the Colonel and his wife.'

'Yes sir,' replied both men, shaking hands with the trio, and saying sympathetically to Willie, 'We are both so sorry to hear that your father and mother have gone missing.'

'Thank you. Did you know my Mum and Dad personally?'

'Yes, we did, Mr William,' said Arthur. 'We were their staff for many years and did dozens of missions with them. They were two very fine people and will be sadly missed.' He looked across to Sergeant Braddock, grinned wryly and said softly, 'We certainly got into some pretty dodgy places with them, didn't we, Jimmy?'

'Yes,' agreed Jimmy. 'But we always managed to get out in one piece, even if it was sometimes just by the skin of our teeth!'

'Ah well, there's nothing too dangerous in this next job, which will be very routine indeed,' said Woody rather quickly, perhaps a little worried that Alfredo and his brothers might hear something they should not. He turned to Alfredo and the rest of the Global Tomotravel Board, thanked them for their hospitality and bade them farewell.

As soon as the Alessandros had left to return to their Board

Room, Woody turned to Arthur and Jimmy and said quietly, 'I want you to take our visitors to Borneo, firstly to visit Governor Beaufort in Jesselton, then down to New Zealand to visit Governor Ranfurly.' He turned to the trio, shook hands with each of them, and said, smiling, 'I'll leave you here now, and wish you well for a safe and successful journey. I'll see you on your return.' He turned, waved, and disappeared up the steps towards his office.

'Come through into the Despatch Office and Storeroom,' suggested Arthur, leading the way.

'Your parents used to use the Storeroom as a preparation room before each journey.' He led the trio through the office to a green painted steel door, fitted with a heavy padlock. Arthur rummaged around in a desk in the office and held up a key.

'The Colonel always asked me to keep a spare in case of accidents,' he said, a little sheepishly. He unlocked the door and gave Willie the key. 'Jimmy and me will get the tomotram ready now for the trip to Borneo. We should be ready to go in about 30 minutes, Mr William.'

'Thanks, Arthur, we'll be ready to go when you are,' answered Willie.

Rather tentatively, Willie opened the door and switched on the light. Although he had no idea of what he might find in the room, he was hopeful that there might be something which would provide him with a clue as to what had led to his parents' disappearance. The room was quite large, with white-painted stone walls and ceiling. Along one side wall was a long cork board, on which had been pasted a mosaic of satellite air photos. The opposite wall was lined with wooden cupboards from floor to ceiling. At the far end of the room there was a kitchen sink and bench, and a large wall mirror hanging above a dressing table.

'We'd better have a quick look round, while we can,' suggested Penelope.

They commenced their explorations slowly and carefully, with Penelope and Gareth examining the contents of the cupboards, while Willie studied the satellite air photos. The cupboards contained an extraordinary variety of equipment: digital cameras, mining helmets, lamps, torches, electric batteries, boots and fluorescent jackets, air-breathing masks, respirators and oxygen tanks, plastic sample flasks, rucksacks and woollen clothing, and piles of laminated maps. It was

Penelope who discovered the most surprising items. She opened one cupboard door to find herself staring at two sets of military uniforms. Both consisted of a field grey tunic, with a high stand collar in blue, white metal buttons down the front, broad, blue sleeve cuffs and a pair of field grey riding breeches. On a shelf above each uniform was a grey felt slouch hat with a blue headband and a red cockade pinned on the right side. She examined the silver braided rank insignias which were fixed to a blue background on the shoulders of the tunics.

'It looks as if your parents were disguising themselves as officers of a foreign army, Willie,' she said. 'I wonder which country?'

'And they were well prepared to protect themselves, if things got sticky,' added Gareth, as he opened another cupboard, obviously a gun cupboard, which contained a pair of 9mm Browning pistols, high-powered rifles with laser-guided sniper-scopes, ammunition and a box of hand grenades.

'Hmm, yes, I suppose so,' replied Willie thoughtfully, as he continued to closely study a particular mosaic of satellite photos.

'Come and have a look at these photos,' he said. 'They're of Borneo, Brunei and Labuan Island.'

Penelope and Gareth gathered around and stared at the mosaic. It had been enlarged so that the ground detail of village houses, jungle, cultivation and rough roads were quite clear. There were markings on the photo that meandered about in no particular pattern. But one group of buildings on Labuan Island had been circled. Printed alongside the buildings was the wording, 'Brittanic North Borneo Coal Mining Co'.

Willie stabbed his finger at the buildings on the map. 'That's exactly where my parents disappeared!'

'So it is,' agreed Penelope, studying the photos carefully.

'So there IS a strong connection between our Earth world and the world of Brittanica after all,' exclaimed Gareth.

'We're ready to go now, Mister William,' Jimmy called.

'We're coming now.' Willie pulled the satellite photos off the wall, folded them up and slipped them into his pocket. He felt sure they'd come in handy when they reached Labuan Island.

They left the room and Willie locked it up, carefully pocketing the key.

Jimmy and Arthur were waiting for them at the door of the

tomotram. Willie felt a surge of excitement as he stepped aboard. He was on a journey of discovery. A very important journey that could yield vital clues about his parents' disappearance.

'This is tomotram 256,' said Arthur proudly. 'Probably the best one we have in the fleet, particularly for longer journeys. Just make yourselves comfortable in the seats. I've made you all a big pot of tea, and there's a large plate of strawberry muffins which Gladys made for us all. This will be a long journey of about 10 hours, so Jimmy and I will get you all some dinner and supper a little later.' The trio settled themselves down and Arthur switched on the motors. There was a powerful hum and the tomotram 256 glided out of the tomotram barn, through tunnel number 5 on its way to Jesselton in North Borneo.

8

THE CROCODILES OF LABUAN

It was early morning on the following day when they reached Jesselton. The heat of North Borneo was stifling and their clothes were wet with perspiration. Arthur drove the tomotram up to the tomotram station which was located just below the Brittanican Residency. Governor Cavendish Beaufort was waiting for them on the platform; a very tall and extraordinarily thin man with long, stick-like arms and legs. He was dressed in khaki shorts, short-sleeved shirt, long socks, brown brogue shoes and wore a Foreign Legion-style hat with neck flaps. He greeted them warmly and with a broad smile acknowledging Jimmy and Arthur whom he already knew.

'Welcome to Jesselton,' he said, shaking their hands. 'I'm Governor Beaufort, but please skip the title and formalities and just call me "Beanpole", as everyone else does.'

The three introduced themselves delighted to receive such a comfortably informal welcome.

'You're just in time to join me for breakfast,' said Beanpole. 'So follow me up these stairs to the house and you can tell me how I can help you. Head Office only gave me a few details of your visit here. They said something about you wanting to visit Labuan and have a look at the coal mining operations there. Come and help me dispose of some scrambled eggs and bacon and you can tell me all about it.'

They followed Beanpole up to the house and into a spacious dining room where the table was already set. There were bowls of fresh fruit on the chiffonier and two bain-maries holding hot scrambled eggs and crispy bacon. A percolator bubbled away at the end of the table, filling the room with the delicious aroma of coffee.

They all tucked in, chatting between mouthfuls about Beanpole's railway, the price of rubber and the terrible weather back in Brittanica. Finally, when they had eaten their fill and were sipping their coffee, Beanpole asked them about their visit to Labuan.

'It's all about a mining survey my parents were doing,' explained Willie. 'They would have come through here a few months ago when they visited Labuan.'

'Ah yes, of course I remember,' exclaimed Beanpole. 'Head Office mentioned that you were Hugh and Sally's son and that you and your friends were continuing an official survey of mining resources which your parents had begun. But where are your parents now?'

Willie was very careful to skirt around the secret nature of his parents' situation and simply said that his parents had died in a recent mining accident. Beanpole was very sympathetic. He pondered for a moment, marshalling his thoughts.

'Your parents came through here about six months ago. Head Office simply advised that they wished to visit the coal mine at Labuan as part of an official survey. They caught the scheduled ferry to Labuan and stayed a couple of days over on the island with the mining manager there, Paddy O'Driscoll, and returned here to get the tomotram back to Brittanica. They seemed happy enough and certainly didn't seem to be worried about anything. Quite the opposite actually, when I come to think of it. They seemed to be very pleased about something.' He smiled. 'Perhaps it was something they'd drunk in Paddy's whiskey. He drinks a lot, you know. Too much for his own good, really. It tends to make him reckless and do things he later feels sorry for. There was a story going round recently that he'd thrown one of his striking miners into a feeding pen on his crocodile farm to teach him a lesson. Never did hear if the miner survived and certainly no written allegations have ever been made against Paddy. However, if it did happen, it certainly hasn't stopped the strikes and riots by his miners. They're a grumpy lot anyway. Some are convicts from India and China, while others are local Malays who can't get a job elsewhere. I believe the mine isn't turning a profit for the Brittanic North Borneo Company and there are rumours that the company would like to cut their losses and sell the mine and the exploration rights over the island. I suppose that's why Paddy is developing his crocodile farm as an alternate employment for himself if the mine's sold.'

'Is Paddy O'Driscoll developing a crocodile farm as part of a zoo?' asked Gareth.

'Heavens no!' exclaimed Beanpole. 'It's a proper farm. He grows crocodiles from when they hatch out of their eggs to a size where he harvests them for their meat and hides. He sells the meat to local butchers and the hides to tanneries. The local leather workers then make all sorts of products from the hides, like handbags, shoes, belts and wallets. Old Paddy must have a bit of a soft spot for the crocs, because he's built up quite a museum about them in the ground floor of his bungalow. Apparently, he has his favourite crocs, which he treats like pets. Even plays games with 'em. Not my cup of tea, thank you.'

'Ugh,' said Penelope with a shudder. 'Nor mine. I think all reptiles are repulsive.'

Beanpole chuckled. 'Well, I can't say they're my favourite creatures either. But here in North Borneo we've certainly got more than our fair share of them.'

He changed the subject abruptly. 'Anyway, I think it's time we got you all down to the wharf to catch the ferry to Labuan. I've arranged for a couple of rickshaws to transport you and your packs down to the ferry, and I've sent a message to Paddy to expect you later this morning. Here's some local money to pay for the ferry, meals and accommodation. Arthur and Jimmy can wait here with the tomotram until you return from the island.'

They thanked Beanpole for his hospitality, loaded themselves into the rickshaws which were waiting for them outside the front door of the Residence and were down at the ferry wharf in about twenty minutes. The ferry was an ancient coal-fired passenger steamer. Its battered deck and superstructure were patched and painted in bright blue and yellow. A grey stained canvas roof was stretched out over the passenger seats to give some shelter from the sun, and from the ash particles belched out from the ferry's funnel. The passengers were mainly local folk carrying cane baskets of chickens, vegetables and strongly smelling fruit. Some sacks of rice were stacked in the centre of the ship and half a dozen scrawny goats were tethered to the metal side rails.

Penelope dug Willie in the ribs and pointed to a large net stored behind the rice and holding about fifty big yellow fruit.

'I bet those are durian fruit,' she said. 'They look luscious on the outside and their flesh is beautifully sweet to eat. But you can only eat them with your fingers pinching your nose closed, as they smell awful. Just like open sewers.'

Willie whispered back, 'They can't smell worse than this boat already smells. I just hope we don't run into any rough weather, otherwise I'll be rushing for the side.'

As it happened, the trip to Labuan was perfect. The sea was flat and glassy. The sea breeze was a cool northerly which took the engine's smoke away from the passengers and took the heat out of the sun's shimmering reflection. They arrived at the wharf at Victoria township just before midday to find Paddy O'Driscoll waiting for them. He was a big brawny man with long reddish hair and pale skin. A wide-brimmed straw sun hat was pulled down to protect his face, and a luxuriant ginger moustache adorned his upper lip. He wore a long-sleeved white shirt, and neatly pressed cream trousers held up by a brown crocodile-skin belt. His brown boots were also made of crocodile skin. He waved to them from the wharf and met them at the gangway with a warm welcome and a crushing handshake.

'Good to meet youse, it is,' he said in his Irish brogue. 'Just jump into these rickshaws here and we'll be away to my bungalow for lunch and out of this sun.'

They did as he instructed and were soon approaching a large comfortable bungalow set majestically on a hill in well-established trees and gardens overlooking the township and harbour below. The bungalow was extraordinarily large and consisted of two stories of living quarters, visitors' accommodation, a study and recreational rooms of a well-stocked library and a billiard room and, of course, the crocodile museum.

'Come inside and meet my business partner, Ah Chee,' invited Paddy, as they dismounted from the rickshaws and entered into the coolness of the bungalow. Ah Chee met them at the front door. She was a strikingly beautiful Chinese woman dressed in a white silk cheongsam embroided with red and gold lotus blossoms.

'How do you do,' she greeted them. 'Please come in. You are very welcome.' She looked at Willie and smiled. 'When Beanpole told us that you were coming to visit us he mentioned that you're the son of Colonel Hugh and Sally. How are they?' Willie repeated the explanation he had given earlier to Beanpole. Both Paddy and Ah Chee expressed their sorrow and regret at his news.

'We will miss them both,' said Paddy softly. 'We all got on so well together when they were last here about six months ago.' He looked across to Ah Chee. 'Ah well,' he said with a sigh, 'that explains a lot. These things happen. We just have to carry on as best we can.' Ah Chee nodded understandingly. Paddy turned to Willie and explained.

'We were hoping to approach your parents about a possible business arrangement Ah Chee and I were planning, but all that can wait.' His face suddenly brightened. 'We are very fortunate to have you three with us now, so we should enjoy the present and not dwell on the past. Let me show you to your rooms upstairs now before we have lunch and then we'll tour the mine and the museum this afternoon.'

'Would you be able to show us your crocodile farm?' asked Gareth.

'Of course, of course,' replied Paddy with a broad grin. 'I've got some real pets among 'em which are really playful. I'll take you there tomorrow morning and show you.'

Lunch was a leisurely affair of yum char washed down with lightly scented green Chinese tea. There was no doubt that Paddy loved crocodiles. The dining chairs were upholstered in crocodile skins, and the walls were adorned with crocodile skins. The table's centrepiece was a massive skull of a crocodile, its gaping jaws bristling with polished yellow teeth and its eye sockets filled with yellow glass. Paddy pointed to the centrepiece.

'Dear old "Hercules" here was a lovely old fella. Died of old age. Must have been a hundred years old if he was a day, I reckon. He was a big boy. Bit like his dinosaur forebears.' He paused for a moment and then mused reflectively, 'It's funny how cr'atures in Borneo can be so massive, like old Hercules here, and then so tiny like the Sarawak Hummingbird. It's almost as if there are spots in Borneo where time stood still for millions of years.'

'Have you always had a liking for crocodiles, Paddy?' asked Willie.

'Yes, pretty much. Ever since I was a young fella and been in the tropics. But I only became interested in crocodile farming since being posted here to the Labuan coal mine.' He sighed. 'Between ourselves, the mine hasn't been doing too well over the last five years, and the future doesn't look too bright either, with the possibility of diesel-powered engines for ships starting to be built. Anyway, we'd better get going and let you have a look at the mine.

We'll walk down to the bottom of the garden to the mine's railway and catch one of the coal trains returning to the mine from the bulk depot at the port.'

The mine's coal train comprised a powerful steam engine, a stores wagon and a line of eight coal wagons. It chugged up and down between the mine head and the bulk depot about six times a day. Paddy waved down the first coal train to appear and they all scrambled into the stores wagon.

Willie felt a growing sense of eager anticipation as they neared the mine. Here at last was his first real opportunity to inspect the site where his parents had disappeared. It was slightly unnerving to go back in time and inspect the area with such a deeply personal interest. Although he knew that a lot could happen in the time gap of a hundred years and he was, after all, in a twin world where things didn't necessarily match up with Earth. He was, nevertheless, desperately hopeful that he would discover some clue, however small, which would explain why his parents returned to this coal mine in Labuan. There must have been something quite special about it.

But his hopes of finding a clue were doomed to disappointment. There seemed to be nothing unusual about the mine. Nothing at all. The tunnel openings and archways appeared to be solidly constructed in brick. There were smaller railway lines leading from the pit head coal heap into the tunnels. The men working the mine were covered in coal dust and were working steadily, hauling small wagons filled with coal from the tunnels to the pit head. There was a tall brick chimney near to the tunnel entrances, but that was unused.

'Where do the tunnels go to?' he asked Paddy.

'Most just go a few hundred yards into the hill. There is a main shaft that drives in about three hundred yards, and then drops down about fifty feet to follow the coal seam. Then there are four side tunnels off the main shaft which go out towards the sea.'

Willie pondered the information quietly and with great disappointment. He wasn't sure what he expected to find. He just felt that there must be something here that would go some way to answering the questions in his mind. He felt greatly dispirited, which must have shown on his face.

'Don't worry,' consoled Penelope. 'We'll find something eventually. We'll just keep looking.'

'That's right,' said Gareth. He turned to Paddy. 'Is there anything special about the coal?' he asked.

Paddy grimaced. 'No, not at all. In fact, as coal standards go, the coal from this mine is second grade. It burns too quickly and is relatively dirty. We've had to lower our prices to meet the market. Most users now are smaller craft or standard freighters picking up just enough to get them across to China, where they can buy higher quality coal.'

Willie wandered aimlessly about kicking the odd lump of coal with his boots. He sat down on some old bricks just inside the chimney and contemplated. He hauled out the satellite photo mosaic and compared the landscape features. There were so many differences and changes that it was only possible to recognise the most obvious. But he refused to give up so easily. There simply had to be a compelling reason why his parents had returned to the mine. Gareth and Penelope watched him in silence, knowing full well that he needed time to come to terms with the realisation that there were no easy or obvious answers at this time. Finally, Gareth went over and sat down beside him.

'Nothing stands out,' he said softly.

'No. There doesn't seem to be anything.'

'Perhaps we could come back at a later date.'

'Yeah. P'haps we could.'

'We could also come down to Borneo and inspect the mine after we get back to Surrenden.'

'Yeah. You're right, Gareth. That's what we'll do.' Willie brightened up. 'Yeah. We'll find a way of visiting the mine when we get back and take photos of it. Then we'll come back here and compare things. We must find something.'

'We will. I'm sure of it.'

Willie stood up with a new sense of purpose.

'OK, Paddy. That completes our survey. We have seen enough. We can return to the bungalow now and see your great crocodile museum.'

Paddy's face lit up. 'Aye, we'll do that and you'll feast your eyes on the only crocodile museum in the world.'

They climbed aboard the coal train and were soon on their way to Victoria township. About halfway down the line they halted at a small stop where the engine took on water.

'I call this stop the Rubba-dub-dub,' said Paddy with a grin, and then, by way of explanation, 'That's Irish for a pub. I use this stop for my crocodile farm down the track there,' said Paddy, pointing to a wide stony track that disappeared into the thick jungle scrub. 'I don't like to advertise it so that's why there are no signs about.'

They soon arrived at the bungalow and Paddy could scarcely hide his excitement at showing off his museum. The museum's entrance was an archway between two stuffed crocodiles with polished black bodies and unblinking yellow eyes.

'These are the "guardians" to the museum,' explained Paddy. He led them into the interior of a huge room filled with display cases, photographs, paintings and memorabilia, stuffed crocodiles of all sizes, dishes of crocodile eggs and hatchlings, skinning tools, dioramas of crocodile nests and of crocodiles killing water buffaloes, crocodile jewellery of necklaces and bangles of teeth and claws, and all kinds of crocodile-hide products such as ladies' handbags, ladies' and men's shoes, wallets, belts, hats and rainproof jackets. On the far wall was a huge painting which dominated the entire room. It was a painting of Paddy wrestling a crocodile. He was holding the crocodile out of the water and under its forelegs. Its exposed white belly contrasted sharply with its dark brown body, black claws and red gaping jaws.

'That's meself and Prince Albert playing about five years ago,' said Paddy, pointing to the canvas. "Berty's about ten times as big now and far too heavy for me to lift, so we have to play other games. In fact, if I tried to wrestle with him now he'd probably finish me off with a "death roll".'

They dawdled about the museum, running their hands over the rough hides and sharp teeth of the stuffed crocodiles, feeling the weight of the crocodile eggs and posing with the crocodile bags. After about an hour of rummaging about the displays and listening attentively as they could to Paddy's endless commentary on crocodiles, Penelope whispered to Willie and Gareth so she could not be heard by Paddy.

'I've seen enough of these horrid animals to last me a life-time. I'm sick to death of blasted crocodiles.'

Both Willie and Gareth nodded their heads in agreement. But there was more to come. When they sat down to dinner, Ah Chee served them with a steaming hot crocodile stew with their rice and Chinese lettuce salad.

'You'll love this,' enthused Paddy. 'The strips of meat are prime rump. It's soft and sweet. You'd pay a fortune for this at the markets.'

The thought of eating a crocodile's rump would be enough to put anyone off eating for a month, but not so for Gareth. He devoured the stew as if the end of the world was coming.

'Great stew, Ah Chee,' he complimented. 'A really great dish. Can I have another helping?'

The other two were anxious not to offend Paddy and Ah Chee, and had to grit their teeth, smile, and disregard the growing nausea in their heaving stomachs. At the end of the dinner they were quick to make excuses about being tired from the tropical heat, and made their way to bed as smartly as they could. Paddy had opened a bottle of Irish whiskey and was keen to drink and talk on into the night, but could see that his guests were very tired from the tropical heat.

'Goodnight and sleep well,' he said. 'I'll wake youse early tomorrow morning so that I can show youse the farm and y'can catch the midday ferry back to Jesselton.'

That night Willie did not sleep well. He tossed and turned, his mind a turmoil of thoughts, his heart a ferment of emotions and his stomach an agitation of crocodile rump steak. He was bitterly disappointed that he had not been able to discover just one tiny clue as to his parents' interest in the mine. He just wanted to leave Labuan behind him now. For him it was an island of disappointments. He'd had enough of it. The stifling heat, his sense of failure and his queasy stomach all combined to make him feel thoroughly miserable. It seemed that he'd just dropped off to sleep when he was woken by Paddy's cheery wake-up call.

'Time to rise and shine. Breakfast in ten minutes.'

He clambered slowly from under the mosquito net and out of bed. He remembered Paddy's obsession with crocodiles and managed a smile. Breakfast was probably going to be crocodile eggs and fried slices of crocodile feet! But it wasn't. Thankfully, Ah Chee served them all a full English breakfast with scalding hot tea. It tasted like heaven, and he perked up to face the day with much greater enthusiasm.

Paddy was brimming with energy and good humour, cracking jokes as he ate his breakfast.

'How many arms has a crocodile got?' he quipped. He answered his own question, before bursting out in laughter. 'Depends how far he's got with eating his dinner!' As breakfast came to an end, Paddy outlined the programme for the morning.

'We'll catch the first train up to Rubba-dub-dub,' he said. 'Then we'll walk down the track to the farm. If you take your packs with you, you'll be able to take the next train directly down to the port to catch the ferry without having to come back to the bungalow. Ah Chee will come with us too. She's got some paper work to complete with the manager.'

They did as Paddy suggested and were strolling down the track to the farm within half an hour. The first indications that there was a crocodile farm ahead came in a series of notices posted on the side of the track. They were written in English and the local Borneo dialect. 'DANGER! DO NOT PROCEED. TURN BACK', they warned. Then a little further on, 'EXTREME DANGER. DEADLY CROCODILES. TURN BACK.' Paddy pointed to the notices.

'Don't want to encourage visitors,' he commented, rather unnecessarily. They were eventually confronted by a high brick wall topped with iron spikes, and entered through a solid wooden door built into the wall. A final warning notice was fastened to the door: 'EXTREME DANGER. DO NOT ENTER UNLESS ON BUSINESS. REPORT TO MANAGER'S OFFICE'.

In front of them was the crocodile farm. It consisted of about twenty large, deep concrete pens, and some open, grassed enclosures guarded by a high stout fence of spiked iron bars. A walkway surrounded the concrete pens and iron fence. Off to one side were a group of low buildings housing the office, storerooms, hatchery, killing rooms, butchery, hide drying areas and staff living quarters.

They dumped their packs in the office and met the farm manager, Kong Shi-See, a slightly built Chinese dressed in grubby shorts and shirt.

'Good morning, Mister Paddy,' greeted Kong, his smile showing a mouthful of teeth stained with betel nut juice.

'Good morning, Kong,' replied Paddy. He motioned to Willie, Penelope and Gareth. 'I'm just going to show the farm to these three friends of mine from the mainland. Ah Chee's got some papers that need your attention.' Kong nodded to the trio and shook hands.

'Have the croc's been fed yet?' asked Paddy.

'Yes, the goats arrived yesterd'y from Jesselton and were fed to

them an hour ago. Pwince Albert had a whole one himself. He's
been a little angwy with the other cwocs, but he seems settled now.'

Paddy nodded in satisfaction.

'That's good. We'll just go out and have a look around.' He
grinned. 'I might even just play one or two games with Berty.'

'OK, Mr Paddy. But just be careful. Pwince Albert is not
himself today.'

'I'll be careful, Kong.'

They followed Paddy out onto the walkway and peered over the
concrete walls down into the water-filled pens. Inside the walls of
each pen was a muddy bank, which provided a place for the
crocodiles to sun-bathe and to feed. Some bones, stripped of flesh,
protruded from the mud. There were dozens of crocodiles in each
pen. Some were almost fully submerged in the dark green water,
their presence only betrayed by their nostrils and eyes protruding
above the surface. A strongly fetid stench of rotting flesh filled the
air.

Penelope shivered as she looked down at the reptiles. 'They look
deadly, they smell deadly, they are deadly,' she said, turning away.

'Oh, they're fine when you get to know them. They do get a bit
cross when they're protecting their nests in the nesting area in that
large forested area over there, but generally speaking they're very
even tempered. We tell everyone to keep out of their nesting area,
just to be on the safe side. Come along to the grass enclosures and
we'll see how Berty is this morning,' said Paddy with a chuckle.

Prince Albert was indeed a prince among crocodiles. He was
huge. His massive black-green bulk was stretched out on the grass
bank near the water. His mouth seemed to be creased in a smile, as
he sunned himself after having gorged himself on goat meat.
Dragonflies danced among the horny bumps on his huge, black
back, feasting on the myriad of tiny water insects.

'Good morning Berty,' called Paddy. 'How's my little Berty this
morning? Had a good big breakfast have ye?' He continued on in
this vein for some minutes, as would a doting mother prattling to
her two-year-old infant. Berty shifted his head slightly towards
Paddy, but otherwise didn't bother moving. Paddy turned to the
trio.

'I'll show you how intelligent he is with a couple of games,' said
Paddy. He unlocked a gate in the enclosure's fence and picked up a
rattan ball lying on the ground. He walked slowly towards Berty and

crouched on his haunches about three yards away from the smiling crocodile. Then he rolled the ball towards Berty's snout. Languidly Berty batted the ball back to Paddy. Paddy was delighted.

'See,' he said with obvious pride. 'If I gave him a tennis racquet, we'd be able to play tennis. Now watch this.'

He carefully climbed to his feet and still talking softly to the crocodile, knelt down and pulled his jaws open. Berty seemed unconcerned. Paddy glanced back at the spectators to make sure they were watching. Then, with both arms keeping Berty's jaws open, he put his head between them. He turned his head so they could see his grin of triumph. Again Berty seemed unconcerned.

That is, until a dragonfly settled on his tongue.

His great jaws snapped shut in a twinkling, trapping Paddy's head and shoulders between them and driving his razor sharp fangs deep into Paddy's flesh.

'*Aghhhhhhh* ...' screamed Paddy. '*Aghhhhhh* ...'

Willie, Penelope and Gareth were stunned, snap frozen in shock. One moment all seemed to be well and then, in an instant, disaster had struck. All that could be seen of Paddy now was his flailing arms and legs, desperately trying to lever Berty's jaws open. But Berty would have none of that now. He had tasted human blood as it spurted from Paddy's wounds and sensed that this was a special meal that he must savour. He took a stronger grip of Paddy's body and started to pull him towards the water, where he could drown his prey and rip him to shreds with a death roll.

It was then that the ghastly realisation of what was happening occurred to the three onlookers. They looked around for a weapon and Willie spied some iron bars which were being used to repair the fence. Without thinking, he grabbed a bar, threw open the gate, and strode into the enclosure. Berty saw him coming and redoubled his efforts to drag Paddy into the water. But Willie was near enough to strike him with the bar. Once, twice, three times, Willie swung the iron bar and brought it crashing down onto Berty's head and body. But Berty steadfastly refused to let Paddy go and resolutely continued to pull him towards the water.

'His eyes. Hit him in his eyes,' screamed Penelope.

Willie swung the iron bar with all his strength onto Berty's skull, just above the eyebrows. The force of the blow halted Berty in his tracks and scraped some flesh off his head. But he still refused to open his jaws.

'Let him go, you black monster,' cursed Willie. 'Let him go or I'll kill you.'

He could see Berty's evil yellow eyes staring at him malevolently. He could sense the cold calculations being made by Berty to let go of Paddy and attack him instead. He brought his iron bar down like a lance, and with one violent thrust plunged its sharp tip deep into Berty's eye. The effect was instantaneous. He let go of Paddy, gave a roar of pain and anger, and turned on Willie, his jaws, now dripping with blood, open in murderous attack. But Willie was ready for him now, and welling up inside him was a sense of fury. He aimed his iron bar carefully and with one powerful thrust he shoved the iron bar as deep as he could down Berty's throat and into his gullet. Berty gave a deep scream as the bar tore into his innards, and he backed off into the water, roaring in pain and shaking his head from side to side in unsuccessful attempts to dislodge the deadly iron javelin. He reached the water, his huge tail thrashing in agony, and swam away towards the other side of the enclosure, the iron bar protruding from the water like a submarine's periscope.

With the crocodile gone, Gareth and Penelope rushed into the enclosure and helped Willie lift Paddy to safety outside the enclosure's iron fence. He was very badly wounded and bleeding profusely from deep wounds in his head, face, neck and shoulders. They cradled his limp body in their arms, his face chalky white and his eyes rolling back in their sockets. Blood bubbled from his mouth and nose from massive internal injuries to his lungs, and bright red blood spurted out from the ripped carotid arteries in his neck. Desperately, Penelope found the carotid artery pressure point and Gareth used his handkerchief as a pad to try and staunch the loss of blood. But they were unsuccessful. Strips of flesh hung from Paddy's face and shoulders. With a colossal effort, he summoned Willie to listen. Willie bent down over his face as Paddy managed to whisper.

'Croc farm … a cover … oil gas seepage … by croc nests … tunnel from mine … hoping your parents … would help … develop … Ah Chee 'n' me … going t' buy … mine … become rich.'

He managed a ghost of a smile and his eyes fastened on Willie.

'I t'ink I'm done for … too clever … my own good … look … after … Ah Chee.'

His head rolled over to one side as his last breath quietly

exhaled, and his whole body went limp. The three continued to hold him, like a marble tableau eternally transfixed with their closeness to their friend's death, their arms and uniforms awash with his blood.

It was Ah Chee's screams of alarm that brought them back to reality. She and Kong had heard the commotion of the fight with Berty, and had rushed out of the office to see what had happened. Poor Ah Chee was inconsolable. She cradled Paddy's head in her arms and wept uncontrollably, rocking backwards and forwards and kissing his lips as if to breathe life back into his body. Penelope did her best to comfort her, hugging her closely as she sobbed.

It was fully an hour before the initial wave of anguish subsided and they began to think of what they should do. At Kong's suggestion, they carried Paddy's body into the manager's office and laid him on a sofa and covered him with a sheet. They washed and cleaned the blood off themselves as best they could and changed their uniforms. Ah Chee then began to think through her mist of grief, sniffing and sobbing.

'I'll have to report ... the accident to the Company ... and to Beanpole as soon as possible. I'll have to get the District Officer to come over later today,' she said. 'We'll have to hold a funeral service for him tomorrow. Oh, my poor dear Paddy.' She dissolved in tears again, and then suddenly realised that Willie, Penelope and Gareth were visitors and would have to leave shortly.

'Thank you for your bravery,' she said, her eyes brimming with tears. 'Without you, I wouldn't have had anything left of my darling.' She paused to recover herself. 'You must go now and catch your ferry to Jesselton.'

'Yes,' replied Willie. 'We'll have to leave now. But we'll be back, Ah Chee, I promise, and we'll do all we can to help you overcome this awful loss.'

They each embraced her and then with tearful farewells left the crocodile farm, caught the train and ferry, and were at the Governor's residence in Jesselton by nightfall. Beanpole was keenly interested in their story. Willie related how they had completed most of their survey of the mine, but would need to return at a later date after the samples they had taken had been analysed. He didn't, of course, divulge Paddy's confession about the presence of oil and gas on the island, and his hopes to purchase the mine and exploration rights from the company.

Beanpole didn't seem at all surprised about the turn of events. 'Dear old Paddy,' he sighed. 'He took his obsession too far and paid the price. Ah well, I'll keep my eye on things at Labuan until a new manager is appointed, and make sure Ah Chee is looked after.'

The three, together with Jimmy and Arthur, had a quick evening meal with Beanpole before climbing into tomotram 256 to continue their journey to New Zealand.

As they settled down in their seats, Willie felt as if he had taken a gigantic step forward in finding answers to the questions he had about his parents' deaths. He now knew why his parents had been interested in the old coal mine. He now knew why they were exploring the old tunnels. It was all about the discovery of a new oil and gas field. At last he had been able to fit some important pieces into the jigsaw puzzle. And he knew he would have to return to Borneo at some time in the future to complete the puzzle.

He reflected on the terrible death of Paddy. He had never been so close to death before. Its finality and Ah Chee's consequential grief impacted deeply on his sensibilities. He knew they had done all they could to save Paddy. But his wounds were so severe and the loss of blood so advanced he knew they had no chance of saving him. He glanced across to Penelope and Gareth, both of whom must also have been going through similar soul searching.

'We couldn't have saved him,' murmured Penelope softly. 'He'd lost too much blood and I just didn't have time to even get the first aid kit.'

The boys nodded in silent agreement. For all of them it had been a sharp lesson on how precious human life was, and how quickly it could be extinguished.

'Beanpole said he would look after Ah Chee,' said Penelope.

Again the boys nodded silently. There seemed nothing more that could be said. They all settled down for the journey, each quietly reflecting on their visit to Labuan Island, the crocodile farm and the tragedy of Paddy O'Driscoll.

They had matured greatly from the events of the last two days.

9

MISSION TO DOWN UNDER

They arrived at the New Zealand Governor's residence in Christchurch just before breakfast time the following day. The tomotram barn was situated in the cellars under the huge rambling house that served as the Governor's house and offices. The Governor, the Honourable Orme Ranfurly, was standing on the platform waiting for them, smiling from ear to ear, and juggling a leather rugby ball in his hands. He was a very large, tall man, with untidy black hair bursting out from under an angler's tweed hat, big bushy eyebrows, and dressed in a brown tweed jacket with matching trousers and brown brogue shoes. He looked like a jolly farmer, full of good humour and, judging from his ruddy complexion, obviously had a strong liking for single malt whisky. He thrust out his massive hand to shake their hands in welcome.

'How do you do?' he asked, his voice booming and echoing in the confined space of the cellars. 'I do hope you had a good trip and didn't find it too tiring. My name is "Scrummage" Ranfurly. I'm Brittanica's representative here in New Zealand.'

'We had a very comfortable journey out, thanks, Governor,' replied the trio, introducing themselves. Willie smiled and pointed to the ball. 'You're keen on rugby?'

'Yes, indeed I am,' boomed Ranfurly. 'Greatest game in the world, no doubt about it. Used to play a lot in my youth, but lost a pin in the eighties, when I was in the Army, so have to be satisfied with coaching now.' He pulled up a trouser leg to reveal a wooden leg and grinned. 'Not to worry though. I can still get about the paddock, and I coach the local team. You don't happen to play rugby yourselves, do you?' he asked, looking hopefully at the boys.

'Well, yes, as it happens, we do,' replied Gareth, nodding his head. 'Willie here is quite a handy No 8 forward, and I play scrum half.'

"Scrum half and No 8 forward, eh? That's marvellous,' beamed Ranfurly. 'What a great piece of luck! My Governor's Invitation Fifteen has an annual rugby match tomorrow afternoon against the New Zealand Wasps. I've invited some good players from the northern teams and from Austronesia, but I'm still short of a couple of forwards, and I could always do with another scrum half. How would you like to play for my Governor's team?'

'That's very kind of you, Governor,' replied Willie. 'But what about Rudyard Percival's flying machine?'

'Ah yes, of course, of course. I hadn't forgotten,' muttered Ranfurly, who clearly had forgotten. His brow furrowed as he pondered, and then he suddenly brightened up.

'I'll tell you what we'll do. You all have a rest now until lunchtime, and then we'll go out and see Percival's machine this afternoon. Then get a good night's sleep, put in a bit of rugby practice tomorrow morning, and play the game in the afternoon. What do you think? Oh, and by the way, please call me Scrummage. It's much less formal than Governor.' He turned to Penelope and said, 'I haven't forgotten you, Miss Pendragon. Tomorrow also happens to be our Pony Club's Show Day. My wife and daughter are both keen riders and I thought you might like to join them, while we get on with our rugby. How does that appeal?'

'Thank you, Scrummage,' replied Penelope. 'I'd love that. I'm not very good though.'

'Right then,' boomed Ranfurly affably. 'That will be our programme. Let's go on up to the house and get you all settled in.'

They followed Scrummage up several flights of cellar stairs, to emerge into a large breakfast room, where his wife and daughter were just finishing laying the table for breakfast. Mrs Scrummage was genial, fussy and motherly. Her daughter, whose name was Meg, was dressed for riding, and had only just got back from taking her pony for a morning gallop. Scrummage introduced the group to his wife and daughter, although, of course, they already knew Jimmy and Arthur from previous trips.

'You've arrived just in time for breakfast,' declared Mrs Scrummage. 'So all of you can just take a seat at the table. Meg and I will get things moving in the kitchen. We're having what they call a "Farmer's Breakfast" around these parts. Hot porridge oats and cream, with lots of brown sugar, grilled chops, sausages and bacon with three fried eggs each, hash brown potatoes, hot buttered toast, apricot jam and honey, all washed down with strong coffee or tea. I guess you'll be famished after such a long journey.'

It was a great breakfast, and when everyone had finished they were ready for a snooze. The tomotunnel travel lag was beginning to take effect. Mrs Scrummage showed them upstairs to their rooms. Their heads scarcely touched the pillows and they were fast asleep. It seemed like only seconds later that they were woken by a thunderous knocking on their doors and Scrummage's voice, 'Wakey, wakey. Show a leg. We're on our way to Rudyard Percival's place in 10 minutes.' They all assembled downstairs, yawning and stretching, but soon became alert, especially after being given a glass of bracing fruit punch by Mrs Scrummage.

'Now,' said Scrummage, chuckling, 'besides rugby, I'm very keen on those mechanical monsters called automobiles. So I had one shipped out from Americana earlier this year. There's just enough room for you, Willie, and myself in the front, and some rear seating in the back for Gareth and Miss Pendragon. I call it my "Puddlejumper" or "Puddles" for short. So get rigged up with a coat, gloves and scarf, and we'll drive out to Percival's to have a look at his flying invention. I've sent word that we are coming to visit him. He's a bit eccentric. The locals call him "Potty Percival" because of his flying activities. They think that the Almighty would have given us wings if we were meant to fly!' He led them out to the front of the house, where an almost brand new car was parked in the driveway. It was painted tomato red, and its brass fittings gleamed in the morning sun.

'Whew!' exclaimed Gareth, appreciatively. 'What a beauty! It looks very much like one of the first Ford Model A Tonneau's ever produced. It's got a horizontally mounted engine in the centre. Probably develops about 10 horsepower. Leaf spring suspension. Electric start. Wooden spoked wheels and brass fittings. Walnut steering wheel with an accelerator lever. Four passenger capacity.' He glanced enquiringly over to Scrummage. 'I'll bet you can get about 20 miles per hour from her.'

'Yes, I can,' agreed Scrummage excitedly. 'I'd be able to go a lot faster, if only the roads were better here. Jump in and we'll get underway.' They all climbed into their seats, and were soon bowling down the narrow suburban streets and out onto the gravelled country roads. Scrummage drove like the Devil possessed. His eyes gleamed fanatically and his gloved hands held the steering wheel with a vice-like grip.

'I just love the freedom and speed,' he shouted, as if to excuse his full-tilt, straight-through-the-puddles driving style. Everybody hung on desperately as they bumped and bounced their way down the road, their scarves flying and their bodies bruised and battered. At last they swung off the gravel road and clattered down a broad clay track that led to a cluster of farm buildings in the centre of an overgrown farm block.

'Here we are,' exclaimed Scrummage, bringing Puddles to a skidding halt outside a small cottage which served as Percival's workshop and storeroom. The trio eased themselves out of the car grateful that their aching muscles could at last relax. They were met at the workshop door by Percival, who was a tall, thin man, with long wavy brown hair, piercing black eyes and thin trimmed moustache. He was dressed in a thick green and blue tartan woollen polo-neck jersey, matching trousers and scuffed brown boots. Over his clothes he wore a rather grimy canvas apron, smeared with oil and grease. In his hands he held an oilcan and spanner. He welcomed them warmly and invited them into his workshop.

'Just be careful what you lean up against,' he cautioned, indicating the glowing forge in the centre of the workshop. 'I wouldn't want you to singe yourselves.' The workshop was in huge disarray. Tools were scattered everywhere on the benches and over the floor. Bicycle wheels shared wall brackets with metal pipes, bamboo poles, wire, tin sheets and cobwebs. Stacked up along the walls were boxes of screws, nuts, and bolts, sacks of coal and cans of grease, paraffin oil and paint.

Scrummage introduced the trio, and then, smiling broadly, but nevertheless speaking with great sincerity and warmth, he announced grandly, 'Rudyard here must be one of the world's most distinguished, yet unacknowledged, creative inventors. Over many years he has persevered in very difficult circumstances, to progress an extremely important project for the advancement of civilisation. This vital project is called "Powered Flight". Working here, in secret seclusion, and using only rudimentary tools and basic materials, Rudyard has made powered flight a reality. Single-handedly, he has created a miracle. He has created the world's first powered flying machine.'

The trio looked around the workshop sceptically. This did not look like the sort of place a miracle could be created. However, at the far end of the workshop, behind two barnyard doors, there did indeed stand a machine of sorts. Rudyard reddened at Scrummage's lavish praise.

'Well, this is just my first attempt,' he protested, rather apologetically. 'But it does work and I have flown it for some distance. Come and have a closer look.'

They all gathered around the machine. It was a simple structure. A lattice-work of metal rods and bamboo formed the fuselage of the aircraft, and this had been mounted on a broad tricycle of bicycle wheels. The lattice-work supported a single, canvas-covered wing, about 20 feet long and six feet wide. Flaps had been let into the trailing edge of the wing to fit in the ailerons. Mounted centrally on the front of the wing was a sturdy motor and a primitive propeller made from curved metal flanges. A cane wicker chair served as the pilot's seat. There were two wooden foot controls for the ailerons and a single metal stick for rudder controls.

Gareth was enormously interested in the technical aspects of the aircraft's construction. His eyes gleamed with admiration as he carefully examined the engine and its mountings.

'It's astonishing,' he remarked, shaking his head in disbelief. 'Absolutely astonishing that such a machine like this can actually fly, as well as carrying a pilot. The engine seems to be made out of cast iron drain-pipes, bicycle sprockets and springs. But essentially it's a double-action, two-cylinder, air-cooled, internal combustion engine, with reciprocating parts and powered by paraffin oil. What sort of power can it develop, Rudyard?'

'I'm not really sure. But I reckon it would be at least 15-20 horsepower. I haven't got the necessary instruments to measure the revolutions. Anyway, it's quite a powerful machine. The all-up weight of the aircraft and pilot is probably close to 500 pounds. With a better cooling system and fuel delivery, I could probably double that power and weight. Come on. Let's take it outside and I'll show you what it can do.'

They opened the barnyard doors and rolled the aircraft out into the open. Rudyard put on a large leather coat, woollen gloves, a leather cap and home-made goggles. He grinned.

'It gets a bit chilly up there.'

He instructed Gareth how to swing the propeller to get the

engine turning over, positioned the aircraft into the wind and climbed into the pilot's seat. When he was ready, he gave a thumb's up sign to Gareth, who swung the propeller and the engine coughed into life. The aircraft moved quickly down the grassy field and took off climbing quite steadily to about 300 feet. Rudyard flew on for about half a mile, turned, landed safely back in a field near to the workshop and switched off the motor.

'There you are,' he exclaimed triumphantly, slipping off his goggles, helmet and coat and offering them to Willie. 'Would you like to have a try?'

'Too right,' replied Willie with enthusiasm. 'It looks as if it would be fun.' He slid into the pilot's seat and Rudyard explained to him how the controls worked.

'It's important to take things quietly,' he cautioned. 'Make your adjustments smoothly and slowly. Don't move your pedals too sharply or hard, otherwise you'll lose control. Keep the nose pointing up to off-set the machine's weight, and keep the motor at maximum power.' Willie nodded as he strove to take in Rudyard's instructions. He felt increasingly nervous and unsure of himself now. He had acted impulsively without thinking things through, when he had accepted Rudyard's invitation. It took Willie and Rudyard two hours of instructions, taxiing, rehearsals and practice on the ground, before he felt confident enough to make his first attempt at flying. Rudyard was encouraging.

'Yes, I think you know enough now to be able to give it a go.' He wiped his hands on a cloth and clapped Willie on the back reassuringly. Gareth and Penelope were beside him, also giving him encouragement and support.

'You can do it, Willie,' whispered Penelope. 'I just know you can.'

'Yes,' agreed Gareth, smiling broadly and oozing confidence. 'You'll find it a doddle. Just keep that motor at full power and it'll be a breeze.'

'I hope you're right,' replied Willie, smiling back and adjusting his goggles. 'See you shortly then.' Rudyard pulled the aircraft into the light wind and swung the propeller. The motor coughed and then settled into a steady rhythm. The aircraft moved forward, gathering pace as Willie steered it downhill to follow the path taken by Rudyard. The wheels bounced against ruts and large tufts of grass. Willie's heart was in his mouth as the control stick lurched this way and that in his hand. At last, after what seemed an age, the aircraft bounced into the air and started to climb, narrowly missing the gorse hedges at the end of the field.

'It's going OK. It's going OK,' thought Willie, as the aircraft continued to climb steadily. His cautious elation grew quickly into thrilling exhilaration with his accomplishment. He was flying! Actually flying! Flying by himself and in the first powered aircraft in the world! He choked back his desire to shout his joy. He wanted to scream, but he daren't. Such delight might invite disaster. On the ground, Rudyard, Gareth and Penelope were jumping with excitement.

'Yee hah, Yee hah,' they shouted. Willie flew on climbing steadily until he had reached a height of about 500 feet. The grassy meadows, trees, and hedgerows slipped away under him like a carpet. The rush of air from the propellers was an icy blast, as if it had just come from the snow-capped peaks of a distant mountain range, which he could now see clearly on the western horizon. The wind was a little gusty but he managed to make gentle adjustments to keep the aircraft steady.

He started to turn the aircraft around to his right to make his return back to Rudyard's field. As he commenced his manoeuvre, a sudden gust of wind caught the tip of the aircraft's wings and threw the whole aircraft on its side. He was unprepared for this and sharply thrust his control stick sideways to compensate. The aircraft responded equally sharply and rolled upwards and over onto its other side. He almost panicked. His mind went blank as the ground and sky seemed to twirl about him. He was about to make a desperate move with his control stick when he suddenly remembered Rudyard's advice.

'Make your adjustments smoothly and slowly.'

He quickly marshalled his thoughts and focused on the immediate task. Gently he stroked the control stick to move the aircraft upright and was rewarded almost immediately. With a huge sigh of relief he brought the aircraft back under control and headed it back towards Rudyard's field, which he could now see looming up in the middle distance. But he was a little breathless now from the shock of the near disaster. His heart was pumping nineteen to the dozen. His blood drained away from his head. The perspiration under his helmet and coat had suddenly chilled into icy droplets. He felt cold, limp and lethargic. His mind seemed to be preparing him to accept the inevitability of yet another disaster, which, this time, would be fatal. But he didn't care.

Then he caught sight of Gareth and Penelope waving encouragingly at the far end of Rudyard's field. It was just the mental spur he needed. It was as if the dark grey blanket of self-doubt, which had started to smother him, had suddenly been ripped away. They believed in him and his ability. He felt a fierce determination surge through his body. The blood rushed back to his head and into his fingertips. He regained control of himself and of the aircraft. It suddenly occurred to him that he was on the home run now. All he had to do was land according to Rudyard's instructions. He tested the responsiveness of the foot pedals and control stick and felt satisfied. He focused intently on his approach, keeping the motor at full power and slightly lifted. The aircraft lost height, cleared the gorse bushes at the end of the field, gently landed, and taxied up to the little throng of gleeful onlookers. Willie switched off the motor and remained sitting in the seat, smiling broadly.

'You've done it! You've done it!' shouted Gareth and Penelope delightedly, slapping him on the back.

'Magnificent, magnificent,' beamed Scrummage.

'That was excellent flying. Couldn't have done better myself!' exclaimed Rudyard enthusiastically. They chattered on together for a minute or two, while Willie pulled himself together, and Gareth discussed possible technical improvements with Rudyard. Finally, Scrummage pulled a fob watch from his jacket pocket, looked at the time, and said, 'Heavens! It's already four o'clock, and we have to get back to the Residence before dark.' He turned to Rudyard. 'You'll remember, Rudyard, that we'd had spoken earlier of the possibility of you lending the aircraft to Brittanica, for further appraisal and possible commercial development. I can see from the reactions of the trio here that this course of action would seem to be very desirable. Are you happy that we now proceed with this proposal?'

'Yes I am, Scrummage,' replied Rudyard, nodding his head vigorously. 'I think that's a very good idea and the best way for the whole idea to be developed profitably.'

They all busied themselves dismantling the aircraft in accordance with Rudyard's instructions and carefully packed it into wooden boxes. These were fitted onto a trailer which would be pulled behind Puddles.

'You'll have to drive very carefully and slowly,' Rudyard cautioned Scrummage. 'That trailer holds my life's work.'

'I will,' promised Scrummage, and he kept to his word. They arrived safely back at the Residence just as the warm, late afternoon sun sank below the horizon. Jimmy and Arthur carried the boxes down to the cellars and stowed them carefully in the tomotram ready for the return trip to Brittanica. It had been a long and exciting day. After a quick supper, everyone bade each other good night and went upstairs to their rooms. Scrummage was particularly keen that Gareth and Willie should get a good night's sleep in readiness for the rugby match the next day.

'Get your heads down now, boys, and sleep soundly. You'll need to be sharp eyed and bushy tailed tomorrow. I'll give you a call in the morning about 9 o'clock, so you'll have time for an hour's practice before lunch. The match starts at 2.30. I've had the programme printed off. Here's a copy for each of you.' He handed them a printed cardboard sheet, which listed the players for each team, their positions and clubs under the imposing heading:

GOVERNOR'S XV v NEW ZEALAND WASPS XV
WEDNESDAY 10 SEPTEMBER
KICK-OFF 2.30 pm

'On the face of it, Scrummage, your Governor's side looks to be very strong,' remarked Willie as he examined the listing. 'You've imported players from around the world! Do the New Zealanders know about this?

Scrummage coughed in an embarrassed sort of way, looked innocently into space and muttered. 'Well, in past years the Governor's side hasn't always won. So I thought that this year I'd make sure we had a reasonable side.' He suddenly looked very serious and said, as if in self-justification, 'This is the equivalent of an international rugby test match, you know. These locals aren't a bunch of babies still in their nappies.' The boys both laughed out loud and nodded understandingly.

'Yes, we know, Scrummage,' responded Willie. 'I believe it's almost like another religion here in New Zealand. We can expect a pretty tough match tomorrow. We'd better get our heads down and get some beauty sleep. Good night.'

10

TESTING TIMES

The next day was crisp and clear. Scrummage was as good as his word and let them all sleep in until mid-morning. After another 'Farmer's Breakfast', Scrummage and the boys jumped into Puddles and drove off to the nearby rugby ground for some practice before the match.

Scrummage led the way into one of the changing rooms, where a group of players were changing into rugby practice gear. The pungent smell of liniment filled the air. Scrummage steered the boys towards a massive, barrel-chested man, with legs like tree-trunks, enormous arms and no neck.

'This is the team's captain, "Pinetree" Meads,' said Scrummage. 'Pinetree, these are the two players from Surrenden, Willie McBride and Gareth Jones.'

Pinetree shifted his bulk to face the boys. 'Aw, yers, we're very pleased to have you fellas aboard. You certainly look pretty fit,' he said with an appraising eye. He turned to face the rest of the team.

'Hey, listen up, you fellas. This is Willie and Jonesy from Surrenden, who have just arrived to join the team. Willie is playing at No 8 and Jonesy at scrum-half. I'll let you introduce yourselves. Now let's get a move on. Be outside in five minutes, so we can put down a scrum and try some lineout moves.' Pinetree pointed to a large canvas bag and said to the boys, 'Practice jerseys and pants are in there. We've got some spare boots hanging over there in the corner. Use your own socks.'

The boys nodded and started to rummage around in the bag. Other players came up to introduce themselves and welcome the boys to the team. They found some rugby gear that fitted and trotted out of the pavilion and onto the field. The rest of the team had already started their warm-up exercises. Under Pinetree's watchful glare the team were doing push-ups, sit-ups, stretch exercises and sprint runs between the goalposts.

'OK, you fellas. Now you're all nicely warmed up, we'll do some set-piece training,' said Pinetree. 'We'll get a scrum down in the scrum machine.' Gareth, as scrum-half, waited off to one side, ready to put the ball in front of the hooker's feet.

'Right,' called out Pinetree as he packed down on the side of the scrum, 'let's get a bit of a go-forward on the count of three. Keep low and maintain a good straight back.'

'One, two, three,' he called. The entire pack grunted with effort and shoved sharply forward as Gareth put the ball in. The scrum machine reluctantly moved back a yard and the ball shot out of the back of the scrum between Willie's feet.

'Not bad. Not a bad scrum,' growled Pinetree appreciatively. 'We'll just do a dozen more to iron out any bugs and then we'll get our line-outs sorted out.' The practice continued for a good hour, before Pinetree seemed satisfied that the team would be able to play effectively.

'Don't underestimate the opposition,' he cautioned. 'I hear that they might even tour Brittanica next year, so they'll be very good. Take a rest now and be back ready for the kick-off at 2.30.'

'I wonder how Penelope is enjoying herself at the Pony Club meeting?' mused Gareth as he and Willie rested on the sidelines. 'I bet she's found a new pony and fallen in love with it.'

'I think you'd probably be right. Another little nag to replace Quirky,' laughed Willie. 'Actually, we may be able to see how she's getting on after the match. Scrummage told me that the Pony Club was just outside the rugby ground.'

In no time at all, it seemed, the Governor's rugby team re-assembled in the changing rooms to get ready for the match. As soon as all the players were changed, Pinetree called them all together and gave them a pre-match booster of advice. Then he led the team out of the pavilion and onto the rugby ground. The pavilion and the sidelines were packed with spectators who cheered loudly as the team ran onto the field. But they gave an even greater cheer for the Wasps team who followed them out of the pavilion. They were dressed in yellow and black jerseys, black pants, socks and boots. The Wasps were a huge team of monster forwards, with a slippery and devious-looking back line, and an energetic dynamo as scrum-half. Willie caught Gareth's eye as they surveyed the opposition.

'Crikey,' he muttered softly, 'this isn't going to be a tea-party.'

'It's going to be a little testing,' agreed Gareth, looking with awe at the opposition. 'But remember, the bigger they are the harder they fall.'

'Oh, sure, sure. I'll try to remember that.'

The first half of the match was an absolute disaster for the Governor's team and they were down 12-nil at half-time. They were slow to get to the break-downs, missed important tackles, knocked-on, lost the throw-ins at the line-outs, and kicked away what little possession of the ball they were able to secure.

They gathered at the sideline for the half-time oranges, battered and bruised and their spirits very much down. Scrummage came down from the pavilion to join them, his face betraying his disappointment at the score-line. Pinetree unbuttoned his headgear, and shook his head mournfully.

'We're going to have to change our strategy and cut down on the unforced errors we're making,' stated Pinetree flatly. 'Anyone got any ideas?' There was an unbroken silence for a few seconds, as the team looked at one another hopefully. It was Willie who spoke up.

'There are one or two things we could try, Pinetree,' he said with bright optimism. The whole team suddenly became very attentive.

'We've got nothing to lose, so why don't we open things up with our backs, pick up the pace and try a few unusual moves in the line-outs,' he suggested. 'If we get the ball away quickly to our backs by getting Gareth to use torpedo-dive passes, pass the ball quickly to our wings, we'll be able to attack them out wide where they're weakest. I can follow up to give our backs support and get to the breakdowns first. That way, we retain possession, and run their big forwards off their feet.' The team now gave Willie their whole attention. 'With the line-outs, we could become much less predictable. We could use the short throw-in much more frequently to burst down the blind side.

'Not bad, not bad at all,' agreed Pinetree, thoughtfully stroking his chin. 'Yes, I think it could work well.' He turned to Gareth. 'How good are you at torpedo-dive passes, Jonesy?'

'OK,' replied Gareth. 'I can get an extra five yards distance in my pass so the backs can stand back a little and have more room to move.'

'Right then,' announced Pinetree, having made up his mind, 'that's what we'll do.'

After a shaky start, the second half was sublime rugby for the Governor's side. The ball shot out from the scrum and into the wingers' hands in a twinkling. The forwards ran forward onto the ball, with pace and strength, to regain possession and resume the attack. The line-outs were a sure platform from which to launch try-making rolling mauls, and breathtaking bursts from the full-back, who cut through the opposition like a knife through butter. Tries flowed from magical reverse passes, dazzling sidesteps and an incredible synergy between the forwards and backs. The Wasps were devastated. What, at half-time, had seemed a foregone conclusion of a victory for them, had suddenly been turned into a thorough defeat at the final whistle. The home crowd at first clapped politely when the Governor's team started to score, but when they began to appreciate that it was superb rugby they were watching, they filled the pavilion with deafening cheers.

With the final score standing at Governor's XV 36 Wasps XV 12, Scrummage was beside himself with joy. He almost danced down out of the pavilion to shake the hands of each of his players as they trooped off the field and into the changing room.

'Well done, well done,' he cried, his face beaming with delight. 'You played like true champions.' He was particularly pleased with the boys.

'The final result was largely due to your second half strategy, Willie, and to your fast and accurate passing, Gareth,' he said, thumping each of them on their backs.

'Great game you fellas played,' boomed Pinetree, shaking their hands with his vast fist.

'Thanks,' replied the boys. 'It was a real pleasure to play in a team with so many good players.' After having showered and changed, all the players congregated in the dining room under the pavilion to talk over the match, and to share a few drinks. Willie took Scrummage aside and said, 'I don't want to be a killjoy, Scrummage, but I think that before the party gets going, my group should slip away and start back for Brittanica.'

Scrummage looked disappointed, but could see the good sense in the suggestion and readily agreed.

'Yes, yes, Willie. You are quite right. We'll go straight back to the Residence now and see that you get away in the next couple of hours. The Riding Club Show will be over now and I expect that Miss Penelope will be already waiting for you along with Arthur and Jimmy.' They climbed into Puddles and drove back to the Residence, singing victory songs, to join the others, who were waiting for them in the lounge. They were drinking champagne! Scrummage burst into the room excitedly, did a little jig (as much as his wooden leg would allow!) and said, 'Ask me. Go on. Ask me how we did!'

Mrs Scrummage smiled calmly, and replied, 'I don't have to ask. It's as plain as the grin on your face. Your team won.'

'*Won*!' exploded Scrummage, 'We trounced 'em. We thrashed 'em. We cut 'em up into little pieces, and fried 'em up for breakfast! 36 points to 12 points. Highest score ever made by a Governor's XV.' He stopped suddenly. 'But hang on a moment. Why are you drinking champagne?'

'Because, my darling, while you males were grubbing about in the mud, Meg and Penelope were winning just about every prize offered at the Pony Club. Best Pony, Best Jumper, Best Groomed Pony. They came away with ten red ribbons.'

'That's astounding, simply astounding,' exclaimed Scrummage. 'Well done, you two.' Meg and Penelope smiled a little self-consciously.

'I've never ridden a grey before,' said Penelope. 'But Meg let me ride her second pony called "Playboy". He's a beautiful grey and didn't misbehave at all. He's just the most beautiful pony imaginable,' she gushed, her eyes bright with excitement. She turned to face Scrummage, Willie and Gareth.

'He's got the most gorgeous, soft nose, lovely big, brown eyes and he's the best natured pony I've ever seen. He's so gentle and obedient. I just love him to pieces! Do you think we could find room to take him back with us?' she said pleadingly. 'Meg said she is happy for me to borrow him for a while.' Scrummage threw back his head and laughed uproariously.

'I think that's a matter for Willie to decide.'

Willie felt flummoxed and very unsure of what to say or do. He turned to Jimmy and Arthur, who were standing beside Penelope. 'Are there any rules or regulations about the carriage of ponies on the tomotram?' he asked. Arthur and Jimmy shook their heads. 'No,

Mr William,' replied Arthur. 'Nothing I've ever heard about. We've carried lots of different things on the tomotram but nothing as big as a pony.'

'My aunt lives down in Kent on a small farm, near a village called Little Chart,' volunteered Jimmy. 'I'm sure she would be happy to offer Penelope grazing and stabling for Playboy. As for travelling back on the tomotram, I'll help Miss Penelope look after him. I used to be a stable-boy when I was a youngster.'

Willie, Gareth and Penelope looked at each other in astonishment. The village of Little Chart was where the Surrenden Riding Club was situated!

'There you are,' burst out Penelope triumphantly and with a knowing smile. 'It was meant to be.' But Willie was not convinced. What if the pony got spooked in the tomotram and went berserk? What if the tomotram was damaged? How would Woody react to them bringing back a pony?

Gareth could see Willie's indecision and understood the safety and the many reasons for his caution. But he could also see how important this matter was to Penelope.

'Woody must have dealt with similar events before,' he said softly to Willie. 'He probably won't be the slightest bit surprised. If we get some bales of clover grass and a tank of water, Playboy should be able to settle down at the front of the tomotram, well out of anyone's way. Anyway, look at Penelope. This is a really big thing for her. I remember my Auntie Dinnie saying that for girls ponies are just as important as dolls.'

Willie nodded his head slowly. 'Hmmm … Yes, I suppose you're right,' he said, without much conviction.

'Oh well. All right then,' he said reluctantly to Penelope. 'But you and Jimmy will have to take responsibility for him.'

'We will, we will, won't we Jimmy?' enthused Penelope.

'Yes, we will, Miss Penelope,' replied Jimmy with a huge grin on his face. 'Come on, we'll get him down to the tomotram now, through the large cellar doors on the back driveway.' They hurried away to get Playboy. The others packed up their kit and loaded it onto the tomotram. As soon as Playboy was safely aboard, and Penelope and Jimmy had packed up their kitbags, they said their goodbyes to Scrummage and his family, and started the tomotram motors for the 15-hour return journey to Whitehall.

The first 8 hours of the journey were uneventful. Except for

Arthur and Jimmy, who were taking turns at driving, everyone settled themselves down comfortably to sleep. Even Playboy lay out to rest quietly on the clover grass scattered on the floor of the tomotram. They had travelled far up through the Oceania tunnel past Australia and into West Borneo when Penelope, Jimmy and the boys had cooked themselves a small 'Farmer's Breakfast' of eggs and bacon, washed down with hot, sweet tea.

'We should be coming up to Kuching shortly,' called out Arthur from the driver's compartment. 'That's where this line meets the Far East Line. Then we head west to link up with the Middle East Line.' He peered into the blackness of the tomotunnel.

'Hello,' he exclaimed. 'There are some lights ahead. It must be a Wormholes maintenance gang at work.'

He slowed down in response to a long line of amber lights set on stands on one side of the tunnel. Ahead, he could see a large set of amber lights, in the form of an arrow, blinking on and off, and pointing down a side-tunnel to the left.

'No, it's not a maintenance gang. It's a diversion. There must be some blockage up ahead on the main tunnel. Ah well, I just hope the diversion route isn't too long. I don't know this area too well.'

He slowed the tomotram speed down to almost a walking pace and proceeded carefully. They soon reached another line of amber lights, followed by a second blinking amber arrow, which again pointed to the left. This led them into a somewhat larger, mainline tomotunnel. By now everyone was peering out of the windows to see what was happening and why they were being diverted.

'That's odd,' said Arthur. 'By my reckoning we're now travelling south when we really want to be travelling west. We now need to get a couple of diversion arrows pointing to the right, I think.'

They travelled for a full minute before they spotted the next line of amber lights leading to the first arrow pointing to the right. This time, however, the arrow comprised a set of green lights blinking cheerily away, and pointing down a rather narrow tunnel. Arthur felt more confident now, and speeded up the tomotram in anticipation of the next green arrow, which he felt should bring them back onto the mainline leading to Kuching.

'Shouldn't be long now,' he announced confidently. The others settled back in their seats, and Penelope went down to the rear of the tomotram to groom Playboy. Suddenly, and without warning, the tunnel ended, and the tomotram seemed about to crash into the wall of the closed end. Arthur was caught by surprise, and was unable to stop the tomotram.

'Brace yourselves,' he shouted. 'We're going to crash!' Instinctively, he crouched behind the shelter of the control panel.

But instead of finding a solid wall ahead, the tomotram slid through a waterfall of black water, and out into an immense grotto-cave of stalactites and stalagmites. Willie and Gareth rushed up to the driver's compartment to see if Arthur was safe.

'I'm all right, Mr William,' gasped Arthur, as he looked around and steered past some colossal towers of shimmering, golden coloured stalactites.

'Put the tomotram into hover mode, Arthur,' Jimmy instructed. 'We mustn't go too far into this labyrinth.' They all peered out of the driver's window and gasped in incredulous disbelief at what they saw.

Before them was a wondrous forest of immense stalactites and stalagmites, as far as their eyes could see. Glistening in the intense, incandescent beams of sunlight entering from the grotto's opening, the pillars formed a bewildering mirror-maze, sandwiched between the dense shadows that shrouded the floor and the roof. The intensity of the light was unbearable, and it became almost impossible to see, even as they shaded their eyes.

Suddenly, dark shadows descended over the tomotram, accompanied by the urgent beating of wings and scratching of a myriad of tiny feet.

'Look, Mr William,' shouted Arthur. 'Those are moths! Swarms of moths! They're all over the outside of our tomotram.' They all looked out through the windows to see a boiling turmoil of thousands of spindly legs, snaking proboscises, and green and orange coloured wings, as dense clouds of moths jostled for a position on the tomotram.

'They're attracted to us because of the reflection of light on the tomotram,' yelled Penelope from the rear of the tomotram. 'They look like Sarawak Hummingbird Hawk moths. We'll have to get into a dark area, so they will fly off.'

'You're right, Penelope,' responded Willie. 'You just stay there with Playboy, and keep him calm, while we do some manoeuvres to get out of here.' He turned to Arthur. 'Take the tomotram slowly down to the floor, Arthur. Once these moths have flown off, we'll get back to the waterfall and out of here.'

'Right you are, Mr William,' said Arthur, as he moved the switches to control their descent.

The tomotram soon reached the floor of the grotto, where it sat rather unsteadily as if resting on a trampoline, as the moths flew off back up into the blinding light. Their spirits rose as they saw that their stratagem appeared to be working successfully. Then, without warning, the front of the tomotram seemed to drop downwards and slide forwards.

'What was that?' Willie asked the others.

They looked at each other blankly. Then there was another slight drop and another forwards motion as if the tomotram was burrowing itself into a hole. There was the sound of branches creaking and cracking. It was quite shadowy now and most of the moths had flown off, leaving a coating of wing dust on the tomotram. A sudden stillness descended. A chilling stillness, that brought a vague, indefinable threat of danger. They continued to look at one another, their senses alert and muscles tensed for instant action. The tomotram slid forward once more as if by an invisible force, which made them almost lose their balance. Then, stillness descended again. They regained their balance, looked outside the tomotram's windows and saw to their astonishment that the tomotram was precariously held up off the ground by the branches of shrubby trees and vines. But these branches and vines were not normal. They were covered in shrouds of grey-white blanket sheets of spider webs. Dense and virtually impenetrable, the shrouds were full of debris and the sludge of insect remains. They each grabbed a torch from their kit and shone the beams out of the windows.

'We're stuck, Mister William,' said Arthur, peering out of the driver's windows into the tangle of branches and spider web shrouds. 'The front of the tomotram seems to be caught up under the branches.'

'Put the tomotram into reverse, Arthur,' called Willie.

Arthur gunned the motors and the tomotram moved back a little and then slid forwards again.

'My God, what's that outside?'

Penelope's urgent call of alarm brought them quickly to the windows. From the light of their torch-beams they could see an army – a tsunami of spiders – advancing towards the tomotram from the sinister drapes of the spider web shrouds. Then the spiders were on the tomotram. They could hear the rustle of millions of spiders' palps sweeping up the wing dust left by the moths like a myriad of tiny brooms.

'Aw, they're just giving the tomotram a bit of a clean-up,' said Gareth with a relieved smile. 'We should ask them to give the tomotram an executive wax while they're about it.'

'I'm not so sure that's all they're doing,' said Willie, peering intently out of the window. 'Look at this.' He pointed to his window. Strands of glistening spiders' web were starting to appear on the window's exterior surface. 'I think these spiders are going to try to sew us into one of their blanket shrouds as a food reserve.'

'You're kidding,' said Gareth in disbelief. He looked out of Willie's window and then some others. Strands of sticky spider's web were also starting to appear on them as well. 'Blimmin' heck,' gasped Gareth. 'Let's get out of here – fast!'

'Arthur,' shouted Willie, 'get us up out of here pronto. Switch on full power.'

'Right, Mr William,' replied Arthur, who had been looking at the sudden emergence of web strands through the driver's windows. 'Damned spideys. Never did like them,' he muttered to himself. He switched the motors to full power and smiled as the motors responded with an accelerating hum. The tomotram heaved itself backward and then stopped, as if held by grappling hooks. The engines strained, but the tomotram was held fast.

'For Heaven's sake, Arthur,' shouted Willie. 'Give it full power!'

'I am Mr William,' shouted Arthur, his voice betraying mounting fear. 'But we seem to have too much weight at the front and we're caught up in these branches.'

Willie looked around. Perhaps if they could transfer weight to the rear of the tomotram it would help free them up.

'Penelope, how about taking Playboy down to the back of the tomotram?'

Penelope went over to Playboy and took hold of his reins. 'There you are,' she said soothingly, caressing the pony's neck. 'There's nothing for you to worry about. We'll soon be out of here.' In fact, Playboy didn't appear to be worried at all. He just stood still quite calmly and watched what was going on. Quietly, Penelope led him down to the back. Almost immediately they could feel the front of the tomotram lift as Playboy's quarter-ton weight started to have an effect.

"Give it full reverse power now, Arthur,' called Willie.

'Yes, Mr William,' replied Arthur, and pulled the controls back.

There was a high-pitched whine as the motors responded, followed by an ear-drum-splitting screech as the tomotram heaved and shuddered its way free from the awful trap of spiders' shrouds and smashed branches.

Released from the tangle, the tomotram leapt backwards. Arthur immediately grabbed the controls, slowed the tomotram down to a gentle cruise and gained height up into the golden light above.

'You wonderful, gorgeous creature,' gushed Penelope as she threw her arms around Playboy's neck. 'You've saved our lives!'

'No doubt about that,' concurred Willie. 'We'd be a spider's lunch in a couple of weeks if he hadn't helped break us free.' He turned towards the driver's compartment.

'How are we going, Arthur? Can you see the waterfall entrance yet?'

'Yes, I can, Mr William,' replied Arthur, his voice full of enormous relief. 'It's just up ahead.'

He steered the tomotram through the black water and into the short tunnel behind. They continued to move slowly forward, until they could see the detour's green arrow blinking away in the darkness. The area beneath the arrow was now brightly lit with lamps, and figures could be seen working with picks and shovels.

'Aha. At last, a Wormholes maintenance crew,' exclaimed Arthur.

'I'll just stop and give them a piece of my mind,' he added, his tone tinged with anger. He stopped the tomotram in the middle of the workers, who could now be clearly seen to be Helvetians. They were all wearing long, yellow coats, with hoods over their heads. The coats bore the company name, 'Maintenance Crew' sewn across the backs. Their faces were smiling mischievously and creased with grime. They all wore long yellow trousers and heavy working boots. They ceased working and leant on their shovels, grinning amongst themselves as the tomotram stopped in their midst. One worker, who was obviously the Crew Boss, stepped forward to the tomotram door as Arthur opened it.

'Looks like you've had a shower,' he said to Arthur, looking round at his crew knowingly. They all burst into gales of laughter.

'That's right,' agreed Arthur evenly, holding back his anger. 'We also had a really close look at the spiders too.' The laughter stopped immediately. The Crew Boss instantly stopped his taunting chuckles and became serious.

'What spiders?' he demanded.

'Oh, didn't you know,' replied Arthur airily, sensing he had found an advantage. 'The floor of that grotto is covered in enormous armies of spiders. They're all damned hungry too. If it wasn't for the waterfall, I reckon they'd be up here after you lot as quick as a wink.' The maintenance crew drew closer together, as if for safety, and looked nervously down the tunnel.

'No, we didn't know that,' said the Crew Boss, his face turning a little pale. 'Look, we were just playing a little joke. We didn't mean any harm for you.' Willie now joined Arthur at the tomotram's door.

'That's all very well,' said Arthur. 'But you've put Mr McBride and my other passengers here in great danger.'

'Mc Bride. Have you got Mr McBride aboard?' asked the Crew Boss.

'Yes, I have,' responded Arthur a little quickly. 'Well, his son actually. Mr William McBride. Colonel McBride and his wife are missing.'

'That's very bad news.' The Crew Boss looked up at Willie. 'My name's Jorvik, sir. We're very sorry to hear about the Colonel and his wife. And we're very sorry that our little joke caused you some trouble and danger.'

Willie shook his hand, smiled and replied. 'That's all right, Jorvik. We managed to extract ourselves OK. Did you know my parents well?'

'Everyone in the company knew your parents, sir, and really respected them,' replied Jorvik. 'I believe they used to travel into some pretty out-of-the-way places.'

'Well, we might also be doing that in the future, so I hope we see more of you and your crew.' He grinned at Jorvik and said, 'But no more false detours!'

Jorvik smiled back. 'I can promise you that, sir. We'll do our best to look after you.' He pointed northwards down the tunnel. 'Kuching is that way.'

With that they shook hands, and waved goodbye. Arthur closed the door, re-set the controls, and accelerated the tomotram down the tunnel. They arrived back at the Whitehall Tomotram Depot about twelve hours later, tired but happy that their first mission had been completed successfully. They unpacked Rudyard Percival's aircraft and stowed it carefully in the storeroom behind the Despatch Office. Jimmy led Playboy off to a wash-down area to give him a drink. He assured Penelope that he would make arrangements with his Aunt for the stabling and grazing for the pony-hero that very day.

Penelope patted Playboy's face and neck. 'See you soon, beautiful boy,' she whispered, and reluctantly joined Willie and Gareth, as they climbed the stairs to report to Woody in his office.

Woody was delighted to hear of their success in securing Percival's aircraft, and promised that his engineers would examine it together with Gareth, who, obviously, had a technical knowledge of such things. Woody opened the cocktail cabinet in his office and brought out a bottle of chilled champagne.

'I think your triumph deserves a little celebration,' he said, as he popped the cork and poured out a glass for each of them. He raised his glass and proposed a toast, 'Here's to the continuing success of Surrenden and Brittanica.'

'To the continuing success of Surrenden and Brittanica,' they chorused.

They chatted on to Woody, relating to him their adventures and experiences. Woody, in turn, listened politely to them, but took particular interest in Gareth's description of the aircraft and how it might be improved to give it greater load-carrying capability. Finally, Willie said that he thought it was time that they returned to Surrenden. Woody escorted them to Gladys's room, assuring them that he would again be in touch with them shortly by coded letter. They opened the green door, entered the Time Thread, and emerged into the Museum Curators' Storeroom.

11

MISSION DEBRIEF – PENELOPE'S LIST

'I still can't believe the size of that crocodile in Paddy's farm,' said Gareth, shaking his head in disbelief. 'It was gi-normous.'

'Yeah, we were lucky all right, dealing with it the way we did. It's a great pity that poor old Paddy didn't survive,' said Willie.

It was Sunday afternoon, the day after the three of them had returned from their successful mission to North Borneo and New Zealand. They had gathered together in the deserted Company Common Room to discuss the events of the mission, and see if they could be better prepared for the next one should Woody ask them. Penelope and Gareth had brought their laptops with them and Willie had his parents' satellite photos of Labuan Island.

'I've got a little list of things I thought I'd like us to talk about,' said Penelope, brandishing a piece of paper. She looked at the boys enquiringly. 'Is that OK?'

'Sure,' they said, a little taken aback at Penelope's organisation. 'Go for it.'

'Well,' said Penelope, 'I've really only got two items, but they're both pretty important. Firstly, could we discuss the "Twin World" idea? I know we've just returned from Brittanica, but could we have all been dreaming? To be honest, it all seems rather like a fairy story to me. It's so unscientific and unreal.'

'Exactly my thoughts,' interrupted Gareth. 'I've been worried about that too. I just couldn't get my head around the idea of twin worlds. I mean … it sounds crazy, doesn't it? Two worlds that are very, very similar, with one world just a hundred years or so behind the other. But then I started to do some internet research on "twins" and discovered that it could happen. Look what I found on the net.'

He fiddled with his laptop and brought up a reference on Wikipedia:

'Identical twins occur when a single egg is fertilised to form on zygote which then divides into two separate embryos. Their traits and physical appearances are not exactly the same due to environmental conditions both inside and outside the womb, and their slightly different DNA structure. Studies have shown that identical twins reared in different environments share similar personality traits, mannerisms, attitudes and interests.'

'Now, I know that this refers to biological twins, but the same description could be made to the birth of twin worlds at the beginning of our solar system, couldn't it? That would explain why both worlds are made of the same materials, have similar volcanic backgrounds and have similar behaviours and environments. What do you think?'

'Yes,' said Penelope thoughtfully, but a little sceptically. 'Yes. That could be true, I suppose. Like … it's got some scientific reasoning behind it … I guess. I'd just like to see some proof.'

'Well, it sounds neat to me,' said Willie. 'It sounds very possible. Tell you what, though. If we can find things that are the same, or almost the same, on both Earth and Brittanica … and stuff … we would know we had real-life identical twin worlds, wouldn't we?' He suddenly reached into his trouser pocket and hauled out the satellite mosaic of Labuan Island and spread it out on the table. 'Let's have another look at these.' They all studied the photos.

'Yes. There it is,' said Penelope, jabbing her finger excitedly on the photo. 'There's that brick tower at the coal mine. Remember?'

'And there are the concrete pens of Paddy O'Driscoll's crocodile farm. They're a bit overgrown now but you can still see their outlines,' said Gareth, pointing to another area on the photo.

'Yeah,' breathed Willie 'You're right. I'd forgotten about the tower. But it's there all right, and so are the crocodile pens.' He paused momentarily. 'Well, what about that huge cavern with the moths and spiders? Was all that real or just a fantasy nightmare?'

'It felt blimmin' real at the time, boyoh,' said Gareth with a grin. 'I can still see those spider webs trussing us up for dinner.' He shuddered. 'Ugh. I hate spiders.' He reached for his laptop. 'Now, let's see. Arthur said we were approaching Kuching just before that tunnel maintenance gang diverted our tomotram, so we must have been travelling through Borneo. I'll Google "Borneo Caves" and see what we get.' His search was rewarded with 143,000 references, with the first listed being www.goborneogo.com, which proclaimed 'Discover Borneo – Mulu Caves Exploration Package'. He clicked on the site.

'Bingo,' exclaimed Penelope, looking over Gareth's shoulder and pointing to a photograph of a gigantic cave on the screen. 'There. Look. The Deer Cavern in the Mulu Caves. Read out the description, Gareth.'

'Mulu is the home to Mulu National Park and one of Borneo's greatest attractions,' read Gareth. 'Deer Cave is the world's largest natural rock chamber that can contain London's St Paul's Cathedral five times over and accommodate 40 Boeing 747s side by side ... hey ... listen to this. Its attractions include the world's largest spider webs and huge swarms of moths. The spiders' webs, constructed by the Stretch spiders, *Tetragnatha bornetorii*, are estimated to spread out over about 100 acres of the cave's primeval forest and vines like massive blankets. The cavern is accessible by plank walks through the jungle and by lighted paths throughout. The cavern is part of a massive cave complex of which about 345 kilometres of paths have been mapped of an estimated 1000 kilometres. Three waterfalls tumble from the cave's roof to subterranean rivers below. At 5pm each day over 2 million bats blacken the sky as they depart Deer Cave in search of food.'

He looked up at the others with a grin. 'How about that, then? The cavern, the waterfalls and the spiders. What more do you want? Looks like the "twin world" theory is starting to measure up.'

'OK, I'll admit that it might look good with physical things ... like caves and towers and stuff. But what about people?' asked Penelope. 'Are there any connections between people? I mean ... if there were people connections, I could really start to believe in it.'

'You're right, Penelope,' agreed Willie. 'If we could find some people connections, the "twin world" theory would almost certainly be true, wouldn't it?'

'You mean that all three of us might have twins in Brittanica?' Gareth teased. 'Or there might even be another Rocky? Or ...' His voice tailed off as an incredible possibility occurred to him. 'Or,' he said in a half-whisper, 'we might find our twin parents.'

The three were silent for a few moments as each wrestled with this bizarre possibility. It was Willie who broke the silence. He shook his head.

'Nah. They wouldn't be our parents. They'd be the parents of our twins, wouldn't they? That would make them some sort of relatives … like cosmic aunts and uncles … our twin Brittanic cousins. They'd be similar but not identically the same.'

'You're right Willie,' agreed Penelope, nodding. 'So what we need now is some connection involving people that we can clearly identify.'

'What about old Rudyard Percival,' suggested Gareth. 'He might figure on the net.'

'Good one, Gareth,' said Willie, clapping him on the back. 'Do a search on him and see what comes up.'

Gareth googled 'Rudyard Percival', but nothing came up. They all felt a bit deflated and disappointed that their expectations hadn't been met.

'I suppose twins don't have to have the same name, do they?' said Gareth. 'What if I do a search for, say, "First Flying Machine" and see what we get.' He typed in his search and selected a Wikipedia site.

They were astonished to see a long list of claims to be the first to have completed piloted flight, some of which were during the 1800s and before. Although most of the early claims had used some form of glider, there had been several attempts using steam engines. It was the attempts in the period 1900-1903 that were of particular interest.

'There he is,' said William excitedly. 'There he is.' He pointed to the list. 'Richard Pearse, New Zealand – 31 March 1903.' Gareth clicked onto the hyperlink.

Richard Pearse
Richard William Pearse (sometimes known as Mad Dog Pearse, 3 December 1877-29 July 1953). A New Zealand farmer and inventor, who performed pioneering experiments in aviation.
Pearse appears to have successfully flown and landed a powered heavier-than-air machine on 31 March 1903, some nine months before the Wright brothers. The documentary evidence to support such a claim remains open to interpretation, however, and he does not appear to have developed his aircraft to match the Wrights' achievement of sustained flight. Pearse himself made contradictory statements which for many years led the few who knew of his feats to

accept 1904 as the date of his first flight. The lack of any chance of industrial development, such as spurred the Wrights to develop their machine, seems to have suppressed any recognition of Pearse's achievements.

List of Witnessed Flights

31 March 1902 – First powered flight flying an estimated distance around 350 yards in a straight line, barely controlled.

? March 1903 – A distance of only about 150 yards.

2 May 1903 – distance unknown: the aircraft ended up in a gorse hedge 15 feet off the ground.

11 May 1903 – Pearse took off along the side of the Opihi River, turned left to fly over the 30-foot tall river-bank, and then turned right to fly parallel to the middle of the river. After flying nearly 1000 yards his engine began to overheat and lost power, thus forcing him to land in the almost dry river bed.

'Wow. That's it all right. No doubt about it,' said Penelope. She was flushed with the excitement of the discovery. 'So it really does look as if we've got "twin worlds", doesn't it?'

'Yep, it sure does,' replied Willie. He lolled back in his chair, feeling triumphant and satisfied with the result of their research. He was conscious now of having felt uneasy and full of doubts when Penelope had first raised the subject of the twin worlds. After all, the whole concept had seemed highly improbable and she had been right to express her doubts. But now their research seemed to prove that the twin worlds did exist and they were part of both of them.

Penelope pointed to her piece of paper with the list of items to discuss. 'Well, my last item is our military mentors. I know that it's quite common for students to have mentors to help them in their careers and education and each of us have our own mentor. But do you think they have any special powers? ... Like ... I mean ... could they protect us from danger?'

'Yeah, that's an important question,' chimed in Gareth. 'The thought image of my mentor came into my mind when we were fighting off those spiders in the Mulu caves, but it was nothing more than that.' He paused and whispered shyly as if he didn't really want the others to hear him. 'I could have been a bit scared.'

'Wow, is that right?' said Penelope with warmth and understanding. 'Me too. The thought image of Dame Amelia came into my mind when we were in the Caves. Then, for no particular reason, I thought of Playboy.'

'Well, he saved us, didn't he?' reminded Willie. 'He really was the key to us getting out of those spider shrouds. Well, I thought of my mentor when I was learning to fly Percival's plane, but I wasn't really in any danger.'

'No. But *we* were, weren't we, Penelope?' said Gareth, giving her a dig with his elbow.

'Yes,' said Penelope, playing along. 'We were in terrible danger from a madman in his murderous flying machine.' They all laughed.

'Well,' said Willie, 'we actually don't know if our mentors have any special powers. I guess we'll just have to wait and see. Keep our fingers crossed that it never comes to that.' He yawned and looked at his watch. "Let's leave it at that for the time being. It's tea-time now and Gareth looks dangerously hungry.'

That night in his room Willie reflected back on the missions to Borneo and New Zealand. They had been very worthwhile. He had made considerable progress on solving some of the puzzles surrounding his parents' deaths. He had discovered that they were trying to explore the possibility of an oil and gas find on Labuan Island. Now he had to find out if the mine explosion occurred from natural causes or not. If it hadn't, then he had to find out who had caused the explosion and why. For some inexplicable reason, his thoughts flashed back to Lucifer-Mortlock and the quarrel with his father all those years ago. Perhaps The Lag would figure in the final explanation of things.

He looked at his Study Timetable and saw that another military training day, called 'Combat Power', was scheduled at the Combat Wing the next day. His memories of the survival training and Exercise 'Chicken Feed' were still very fresh in his mind, and he supposed that the lessons were going to be more of the same.

But then again, Rocky always had a surprise up his sleeve.

12

COMBAT POWER

Major De Roche stood behind the lectern in No. 1 Lecture Hall, in the Rutherford Science and Technology Laboratory Block, and gazed up at the rows of cadets in the tiered seating. It was three weeks after Exercise 'Chicken Feed', and the junior cadets had assembled for a full day of military training. It was rumoured that Rocky had been delighted with the cadets' performance on Exercise 'Chicken Feed', but if that was the case, he was hiding his pleasure well. His face was impassive, and his manner was analytical and detached, like the coach of a Lion's rugby team. He rapped his knuckles on the lectern to get the cadets' undivided attention.

'Battles are won by the side that deploys overwhelming "Combat Power",' Rocky stated without emotion. 'Today's lessons are about "Combat Power", so if you want to know how to win battles, then you'd better pay attention.' He paused briefly and looked directly at the cadets, a ghost of a smile on his face. He went on.

'Combat Power is the most appropriate mixture of firepower, mobility and morale to win the battle in the situation at hand. Let me give you a few examples. If you have masses of firepower, but you cannot see the targets, then your firepower cannot be used to destroy the enemy. If you have a huge army, but your soldiers are starving, have poor equipment and bad leadership, then their morale will be low, and they will have no will to fight the enemy. On the other hand, if you have masses of firepower, and a huge, well-fed, well-equipped army with high morale, you may still lose the battle, if you are immobile and cannot manoeuvre your forces to avoid destruction from the firepower of the enemy.

You can see, then, that getting the best mix of combat power is quite tricky, and is highly dependent on your objective. Once you have determined your objective, you should complete your military appreciation, and tailor the combat power of your forces to give you the best chance of victory. You should also be aware that it is always cheaper, and easier, to "Win the hearts and minds of people" than it is to "Search and Destroy" them. It might take longer, sometimes much longer, but in the end those that started out as your enemy could end up as your friends. So your objective should always include the notion of "temporarily disable", rather than "permanently destroy".' Again he paused, and glanced off to a side door leading into the lecture hall.

'We are very fortunate today to have a guest lecturer from the Weapons Advanced Research Technologies Establishment (WARTE), based at Sedlescombe, to talk to us about how science and technology can help us obtain the best mix of combat power. Ladies and gentlemen, Professor Zharkov.' As he spoke, Rocky turned, and motioned with his arm to the side door.

Professor Golka Zharkov, dressed in a white laboratory coat, bounded into the Lecture Hall, carrying a large metal suitcase, which he placed on a small table beside the lectern. His face was lined and creased, and his eyelids were saggy, and slightly bloodshot. His worried looks belied a man who exhibited enormous energy and enthusiasm for his work. He leaned on the lectern and smiled beamingly up at the cadets like a modern-day Albert Einstein.

'Good morning, ladies and gentlemen, and thank you Major De Roche for that introduction.' His voice was warm with a slight guttural quality. 'This is the tenth year I haf had the pleasure of introducing Surrenden cadets to the marfels of adfanced science and technology, and collaborating with the School in conducting faluable equipment user trials. I intend to follow this tried and proven procedure again this year. I will also leaf with your Museum Curator, Lt Shrewdfellow, as I haf done before, some examples of the new equipments to be added to the exhibition gallery now being constructed.

'This year, I wish to introduce you to three new technologies, and their combat equipments. You will then be able to use them in your future combat power mixes. Firstly, let's look at the exciting new advanced science of nanotechnology. This technology deals with the manufacturing and the measuring of objects of microscopically small size. Extremely small size, in fact. The basic unit of measure is the nanometre, which is one thousand-millionth of a metre! We are now talking about objects so small that they merge into, interact with, or pass through, the very structure of other materials. These qualities have enabled us to create a new generation of materials, called "meta-structures", which possess quite unusual electrical, optical and magnetic properties. The prefix "Meta" means "change", or "transformation to a higher order".

'We have developed one meta-structure, called **"See-through"**, which transforms our ability to see objects. Because this new meta-structure is smaller than the wavelength of light, it is able to interact with the light's photons. When we coat, or paint, an object with "See-through", it directs light around the object and streams it to exit in the same direction it was travelling before. Consequently, an observer sees nothing of the object. Of course, this has enormous advantages for military combat power.'

He paused, and smiling broadly, gestured with his arm towards the empty space at the rear of the lectern.

'Let me demonstrate with my colleague here.'

He looked around behind him. There was nobody there except for Rocky who was sitting in a chair by the entry side door.

'Good heavens,' exclaimed Professor Zharkov, in surprise. 'My colleague has gone.' He turned to the cadets. 'You haf all been here for the last half an hour. Has anyone seen my colleague? His name is Captain Dreadnought.' There was no reply from the cadets, who looked at one another enquiringly. The Professor looked at Rocky appealingly.

'Haf you seen him, Major?'

Rocky shook his head. 'No, Professor. I haven't seen anybody here other than yourself and the cadets.' The Professor turned back to the class.

'Hmmm,' he mused. 'No-one here has seen Captain Dreadnought. Perhaps, if I shake a little "Pixie Dust" in the air, he might be persuaded to appear!'

He took out a can of ordinary supermarket talcum powder from his suitcase, stepped towards the rear of the lectern, and shook the talcum into the air. Instantly, as if by magic, a figure appeared as the talcum powder settled. It was the figure of a giant-size robotic soldier, his automatic weapon at the ready. It looked like a sculptured ice figure, cold, efficient and lethal.

'Ah, there you are, Captain Dreadnought,' said the Professor in mock surprise. He moved again to his metal suitcase. 'Would you please introduce yourself to the cadets?'

'Yes- Professor,' said the robot haltingly. It raised its left arm in a salute, while its right arm continued to hold its weapon. 'Hello- cadets.- My- name- is- Captain- Dread-nought.- I- am- a –Mark-Eight- Auto-mated- Troop-er- design-ed- for- the- mod-ern- battle-field.'

'Of course you are, Captain Dreadnought,' agreed the Professor, heartily. 'And a jolly good automated trooper you'd make too, I'm sure. But the only reason we can see you now is because the light is reflecting off the talcum powder.' The Professor turned to face the cadets. 'So you see from that demonstration that the "See-through" paint did not react with the talcum powder, and the ambient light was reflected off each particle of dust. Accordingly, we were able to see the *shape*, but not the *detail* of Captain Dreadnought. We are continuing to work on improving the unique properties of the "See-through" paint, so it can integrate with other materials it comes in contact with.' He reached inside his metal suitcase again and withdrew a large torch-shaped object with a large cylindrical head.

'Let's now turn to our second advanced technology – that of Lasers. The letters in the word "Laser" stand for Light Amplification by Stimulated Emission of Radiation. Lasers are devices that generate an intense narrow beam of light, or other electromagnetic radiation of a single wavelength, by using the natural oscillations of atoms or molecules. Because the laser light is so concentrated, its energy can be used to cut through all kinds of materials, including metal. They are also used in surgery where surgeons can cut through tissue with incredible accuracy, and the laser beam seals small blood vessels around the wound.

Today, however, our interest in laser technology is not for its life-saving surgical capabilities, but for its ability to temporarily blind the enemy. We haf to be very careful here, to use only low-powered lasers, in order *not* to cause permanent blindness, which is contrary to Protocol IV of the 1980 United Nations Convention on Certain Conventional Weapons.' He held up the torch-like device in his hands to show the cadets.

'Our laser device, called a **Laserlance**, is a solid state laser, and has three settings to control the power of the laser beam: low, medium and high. It's also equipped with an optional array of lamps which give off white light, so that the operator can see where the laser beam is pointing. With the help of Captain Dreadnought here, I'll now demonstrate the capabilities of the Laserlance. But before I do, each of you will have to wear a set of these specially modified safety glasses, which we call **Beam-blockers**.' He dug into his suitcase again and brought out a set of black, broad-banded, protective eyepieces for each cadet.

'Make sure you cover your eyes completely with your Beam-blocker. If you don't, you may end up being temporarily blinded.' He then went over to the robot, dusted off the talcum powder coating its Vision Visor, and slipped a Beam-blocker over his own head and eyes.

'Now, Captain Dreadnought,' said the Professor. 'Tell me what you can see.'

'I- can- see- twenty- one cad-ets,- Professor,' stated the robot tonelessly. "Six-teen- males,- and- five- fe-males. One- male- is- pick-ing- his- nose.' The cadets all sniggered and looked quickly around to see who could be so bad mannered.

Professor Zharkov grinned and replied, 'Thank you, Captain Dreadnought.' He turned to the cadets and pointed the Laserlance at the bottom of the robot.

'Now I have set the Laserlance's power at Low. Watch the red spot of the laser beam as I move it up the Captain's body from his boots to his Vision Visor.'

He did so, and let the laser's tell-tale red spot dwell over the robot's Vision Visor for a moment before switching the Laserlance off.

'Now, Captain Dreadnought, tell us what you can see,' instructed the Professor.

'I- can- see- noth-ing,' responded the robot without emotion. 'My- light- sen-sors- are- disabled.- My- auto-matic- circuit- Audit- and- Repair- sys-tem- reports-slight- dam-age- to- my- light- sen-sors- requir-ing- twelve- hours- to- recover.'

'Thank you, Captain Dreadnought,' replied the Professor. He turned to face the cadets.

'There you are. The robot is *not* permanently blinded and will recover in twelve hours. However, until that happens, he is useless as a battlefield trooper, as he cannot move safely and cannot fire his weapon effectively.' He put the Laserlance away in the suitcase.

'Now, let us look at the third new technology. This technology has had an enormous impact in the science of psychology. Psychology, as you may know, is concerned with the study of all forms of human and animal behaviour. This new technology is a gas, which causes the inhaler to have temporary hallucinations, fantasies, delusions, illusions and phantasmagoria of all kinds. We call this new gas "**Dream**". It is made from derivatives of the toxins found in the so-called "Magic Mushrooms", the Death-Cap mushroom, and a chemical substance called 3-quinuclidinyl benzilate, or BZ, as it is known. This new gas is made for crowd control and law enforcement, rather than for warfare as a chemical weapon. The gas takes effect almost immediately it is inhaled, and takes some weeks to naturally wear off. It is therefore very useful in, say, anti-terrorist operations. In fact, a very strong form of "Dream" has already been used by the Russians against Chechen terrorists, to end a hostage crisis at a Moscow theatre in late 2002. Of course, to protect oneself against the nightmarish effects of "Dream", one would need a suitable gas mask and a gas suit. I have a gas mask and a gas suit here to show you.'

He rummaged around in his suitcase, and triumphantly held up in one hand a dark green, full-face rubber gas mask, with huge goggle-eyes, a nose flange and double air respirators. In his other hand he held a dark green, one-piece plastic suit, with a hood and zipper. He hung the gas mask over the lectern, unzipped the gas suit and climbed into it, pulling the hood over his head.

'Does it fit me?' he asked. 'They come in four sizes – baby, small adult, medium adult and large adult. Actually, I probably need an extra small adult size.'

There was little response by the cadets, who were still more interested in the gas mask dangling from the lectern.

'Do I look beautiful then?' enquired the Professor appealingly, pirouetting like a ballerina.

'No. Not at all,' chorused the cadets laughing, who now had sufficient time to re-focus on the gas-suited figure.

'You look like a frog,' said one.

'More like a warty toad,' quipped another, making a reference to the initials of the Weapons Advanced Research Technologies Establishment.

'OK, OK,' replied the Professor, grinning and nodding. 'But you do realise that this little green number is high fashion in the gas-suit world?' Without waiting for a reply, the Professor continued. 'High fashion or not, warty toad or not, it's very important, as you will find out later, that your gas suit and gas mask fit perfectly.'

The words, 'as you will find out later' hung in the air like Damocles' sword. The cadets fell silent and they suddenly became extremely attentive. It dawned on them that they may shortly be donning a gas mask and gas suit. And so it was.

'Now, I would like each of you to pick up a gas mask and a gas suit from the boxes on the table beside the door, and move outside to the Gas Training Chamber,' invited the Professor, indicating with his arm towards the entrance to the Lecture Hall.

'But there's nothing there, Professor,' exclaimed a cadet. 'Are the boxes outside the room?'

'Aha,' replied the Professor, grinning broadly. 'The boxes are in the room all right. I put them there myself earlier this morning before my presentation. Perhaps we have to use a little more "Pixie Dust" to make things clearer.' He held out a can of talcum powder towards the class.

'Do I have a volunteer to help me?'

'Yes,' said Willie. 'I'll give it a go.' He walked quickly up to the Professor and took the can of talcum powder.

'Where should I sprinkle this "Pixie Dust", Professor?' he asked.

'Over here in this direction, Mr McBride,' responded the Professor, indicating an area to the left of the entrance door.

However, instead of immediately sprinkling the talcum powder, Willie searched the area with his hands. His fingers felt the outline of two large cardboard boxes on what felt to be a wooden table, and yet he could see nothing. He lifted the lid on the first box and looked inside. The contents were not coated with the See-through paint, and he could see that it was full of gas masks. He pulled one out with a flourish, just like a magician pulling a rabbit out of a hat.

'*Yes,*' exclaimed the Professor, chuckling approvingly. 'Maestro McBride thrills the crowd with yet another illusion. Thank you, Mr McBride. Would you please take your gas mask and a gas suit, and lead the way to the Gas Training Chamber. Each member of the class, now pick up a mask and suit and follow Mr Mc Bride.'

The cadets did as they were instructed and Major De Roche,

together with Company Sergeant-Major Larkin, met them outside a nearby red brick building, which had been specially built as a Gas Training Chamber. When they were all assembled, Rocky gathered them around him for a briefing. For once, he was smiling, and his whole attitude was one of re-assurance and encouragement.

'Now,' he said warmly, 'I know this training exercise is not everyone's cup of tea. Some of you may even be a little frightened following Professor Zharkov's presentation, and what you imagine will be the possibility of risking hallucinations from inhaling Dream gas in the Chamber. But let me reassure you that this is not the situation. We are *not*, I repeat *not*, using Dream gas this morning, but a harmless irritant called CS gas, which is sometimes used by the police for crowd control.

This Gas Training Chamber is for training only and has built-in safety features. Firstly, it has a Preparation Room immediately inside this exterior door. The Preparation Room is separated from the gas-filled chamber by a clear plastic door. At the other end of the gas chamber is another clear plastic door leading to another room, called the Safety Room. This in turn has an exterior door. The gas chamber itself has a line of windows to the exterior, which can be broken to give immediate access to the outside. Company Sergeant-Major Larkin will be in the Preparation Room and Company Sergeant-Major Truscott is already waiting in the Safety Room and will be watching each of you as you move through. Are there any questions so far?'

'Yes sir, I have,' said one of the cadets, whose face was ashen, and who was clearly not relishing the prospect of going through the Chamber. 'Why do we have to do this training?'

Rocky nodded and continued smiling. 'That's a very good question. The answer concerns the future trend of global military operations. You will recall that I spoke earlier of the desirability of "temporarily disabling", rather than "permanently destroying". The use of disabling gases is going to be much more widely spread in the future, and you should have a better understanding of the possible effects on those people on the receiving end, as well as the necessary protection measures. There is also the wider matter of familiarity. The more knowledge you have about emerging situations, the better equipped you will be, to be successful. In short, the more one knows, the less likely one is to be afraid. This gas training is the only opportunity you will have to participate in practical training in this useful technology during your time at Surrenden.' There was a hushed sigh of relief from the assembled cadets. Rocky looked around the group.

'Any more questions before we continue?' There were none, and so Rocky continued.

'You will get into your gas suits and gas masks now, and enter the Preparation Room one at a time, and only after I have checked the fitting of your equipment. You will walk slowly through the gas chamber, breathing normally, and exit out into the Safety Room. Sergeant-Major Truscott will let you out into the open, where you will take off your mask and suit. You will wait until we have all been through, when we will have a quick debrief, and return to your rooms for a shower and clean-up.' He turned to face William and said with a smile, 'You can be first, Mr McBride.'

Willie nodded. He felt quite confident about what he had to do, but his whole body was tense and alert. He unzipped his green gas suit and climbed into it, aware of its soft texture and folds. He pulled the zipper up, and was immediately aware of a build up of body heat as the suit started to insulate him from the outside environment. Rocky helped him don his gas mask, pulling the adjustable rubber straps around his head to achieve an air-tight fit around his face. He found he could breathe quite easily, and he could see clearly through the mask's eye goggles.

Rocky was smiling at him. 'You look OK, Mr McBride. How do you feel?'

'I think I'm all right,' replied Willie, aware of his rather muffled voice echoing in the mask.

'Very good then,' responded Rocky. 'We'll just pull your hood over your head, and you can get on your way.'

Willie entered the Preparation Room to find 'Larry' Larkin, dressed in his green gas suit and mask, waiting for him, grinning and giving him the big thumbs-up sign. The Preparation Room was shadowy and slightly threatening. Willie's mask obscured his peripheral vision and he found he had to consciously turn his head to see about him and where he was going. Larry pushed open the clear plastic door to the gas chamber. Willie entered and looked around. The chamber was about 20 yards long and five yards wide. Despite the light entering from the line of safety windows, the chamber was very gloomy. He could see the concrete floor and walls, and some piping and nozzles, through which the gas was introduced. There was a white haze of gas filling the chamber. He walked slowly towards the other end, breathing as normally as he could. He could smell nothing unusual, but he could hear his breathing, and the movement of the valves in his respirators regulating the flow of the toxic air through the filters. He was aware of his feet shuffling as he walked. He looked about, and could well imagine the terror felt by a victim of a gas attack. At last he reached the other end of the chamber where he could see 'Trusty' Truscott through the clear plastic door. Trusty was also grinning and giving him the thumbs-up. He entered the Safety Room, where Trusty gave him a victorious slap on the back and opened the exterior door for him to exit out into the open. He felt an immediate surge of relief, pulled back his hood and carefully took off his mask.

'Well done, Mr McBride,' said a woman's voice. Willie looked around in surprise to see Matron Sweetingham and Corporal Jenkins standing beside the School's ambulance, its back door open, ready for any casualty.

'Well done,' repeated Sweetie, with a warm, welcoming smile. 'Take your gas suit off, and come over here and wash your hands and head in this basin of water.'

Willie looked at Sweetie and Corporal Jenkins thankfully. 'Major De Roche didn't say anything about having an ambulance waiting for us!' he said with some surprise.

'Probably didn't want anybody to be alarmed,' said Sweetie gaily. 'We're just here as a safety precaution, aren't we, Corporal Jenkins?'

'Yes, Matron,' agreed Corporal Jenkins, lightly and with a grin. 'We're just a belt and braces safety precaution.' He turned to Willie and said quietly, 'What was it like Mr McBride? I've never actually done any gas training yet.'

'Not too bad, Corporal. Just a bit dark and gloomy,' replied Willie, getting out of his suit. 'I seemed to be unaffected, although I think I can feel a little irritation around my neck where the mask and clothes didn't quite meet. What do I do with this suit and mask?'

'Give them to me, sir,' said Corporal Jenkins, regarding him with new respect. 'They get washed, and checked for serviceability. If they are re-useable they get re-boxed. I think this lot is to be taken to the Museum, for use as exhibits in the new display they're building for the Research Establishment. Lieutenant Shrewdfellow is organising that.'

As soon as all the cadets had gone through the Gas Chamber, Major De Roche and Company Sergeant-Majors Larkin and Truscott joined them for a final debrief.

'Now, that wasn't too bad, was it?' said Rocky, still exuding warmth and re-assurance. 'You can see now how important it is to be well prepared, with knowledge and protective equipment. We'll finish off our gas training here, and I'd like you all to return to your rooms and have a good shower to clean off any CS gas residue. Do not wear your present uniforms again until they have been laundered. If anybody feels the slightest bit unwell they are to report to Matron immediately, and particularly before you go off tomorrow on this long weekend holiday. Thank you, Sergeant-Majors Larkin and Truscott for your assistance today.' He looked enquiringly at the cadets.

'I just need two or three volunteers to help me take Professor Zharkov's presentation equipment to the Secure Store in the Museum for temporary storage until transport from WARTE arrives. Oh yes, Mr McBride, Mr Jones and Miss Pendragon, you're the Museum's Assistant Curators, aren't you? How about giving me a hand?' The trio followed Rocky back into the Lecture Hall, where Professor Zharkov had collected all his equipment to take back to WARTE.

'Ah, there you are, Major De Roche. And with some porters too, I see,' exclaimed the Professor. 'I seem to have quite a lot of items this time. Let me see, now. A couple of boxes of Laserlances and Beam-blockers, half a dozen pails of See-through paint, and half a dozen boxes of Dreamshells and Dreambombs. For some field trials we held earlier, we packaged the Dream gas into some short-range, small calibre 4-inch artillery shells and some bomblets. They seemed to work all right. They'll make excellent Museum exhibits in future years.'

'Thanks very much, Professor,' responded Rocky. 'I'm sure Lieutenant Shrewdfellow will value these exhibits when they are donated by WARTE. Perhaps you would like to join me for lunch. These cadets will take everything up to the Museum's Secure Store.' And with that, Rocky smiled at the trio, grasped the Professor by the arm and steered him out of the Lecture Hall towards the Staff cafeteria.

'Crikey,' breathed Gareth, as he surveyed the heap of equipment. 'I hope the WARTE forgets to send transport. These little treasures would come in handy for us to use in Brittanica.'

'You can say that again,' agreed Penelope. 'Let's hope that Zharkov turns out to be the absent-minded professor!'

'Wouldn't it be great if they did forget?' whispered Willie. 'We'd better take great care and lock them away safely in the Curators' Storeroom. Then, if WARTE still haven't collected them, we'll take them through the Time Thread when we get a call for our next mission.'

It took a couple of trips for them to ferry the boxes and pails safely into the Storeroom, and store them by the Time Thread door. Just to be on the safe side, they threw a large camouflage net over the equipment, so that it was less obvious.

It was only two days later when Gareth, whose turn it was to check the Storeroom for mail, came into the Company Common Room to meet Penelope and Willie.

'We've got another letter from Woody,' he said, in scarcely concealed excitement. 'I'll take it up to my room and decode it for us.'

After about half an hour he returned in great triumph. He opened up the brown manilla folder so that the other two could read the decoded message it contained.

Woody's message read:

HAVE LONGER JOB FOR YOU stop PLEASE MEET ME TOMORROW MORNING IF POSSIBLE stop WOODY

'That couldn't have been better timing,' said Penelope. 'We start our long weekend tomorrow. We could go straight after breakfast.'

'Yes we could,' agreed Willie, 'and we'll take those extra little toys left by Professor Zharkov and haven't been collected by WARTE yet.'

They sat and talked in the Common Room, wondering what sort of mission Woody had in mind for them. Penelope was beside herself with the anticipation of possibly seeing and riding Playboy again. Gareth was even more imaginative.

'I bet he wants us to travel to somewhere like Outer Mongolia, to pick up a yak for scientific analysis,' he joked.

'Possibly,' said Willie thoughtfully. 'But I reckon it's got to be something quite important. Woody does say a "longer" mission, after all. Whatever it is, you two had better take your mentors' badge and shell-case, and I'll take my mentor's ring. We may have to test our mentors to help us get out of any trouble.'

Willie was also keen to return to Brittanica and to visit those places where his parents had been. After his success in Labuan, he felt that the more he travelled following his parents' footsteps, the more likely he was to find out who could have blown up the coal mine. It seemed clear to him now, after having thought over the technical advice given by Sergeant Routledge, and having actually visited the coal mine, there could be little doubt that the mine had been deliberately blown up.

Immediately after breakfast the following day, they went up to the Museum, stacked the Zharkov equipment and their packs onto three parcel trolleys, and entered the Time Thread. Although they were feeling more confident now, all three had butterflies in their stomachs. After another weightless, soundless journey though the Time Thread, they emerged into Gladys's Cleaners' Room. The room was empty, but it wasn't long before she appeared.

'Hello, it's so nice to see you again, Mr Willie, Miss Penelope and Mr Gareth. Oh my, you have bought a lot of boxes and things with you this time, haven't you?'

They all cheerily acknowledged her greeting.

'Well, yes, we DO have rather a lot of luggage, Gladys, which we will need to take with us on the tomotram. But first we have an appointment with Woody, so we'll just quietly slip along the corridor with these trolleys and stuff to his office.'

'Yes, of course,' replied Gladys, opening the door so they could continue wheeling their laden trolleys into the corridor.

'Mr Woodhouse is waiting for you.'

13

MISSION TO SARAWAK

Secretary Woodhouse was not alone in his office.

'Allow me to introduce two colleagues of mine,' he said, rising from his desk chair. 'This is our Head of External Intelligence,' he said, motioning towards a grey-suited staff officer. 'We simply refer to him as "J" in order to avoid mentioning his name for security reasons.' He gestured towards the other.

'This is General Clarendon, our Chief of Army General Staff,' he said, introducing a very large military officer with a chest full of medals.

'How do you do,' chorused Willie, Penelope and Gareth.

'I thought I would ask these two gentlemen to assist me in giving you a briefing,' continued Woody. 'It's about a rather interesting mission we would very much like you to undertake for us. If you would like to sit down on these chairs facing this map of the world, we can get started.'

The trio sat down in the plush leather chairs and waited attentively as 'J' and the General eased themselves into the leather couch off to one side. 'J' fished out a silver cigarette case, selected a Black Russian Sobranie cigarette and lit up. A thin cloud of pungent, highly scented smoke swirled slowly around his head. Woody pulled a curved meerschaum pipe from his pocket, and looked thoughtful as he lit the tobacco, and took a couple of puffs. He moved to the wall map.

'Hmm,' he started slowly. 'It's all a bit delicate, really. We haven't many options, and we can't be seen to take direct action at this time. Simply put, we in Brittanica are in competition with other countries for secure access to scarce resources. We need 'em, and so does every other developing country. Unfortunately, these valuable resources, like precious metals and diamonds, aren't just down the road waiting to be picked up. No, sir. They're overseas in some pretty far away places. They're wild, undeveloped places, with few roads, ports or sanitation. And the inhabitants of these regions are likewise rather wild and backward. However, our country and some other countries of Europe have been quite successful over the past 50 years in coming to terms with these inhabitants. They in turn have permitted us to have access to the valuable resources in their territories. We have all used these resources for the betterment of our citizens, and have invested a portion of the profits into building roads, bridges, hospitals, ports and so forth for the inhabitants of the territories.' Woody paused for a moment and took another puff on his pipe.

'But now we come to the fly in the ointment. Simply put, it's the sudden emergence of the Teutons as strong new competitors for these valuable resources. They have established footholds in equatorial Africa, North Africa and the Far East. We are particularly concerned at the moment with their progress in the small state of Sarawak. It's in Western Borneo and it seems to be brimful of high quality diamonds. Now, I'm aware that none of you will know anything yet about the Teutons, so I'll ask "J" to give you some background.'

'J' sprang quickly to his feet and extinguished his Black Russian cigarette in an ashtray. He was elegant in his dark grey suit, white shirt and bright yellow, velvet bow tie. His greying hair, upright stance and thoughtful brown eyes gave him an air of forthright maturity and wisdom. He pointed towards Europe on the wall map and began. He spoke quietly, but incisively, using his hands to emphasise important points and indicating geographical areas on the wall map.

'Firstly, a little bit of history,' he said. 'The present Teutons are descendants of an ancient Germanic tribe of Teutones who were originally settled in Jutland. About 2000 years ago they invaded the warm, southern kingdoms of Europe. 'Sweeping down from their dark, gloomy lands in the wintry North, they defeated the inhabitants in the southern lands, and created a number of feudal states and minor kingdoms. For the next 2000 years these states and kingdoms were always at war with one another, until about 40 years ago when they were successfully unified under a Chancellor,

Leopold Schonhausen, the so-called "Iron Chancellor", as the Kingdom of Teutonia.

'The kingdom also has a young hereditary ruler, Emperor Wilhelm IV, who succeeded to the throne about ten years ago. The Teutons have very large, well equipped armed forces, and are now developing their heavy industries as quickly as they can. They need to find and import raw materials to fuel this development. Until recently they have been content to stay within their borders and to trade with the rest of the world. However, under their Emperor, Wilhelm IV, there are signs of aggressive nationalism and strengthening of their Armed Forces.

'They would like to expand their influence, particularly into countries where they can acquire raw materials, such as coal for their armaments factories and diamonds for their instruments. They have their diplomatic representatives in all major countries around the globe and an excellent Military Intelligence Service called the BND. There are about 30 million Teutons living in the Kingdom, but many millions more living abroad who have family connections back to the Kingdom, and who speak Teutonish.

'The Teutons have no state religion as such, but worship a number of Gods and Goddesses, such as Smertrios, their God of War, and Dispater, their God of the Underworld. They believe in magic and the influence, good or bad, of their Gods. They are particularly fearful of Zeust, the God of all Gods, who they believe appears in the form of a flying dragon.'

'J' reached down to a small briefcase propped up against the end of the sofa and pulled out a large framed black and white photograph.

'Here is a picture of the Emperor Wilhelm IV in his full uniform of a Field Marshal of the Teuton Army. As you can see, he is quite a handsome looking fellow with his well-groomed hair, upright manner and large handle-bar moustache. Unfortunately, there were difficulties when he was born, and so his left arm is withered. He was educated at Friedrich University. He is considered to have a quick intelligence but unfortunately an even quicker temper. He is the main driving force for this aggressive expansionism by Teutonia to conquer the world.'

"J" chuckled as he returned the photograph to the briefcase.

'Let's hope that Zeust, their God of all Gods, doesn't have a similar need to expand!

'Now, let's turn to the Teuton people themselves. Generally speaking, they are a very intelligent race, with some excellent characteristics. They are considered to be diligent and hard working, innovative and inventive, virtuous and incorruptible, young and vigorous. In short, they would be excellent citizens. However, they have two major failings. Firstly, they consider themselves to be superior to any other race on this planet, and, secondly, they are very inclined to force their opinions on everyone else – mainly by military force! I'll now ask General Clarendon to brief you on the Teuton Army.'

He resumed his seat on the sofa, as the General heaved his bulk up to stand in front of the wall map. The General was very large and impressive. His splendid uniform was that of the 13th Hussar Regiment in dark Sherwood green with gold piping on the tunic front and on his sleeves. He wore the blood-red gorgettes of the General Staff in the front of his throat, and red epaulettes on his shoulders, on which he carried the rank insignia of a Major-General. His voice was deep and firm, resonating with confidence and determination. He looked directly at them and started with the announcement:

'The Teuton Army is the largest in Europe and outnumbers our own Brittanic Army by ten to one. It is only by combining our forces with those of our allies that we are able to match their numbers. However, as big as they are, their present combat power is comparatively low, with limited firepower and mobility.'

'What actually do you mean by that?' asked Willie.

'Well,' replied the General, 'while they may be able to deploy many soldiers on the battlefield, those soldiers don't have many supporting cannons, and what ones they do have will be old, inaccurate and have short ranges. They don't have many vehicles and the ones that they do have will be slow, small and break down easily when the going gets tough.' He paused briefly, then carried on, while gently tapping his swagger stick on the arm rests of the couch as if to emphasise his next points.

'However, they are now starting to change things by introducing new weapons based on fresh science and technological discoveries. These new weapons are being issued to their Home Forces initially and have not yet been seen in their Colonial Forces in Africa or the Far East. But I suppose it will be only a matter of time before they, too, will be better equipped. Presently, their Home Forces number about ten infantry divisions. The Colonial Forces are much smaller at two infantry brigades, generally comprising battalion groups of infantry, artillery and engineers, with supporting transport, stores, repairs and so forth.' The General glanced across to Woody, who took his cue.

'Thank you, gentlemen, for those informative briefings,' he said. He turned to the trio. 'I hope that has given you a good idea of the background, strengths and weaknesses of the Teutons. You can see that their expanding colonial ambitions are on a collision course with our own objectives.

'I'd like us to look now at the situation in Sarawak. We are very concerned that the flow of diamonds from this country will accelerate the modernisation of the Teutons' armed forces. We know that their colonial forces in Kuching, the capital of Sarawak, are using the local Iban tribesmen as slave labour in their diamond mine.' Here Woody paused and, looking directly at them, said softly, 'We need you to find a way of destroying the Teuton military forces in Sarawak and freeing the Iban people from slavery!'

The three drew in their breath, gulped and looked at each other. This was a real challenge indeed. A really, really, big challenge! General Clarendon and 'J', having resumed their seats on the couch, watched them intently. The room was suddenly very still and quiet. Woody propped himself on the back of a chair and waited. Penelope and Gareth looked to Willie for a lead. He was thinking furiously, his face a study of intense thought.

The objectives of the mission were honourable with desirable outcomes; although how they fitted into a bigger, broader plan was unknown. The Teutons would be a formidable force, well organised and well established. They should not be underestimated. Nevertheless, the trio did have access to sophisticated equipment which could prove to be battle winners – Percival's aircraft, the Laserlances, the invisibility paint and the hullucinary shells. And they also had the element of surprise in their favour. If they could have a safe base to work from in Sarawak, and be assured of the support of the Iban tribes, there was a very good chance they could be successful.

But by far the most important factor for Willie was that the mission would probably be based in Kuching, the capital of Sarawak, and the birthplace of Lucifer-Mortlock. Oh, yes: Lucifer-

Mortlock. The old Lag. He might just be the vital clue in Willie's quest to uncover what really happened to his parents. He knew it was a long shot, but he was suddenly seized with an intense desire to visit Kuching, explore its surroundings and meet its people, if he could. It would be an excellent start in finding out as much as he could about the Lag and his background. Who knows? He might stumble across a fact vital to solving the puzzle.

His face cleared, and, glancing across to Penelope and Gareth, he raised his eyebrows in the unspoken question, 'I think it's OK, but what do **you** think?' Both responded with a quick nod and a grin.

'Yes, Woody,' said Willie with a slight smile, 'we'll give it a try!'

Immediately, 'J' and the General scrambled to their feet, and energetically shook hands with the trio, their faces wreathed in smiles.

'That's an excellent decision,' boomed the General. 'We'll give you every support we can.'

'Yes, absolutely,' nodded Woody. 'I thought this mission would interest you.'

'Well, we will need to take all our equipment with us,' replied Willie. He paused momentarily as he remembered their previous mission to that part of the world in Labuan Island. He grinned. 'We'll call this mission "Operation Crocodile" in memory of Paddy O'Driscoll. And we will need to use the most powerful tomotram you have. We will also need a good in-country briefing of the situation in Sarawak when we get there.'

'You shall have it, of course,' agreed Woody. 'Our Consul in Sarawak is the Honourable Edward Spring-Rice. We call him "Porridge" because he's always so energetic and full of oats. He's been knocking around the Far East for years and knows the Iban locals and the country like the back of his hand.'

With that, the briefing came to an end. After shaking hands with Woody, 'J' and the General, and receiving a chorus of good wishes, the trio made their way down to the Tomotram Depot to pack and prepare.

14

THE SLAVE MINES OF BATU LINTANG

While Willie studied the maps of Sarawak given to him by Jimmy, Penelope and Gareth busied themselves checking and packing the equipment. There were boxes of Laserlances with spare batteries, large pails of Seethrough invisibility paint and brushes, boxes of Dreamshells and Dreambombs, full-face gas masks, first aid supplies and survival kits. As soon as all was done, they boarded the tomotram and Arthur set the instruments for Kuching. He flicked the starting lever and with a whir the engines sprang to life. The tram moved smoothly down the tunnel gathering speed as it went and they were on their way.

Their journey was uneventful, and within a matter of hours they arrived in a small, brightly lit cavern that was the tomotram terminus under the Brittanic Consulate of Sarawak. Waiting for them on the platform was a thin, rather tall man in neatly pressed light grey planters' order, wearing a matching light grey helmet, rugged brown boots and leggings, and smoking a cigar. He introduced himself, shaking their hands in turn in a quick, urgent manner.

'Spring-Rice,' he exclaimed and, grinning, added, 'welcome to Sarawak, the armpit of Borneo! And please call me Porridge. Everybody else does.'

'Why do you call Sarawak the Armpit of Borneo?' asked Gareth.

Porridge laughed out loudly and replied, 'Most people think of it as being rather smelly and very hot! But after a while one gets used to it, I suppose. Now then, after such a long journey you must be starving. Follow me upstairs and join my wife and I for morning tea.' With that he marched briskly along the platform to an exit doorway and skipped up the stairs. The trio hurriedly followed and emerged into the basement of a large house.

Already the tropical heat was overwhelming, hitting them like a blast of heavy steam. They proceeded up some further stairs and entered into a lovely breakfast room, with large open windows overlooking a sweltering vista of trees, palms and ramshackle buildings sloping down to the sea. To their left, a large jungle-covered mountain heaved itself up from the coast and into the clouds.

'Whew, is it always as hot as this?' asked Gareth, taking off his woollen jersey.

'Absolutely,' replied Porridge. 'But don't worry. I've got some thin, cooler clothing for you to change into. It gets hotter downtown, but it's quite cool further up on Gunong Niyut. We're just on the outskirts of Kuching, the capital of Sarawak, and located on the foothills of Gunong Niyut.' Mrs Spring-Rice was fussy, motherly and rather chubby. She welcomed them warmly.

'Now, I do hope that you like chocolate biscuits and iced lemonade, Penelope,' she gushed. She smiled at the boys. 'I've just baked a lemon sponge cake with passion fruit icing topped with cherries. There's a bowl of fruit with bananas, paw-paws and loquats. You just help yourself,' she invited, pointing to a table covered in an apricot-coloured tablecloth and plates of cakes and biscuits. 'There's some freshly made Earl Grey tea in the pot, too,' she said, pointing to some blue and white willow-patterned cups surrounding a huge, fat teapot and matching milk jug.

'Thank you very much indeed, Mrs Spring-Rice,' chorused the trio and without further ado they sat down at the table and attacked the offerings with gusto.

'While you're eating,' said Porridge, 'I might as well tell you a bit about the situation here in Kuching, the Teuton diamond mine at Batu Lintang, and the local Borneo Revolutionary Armed Freedom Forces, or BRAFF, as it is known here. Then, when you're ready this afternoon, I suggest we do a recce of the diamond mine and see just what the Teutons are up to.'

'That sounds like a great idea,' mumbled Willie, his mouth full of sponge cake.

Penelope and Gareth nodded in agreement.

Porridge pulled up a chair to the table and used the salt cellar and cutlery to illustrate his briefing. 'Well, the Teuton forces here in Sarawak comprise about 800 officers and other ranks. They are organised into four infantry companies, each numbering about 100 soldiers, two artillery batteries each armed with six 4-inch field guns, a company of guards for the diamond mine, an engineer troop looking after their tomotram terminal in the diamond mine, and some supporting administrative troops.'

He positioned the cutlery in a line underneath the salt cellar to represent the infantry companies, artillery and engineers.

'Except for the field guns, the Teutons' only other weapons are general issue "Kommisar" carbines. The rank-and-file soldiers wear regulation khaki tropical uniforms with riding breeches and riding boots, and standard-issue black and silver spiked helmets, called "Pickelhaubes". They are normally armed with a carbine and carry ammunition in pouches fastened on a leather belt. Most of their forces are based here in Kuching. They are badly behaved conscripts in the main, and they treat the local Ibans abominably.'

He positioned the bowl of fruit ahead of the salt cellar and pointed to it.

'The Teuton military commander here is a Colonel Goroka, who is a really tough customer with a fierce, unpredictable temper. His nickname is the "White Rajah", and his headquarters is located in a replica Teuton castle called a "Schloss". The locals are terrified of Goroka, and even his own soldiers are very fearful. He is a huge man with longer than normal arms, a scarred face and over-developed teeth. He's not a pretty fellow!'

Porridge positioned the plate of biscuits to one side of the fruit bowl.

'The Teutons have developed the diamond mine here using the local able-bodied men and women as slaves, kidnapping them from their homes and forcing them to work in chain gangs. They have even kidnapped some of the young teenage children. The locals are powerless. Although they are a naturally peace-loving people, they are very territorial and will fight to protect their patch and their families. However, they only have spears, blowpipes and bows and arrows, which are no match for the Teuton Army's rifles and field guns.'

Porridge pointed to the lemon sponge cake. 'The BRAFF, on the other hand, do have some field guns and rifles. They are based in the jungle villages, just north from here on the other side of a steep gorge separating the town, and the mine from the densely covered foothills of Gunong Niyut.'

He paused briefly.'Ah, I see you've finished tea now. How about us having a quick look at the diamond mine? We can use the tomotram for most of the way, but we'll have to do the last bit on foot so we aren't seen by the guards.'

'That's a good idea,' replied Willie. 'But we've bought something in our bag of tricks which I think will help us use the tomotram all the way and, hopefully, will let us see more of the mine.'

Porridge looked at him sceptically, but said nothing and led the way down to the tram terminus. He took down a basket of the cakes and fruit for Jimmy and Arthur, knowing that they would have helped themselves to some bottles of cider.Once there, the trio unloaded the Seethrough paint and brushes and they all set to work painting every inch of the outside of tomotram 256 with the clear, magic liquid.

As they painted, the tomotram started to disappear from view, except for the end doors, which were left till last. They also left some very small pinholes on four or five of the windows which they could use as spy-holes to look out from the inside.

'Good heavens,' exclaimed Porridge, 'this stuff is simply miraculous!' He put out his hand to feel the now-invisible metal exterior of the tomotram. 'How long will it last like this?'

'As long as you like, pretty much,' replied Gareth. 'Just so long as we don't get too much dust or dirt on it so that light is reflected.'

Having painted the tomotram to Willie's satisfaction, they all climbed aboard and Porridge helped Arthur set the instruments for the diamond mine. With scarcely a sound, the tomotram's motors hummed into life and they glided down through a maze of black tunnels until, almost without warning, they emerged into the gloom of a gigantic cavern's roof and drew to a halt. Around them were thousands of bats hanging upside down from the crevices like black shrouds. A nauseating odour of guano penetrated everywhere like smog. The cavern was massive. It was large enough to hold Westminster Cathedral. A black underground river flowed through the centre, reflecting gigantic rock formations, dimly lit from the natural light of the cavern's entrance. The entrance was a huge, jagged hole through which could be seen a patch of sky fringed by thick green jungle. Inside the entrance, streams of water cascaded down dark brown stalactites. Centipedes feasted on the thick coating of bat guano on the lower rocks. Below was the Teutons' diamond mine.

It was a picture of satanic hell. One of the inner cavern walls was lined with ledges riddled with black tunnel cavities. Perched on the ledges were hundreds of Iban slaves, their toiling, exhausted and aching bodies caked in dirt, their legs shackled to lengths of chain, as they dug out the diamond concentrate with hand shovels. Their only light came from the hellish red, flickering flames of fire-torches held upright in iron stands. Smoke from the fire-torches filled the cavern with a fine, choking haze. Teuton soldiers armed with thick whips and bayonets moved among the Ibans, swearing and cursing, prodding at any slave who was too slow, and whipping those who were too weak to move.

Those working on the ledges loaded up wicker baskets, which were sent by a spider's web of aerial rope-ways, down to piles on the cavern floor. Here, more Iban slaves carried the concentrate to washing pans, where it was sieved with water from the underground river. Near the entrance to get maximum light were a small group of slaves who were examining the remaining heavier concentrate in the washing sieves for the diamonds. They were scantily clad, so they could not steal any diamonds they found. Teuton guards surrounded them. Whenever a diamond was found, the slave raised his hand and a guard took it, and placed it in a black leather bag. On the cavern floor, beside the entrance and a large black tomotunnel, two dark red Teuton tomotrams were parked. Packed in one of them were stacks of black leather bags containing more diamonds, ready for transport to Teutonia. Towards the centre of the cavern's floor was a pile of earth concentrate on which a large black iron tripod had been erected. Suspended from the tripod's top were three whimpering Ibans, their thin, pathetic bodies spread-eagled, their backs bloodied from whip-lashes.

Without warning, there was a commotion among the guards, and some lined up at the cavern's entrance ready to welcome a visitor. They stood to attention and in strode a huge Teuton officer. Porridge nudged Willie.

'That's the military commander, Colonel Goroka,' he whispered. 'I wonder why he's come here.'

The Colonel carried some maps and papers, and motioned to the officers to gather around him. They all started to examine the maps and talk among themselves, when, suddenly, the Colonel held up his hand for silence, straightened himself and looked around suspiciously. He sensed that something was not quite right, and sniffed the air carefully.

'Oh, no,' thought the trio, 'he can smell us perhaps, or see a patch of the tomotram we missed painting.'

The Colonel seemed to stare in their direction for a long, long time. The trio held their breath and waited motionlessly. Then, shaking his head slowly, and reluctantly, as if not quite convinced, the Colonel turned back to his officers to concentrate on the maps and began giving them orders. The trio began to breathe again in cautious relief.

Very, very quietly Willie whispered, 'I think we should move out of here and return now while they are otherwise engaged.'

'Absolutely,' mouthed Porridge, nodding assent. Very gently, Arthur and he reset the instruments for the Consulate, and switched on the motors to silent mode.

Soundlessly, tomotram 256 glided back to the tunnels from which they had entered the cavern and re-entered the tunnel maze.

'Phew, that was a close call,' said Penelope rather breathlessly. 'Aren't those Teutons brutal?' Everyone nodded silently in agreement.

'And so cruel and viscous too,' added Willie, thinking of the Iban slaves strung up on the metal tripod.

'Those poor, poor Ibans,' continued Penelope. 'That was an unbelievable hell-hole. We really must try to free them from these damned Teutons.'

They soon arrived safely back at the Consulate's terminus and again followed Porridge up into the house. Mrs Porridge had dinner already laid out on the table.

'I thought you might enjoy some local delicacies,' she beamed, 'after such a hard day's work.' She served each of them a steaming bowl of goats' eye soup, followed by hot dishes of roasted parrot, jellied snake, thin rashers of braised goat rump, creamed corn and boiled broccoli. A dessert of guava pie followed, and all of this was washed down with some bottles of local 'Tiger Bay' beer.

'That was delicious, thanks, Mrs Porridge,' said Gareth, 'I couldn't eat another mouthful, I'm so full. You're a really terrific cook!'

The others nodded in agreement, murmuring their approval of

such a wonderful dinner and starting to yawn as their bodies and senses relaxed after the day's experiences.

'That's so nice of you to say so, dear,' replied Mrs Porridge, smiling warmly at the compliment. 'Now, upstairs there's a room each for you. I suggest you all get some sleep now, as you'll probably have a full day ahead of you. Don't forget to tuck your mosquito net in under your mattress. The mosquitoes here are really quite ferocious.'

'That's right,' said Porridge, grinning. 'Keep all your blood to yourself. Don't give any to those little blighters. Tomorrow I'll take you up to the Iban village in the jungle and introduce you to their Chief Hassan. It will be a full day, so you'll need to get a good night's rest.'

The trio looked at him with gratitude. The oppressive tropical heat, the long journey from Whitehall, and the high tensions of the nightmarish Teuton's diamond mine had all taken their toll. They were absolutely exhausted, and they were determined to get a good night's sleep, mosquitoes or not.

15

THE IBAN REBELLION

The next day dawned slowly, the morning coolness reluctantly giving way to the gathering heat from the sun, still hanging below the horizon. The stillness of the night was broken by the sudden fluttering and calls of the birds. The first grey light of day grew clearer and sharper, quietly urging all to awake. The air was crisp and clean, like fresh bed-sheets. A light cool breeze shivered through the tree-tops, and through the open bedroom windows, stirring the mosquito nets. A new day had arrived, full of promise and optimism.

Willie awoke, slid from under the mosquito net, and walked over to the bedroom window. The view over Kuching was spectacular, with the palm trees sloping down to the dark blue line of the sea beyond. The red furnace of the sun was just rising above the horizon, its rays lighting up the higher, jungle slopes of Gunong Niyut. He could see a sprinkling of small stone and thatched houses through the palm trees, and some early rising Iban men lighting their outside fires. Some wives carrying babies slung over their backs emerged from the houses and began preparing the morning meal. The rhythm of peaceful domestic chores had begun, as it did every morning, all over the world. It felt good, comfortable and orderly.

Suddenly, he spotted a squad of Teuton soldiers marching down the road towards the sea. The spikes on their pickelhaubes glistened in the morning sun like a thicket of dancing daggers. Their carbines were slung carelessly over their shoulders. They were talking and laughing loudly among themselves, their harsh guttural tones shattering the morning peace. Willie frowned as the reality of the

Teuton occupation of Sarawak, the awful diamond mine and their mission flashed into his mind, quickly dispelling his enjoyment of the morning.

He checked his personal equipment in his pack. For the next ten minutes he completed his routine morning stretch exercises of 50 sit-ups, 100 push-ups and 20 bend-overs. He went downstairs to find that all the others were already seated at the breakfast table with Mrs Porridge fussing over them with boiled eggs, toast and tea.

'Have some more marmalade, Jimmy,' she said, and turning to Penelope and Gareth, 'Do try this lovely frangipani honey. It's delicious.'

They all nodded absent-mindedly, murmuring their thanks, but with their thoughts focused ahead towards the forthcoming events of the day. Porridge was as perky as ever.

'Hope you all slept well,' he chirped, as he bounced into the room. We've got a big day in front of us. I've already sent word to Hassan that we're coming to visit him today.'

They finished breakfast and checked their packs. Jimmy and Arthur went down to the tomotram terminal to do their daily mechanical checks. The Seethrough invisibility paint was still effective and all was secure. Porridge fished around in a cupboard and brought out some maps of the area and spread them out on the table. The trio gathered around him as he pointed out the important features of the terrain.

'Here's the town,' he said, jabbing his finger onto the map. 'Here's our Brittanic Consulate, there's the Teuton's diamond mine at Batu Lintang, and there's Colonel Goroka's Schloss Headquarters.' He then pointed to an area west of the town and part way up the slopes of Gunong Niyut. 'This is the Ngaio Gorge,' he said. 'It separates the town and the diamond mine area to the east under the Teutons' control, and the dense jungles and grasslands to the west controlled by the BRAFF. If the Teutons are to make sure that their diamond mine is safe from attack, they have to occupy and secure at least part of the area west of the Ngaio Gorge. I'm positive that they would like to do this sooner rather than later, before the BRAFF get stronger.'

'Can we get the tomotram up into the area controlled by the BRAFF?' asked Willie.

'Yes,' replied Porridge. 'This area is volcanic, and Gunong

Niyut is still a live volcano. There are tunnels leading up to the
Gunong from here into a small cave system not far from Hassan's
village.'

'That sounds as if it could provide us with a handy forward
base,' suggested Gareth. Willie and Penelope nodded agreement.

'Right,' decided Willie, 'we'll take all our equipment with us
and set up in the cave.' They moved down to the tomotram terminal
and boarded the tram. Jimmy and Arthur had already completed
their checks.

'We're all set to go, Mister William,' reported Arthur, wiping
some grease smears off his face.

Once again Porridge and Arthur positioned the instruments, and
tomotram 256 glided off into the blackness of the tunnels leading
up to the cave on Gunong Niyut. Within minutes, it seemed, they
had arrived, and drew to a halt behind some rocks, in the dark, deep
shadows in the rear of a large cave. A faint glow of light filtered
into the space from the entrance, which was screened by low scrub.

'This is it all right,' said Porridge, in a half-whisper, as if
frightened he might be making too much noise.

'It looks excellent,' replied Willie, peering out of the tomotram
door. 'But there's that terrible guano smell again. I do hope it's not
more bats.'

'What's guano?' asked Gareth.

'Bat pooh,' said Willie, holding his nose as he jumped down
onto the cave floor. 'Let's have a quick look around and then go
and meet Hassan.'

They all dismounted from the tomotram and set about exploring
the cave. It was about the size of a large warehouse, with a hard,
flat volcanic rock floor, with a metre-wide perimeter of guano at the
bottom of the cave walls. The entrance was rectangular with a low
rock overhang just high enough for a person to walk upright. A
small stream of clear water flowed down one side of the entrance
way. As they moved about they disturbed clouds of nesting brown
birds, which swirled soundlessly in great agitation around the
cave's roof.

'Aha,' exclaimed Porridge excitedly, pointing up to the birds.
'They're white-nested swiftlets. Their nests make really tasty soup.'
He waved his arm towards the cave walls, which were bristling
with a multitude of tiny, dark green nests attached like shelf
brackets.

'Ugh,' grimaced Penelope. 'I think we might give them a miss this time. We'll just keep them in mind as a possible food reserve for later – much later.' They finished their exploration of the cave, noting that there was ample room for them to spread out and assemble their equipment.

'Right ho,' Willie said briskly. 'This will be ideal for us. I think we should go on down to the village now, Porridge, and meet Hassan.' He turned and smiled. 'Jimmy, would you and Arthur unload the tomotram and make camp while we're away?'

Jimmy and Arthur nodded quickly and started moving the equipment from the tomotram to the cave's floor. The trio shouldered their packs, and followed Porridge out of the cave and out onto a flat grassy field about the size of a football field. The cave faced west away from Kuching, and was above the line of thick jungle of scrub, palms, vines and trees below the field.

'The village is about half a mile from here,' commented Porridge. 'But we'll just take it slowly and quietly. The track through the jungle will be a bit rough here and there, so watch your step. Also, be careful you don't tread on the scrub leeches! Try to avoid 'em if you can.'

The leeches were there all right, reacting to the vibrations of their footfalls. Standing upright on their sucker bases, like thin, grey sausages, they strained to attach themselves to any part of clothing or footwear. Once attached, they would slither about until they found some flesh into which they could fasten their jaws and commence sucking the new host's blood.

The group soon entered the jungle and tramped silently along the soft, leafy path, scrambled over outcrops of rock, or pulled themselves up inclines, using small saplings. It was hard, physical work and they were soon very hot and sweaty. The jungle itself fell silent, as if all its creatures had suddenly halted what they were doing to watch this strange procession. The group themselves fell quiet. Each member had their head down, fully concentrating on their own strenuous efforts to keep moving forward through the thickening vegetation.

Then, quite suddenly, the vegetation itself sprang to life alongside the track, to reveal an ambush of fierce, Iban warriors daubed in war-paint. Wearing hideous masks and carrying razor-sharp spears and buffalo skin shields, the warriors stood shoulder to shoulder – a menacing wall of death. From the plaited belts around their waists dangled shrunken human heads. These were the head-hunters of Borneo! Instantly, Porridge and the trio stopped still, their hearts beating furiously.

'Just remain calm and still,' warned Porridge in a loud half-whisper. 'This is just a welcoming party, I think. This will just be their ... um ... normal procedure.' He cleared his throat. 'Ah ... em ... nothing to get worried about, I'm sure.' Porridge's voice trailed off into uncertainty and without a trace of re-assurance. Nevertheless, the trio edged closer to Porridge, and stared back at the circle of silent death masks and shields. Then, as if a signal had been given, all the warriors began to stamp their feet in time and clash their spears aggressively against their shields, moving as if to separate Porridge to one side.

Stomp, stomp, stomp and clash ... Stomp, stomp, stomp and clash ...

'Don't be frightened,' shouted Porridge to the trio above the din. 'I'm *sure* all this must be quite normal procedure.'

Stomp, stomp, stomp and clash ... Stomp, stomp, stomp and clash ...

The tempo started to get faster and faster.

'I sincerely hope you're right, Porridge,' gritted Willie, looking as unconcerned as he possibly could so as not to alarm Penelope and Gareth. 'They look blimmin' upset to me, and we're completely at their mercy.'

'That's an understatement, boyoh,' whispered Gareth to Penelope, whose face was now very pale.

Stomp, stomp, stomp and clash ... Stomp, stomp, stomp and clash ... stomp, stomp, stomp and clash. The menacing tempo and noise was reaching a crescendo. What ever was going to happen was going to happen in the next few seconds. Suddenly, all was still. The last echoes of the crashing shields died away. For a few moments that felt like eternity there was absolute silence. Then, with screams of murderous rage, the Iban war-party pointed their spears at Porridge and the trio, and charged.

'We're goners,' thought Willie, as he closed his eyes and waited for the searing pain of a spear being thrust through his body. But there was no spear thrust. There was no pain. Abruptly, the warriors ceased their howls and stood quietly in a close circle around the group, their spears now held upright. Slowly, Porridge and the trio opened their eyes and looked at the warriors' unblinking death masks that surrounded them.

Then a voice from behind one of the masks said, 'Good morning, Porridge!'

'Good heavens,' exclaimed Porridge with enormous relief, 'is that you, Hassan?'

From behind a large death mask, an older man emerged, grinning from ear to ear.

'Yes, it's me,' he said, as all the other warriors suddenly put aside their masks and broke into gleeful laughter, delighted with the huge impact that their demonstration had had on the group. Despite his age, Hassan was as sprightly and alert as a youngster. He was wearing a full, red Iban shawl which covered his body from shoulder to kneecap.

'Sorry about this little welcome, but I hope you were scared stiff!' said Hassan, shaking hands with Porridge and the trio. 'I wanted to show your new friends here that we Ibans are not a pushover when it comes to protecting our rights and freedom.'

'Well, you almost scared us to death!' exclaimed Willie, shaking hands with Hassan. He introduced Penelope and Gareth. 'We thought we were done for.'

'Well, and so are we, what with the way these damn Teutons are treating us,' responded Hassan. 'Porridge has already told us that you were coming and that you may be able to help us get rid of them. We have been looking forward to meeting you and seeing what might be done. Let's go down to my village now and discuss how we can defeat these brutes.' With that, he motioned to his warriors and led the way downhill through the jungle to the village.

Their approach was announced by the barking of the village dogs, some of which ran out to greet them. More importantly, however, were the sentries who guarded the entry tracks from well-camouflaged bunkers surrounding the village. These were not like the warriors armed with spears and clubs, who had ambushed the group earlier. These were real, combat-ready soldiers, clothed in green fatigues, brown boots and puttees, brown leather belts carrying ammunition pouches, and armed with M98 Mauser carbine rifles. These soldiers were the BRAFF. There were other groups of well-armed BRAFF soldiers sitting quietly inside the village longhouses. The muzzles of field guns were visible in their hiding places in some other innocent-looking huts.

'Ah, Mr McBride,' observed Hassan chuckling quietly. 'I see you've noted some of our other preparations.' He pointed to the painted warriors with the spears. 'We have some for window-dressing and deception;' then, pointing to the BRAFF soldiers, 'and some for the real business of fighting. We've gone to considerable lengths to give the Teutons the impression that we are only armed with spears and clubs.' Then he turned towards a uniformed tribesman, who had approached quietly from a group of BRAFF officers.

'I'd like you to meet the BRAFF commander, Major Mamood.'

The Major was impressively tall and wiry. His head was large and his dark brown eyes extraordinarily bright and alert. He wore the dark green tropical tunic uniform of the BRAFF officer corps, green belt, ammunition pouches and a leather pistol holster carrying a 9mm Colt revolver. His trousers, with dark red piping, were tucked into bright black leather boots and khaki puttees. His left hand was missing. Instead, the Major had a fitted black metal hook which protruded slightly out of his uniform's sleeve; a legacy from previous battles against the Teutons. The Major shook hands firmly with Porridge and each of the trio.

'Pleased to meet you,' he said, smiling at Willie. 'I hope you're able to help us.'

'We'll do whatever we can,' replied Willie. 'But your soldiers look very impressive and business-like.'

The Major was delighted to receive this praise, and murmured self-effacingly, 'We have been recruiting and training hard.'

Hassan led the group into a large rectangular stone building with open windows and wooden shutters, surrounded by about a hundred longhouses constructed from bamboo and thick thatched roofs.

'Come through here, and make yourselves comfortable while we have lunch,' he said welcomingly, motioning towards some large cane couches, which were covered in comfy blue cushions, and set around a low wooden table. Hassan seated himself on some soft silk tasselled cushions in a huge, heavily carved, ebony chair at the head of the table, which had all the appearance of a king's throne. Major Mamood settled himself in a smaller chair beside Hassan. The group accepted Hassan's invitation with gusto, spreading out over the cushions so as to best feel their comforting softness. Lunch was served and placed on the table in wooden bowls.

When all had eaten their fill and lolled contentedly back in their cushions, Hassan began to tell them of the Iban's dreadful plight.

'It all began about twenty years ago with a visit from an ambassador from Teutonia to my father, Chief Emberly, who was the Chief of the Ibans at the time. The ambassador offered trade opportunities, medical treatment and facilities, better roads, a bigger port, guaranteed markets for our farm products and some village schools. In return, all that the ambassador asked for was a small amount of land to enable these developments to take place and exclusive trading rights.

'For a time the arrangement seemed to be working well. A start was made on the road and port developments and our farm produce, particularly bananas, was bought by the Teutons. Then they asked for more land to establish their own farms and brought in their Colonial Forces, supposedly to guard the developments. Then they began to take land forcibly and with little or no compensation. Resistance was put down by their troops and my tribe was forced up into the hills, where we are now. When diamonds were discovered in the Great Cavern at Batu Lintang, the Teutons press-ganged able-bodied males to work in the mine for a pittance of payment. Soon their demands for labour in the mine became impossible to meet, and they introduced slave labour. Since then we have lost our freedom, we have been forced off our farms, our food supplies are scarce and my people are getting sick and lack education.' He paused for a moment and then continued, his voice faltering and strained with emotion.

'We can only look towards a terrible future with these cursed Teutons, particularly under their military commander, Colonel Goroka, the self-styled "White Rajah". We must get rid of them as quickly as we can, so we can return to the peace, freedom and prosperity we once had.' Hassan's eyes glistened with tears and he turned to Major Mamood. 'Tell them what we know about the Teutons' military plans.'

Major Mamood skipped to his feet and unrolled a map fixed to the wall behind his chair. 'We think the Teutons intend to attack us within the next couple of days, probably the day after tomorrow. Their objectives will be to invade this village here and push us even further up the mountain and into the volcanic wastelands.' He pointed to the wall map. 'To do this, they intend concentrating their units just west of Kuching, move them across the Ngaio Gorge, and assault the village from the east about here. They intend using most of their infantry and artillery forces for this operation. So, by my reckoning, they will probably use about 600 troops.' He looked directly at the group and said quietly, 'We have only 300 BRAFF soldiers to confront them, so we will be outnumbered two to one. This means that we will have to fight cleverly, and use the natural obstacle of the Ngaio Gorge to our maximum advantage.'

'How deep is the Ngaio Gorge?' asked Willie.

'Between 300 and 400 yards,' replied Major Mamood. 'It's also quite narrow and steep, with areas of loose shingle scree, and with little or no cover. If we can hold the Teutons there, and stop them crossing, we should set back their plans quite a bit.'

'Yes, that's right,' agreed Willie. 'But it would be better still if you could deal them a really severe blow while their forces are concentrated. It could hasten you overthrowing the Teutons completely in Sarawak.'

Major Mamood nodded his head in agreement. 'That's absolutely right,' he said, looking a little surprised that such a sound military judgement could come from such a young man.

'Very good,' mused Willie. 'We'll obviously have to focus our efforts on the Ngaio Gorge to support your troops. We can also give you some rather special shells for your gunners to use.'

'Your guns are 4-inch Mark 1, light Oerlikon field guns, aren't they?' enquired Gareth.

'Yes, that's right,' said Major Mamood, again surprised and impressed that such detail was known by the visitors. The group gathered round the wall map and continued to discuss further planning details until all were satisfied as to the parts they were to play.

Finally, Willie decided that the group should return to the volcanic cave and make their preparations for the coming battle. Major Mamood provided them with a small escort of ten BRAFF soldiers, and, bidding farewell to Hassan and the Major, the group made their way back to the cave, just as the sun started to dip over the horizon.

16

THE SIX Ps

The new day's dawn was grey and crisp, its half-light illuminating the first stirrings in the small encampment outside the cave. While Porridge, Jimmy and Arthur had slept in the tomotram, the trio had passed the night sleeping soundly in camp stretchers fitted with mosquito nets, which had been placed outside the cave, around a large camp fire. The BRAFF soldiers were already up, packed, breakfasted and standing-to at their defensive posts. A delicious smell of bacon and eggs drifted from a long-handled frying pan held by Jimmy over the refuelled camp fire. A pot of coffee simmered, its invigorating aroma adding to the call to start the day. The canvas camp chairs surrounding the fire absorbed its warmth and invited someone to sit and share their comfort.

The group roused themselves as Jimmy called out, 'Wakey, wakey. Rise and shine. Breakfast in five minutes.'

'Oh, your blood's worth bottling, Jimmy,' murmured Penelope, snuggling further into her blankets as she summoned up enough motivation to get out of bed.

'Great way to start the day,' said Gareth, stretching and yawning, as he pushed aside the mosquito net and perched on the camp stretcher to clear his thoughts.

'Thanks, Jimmy,' said Porridge, emerging from the cave, and helping himself to a mug of coffee. 'Where's Willie?'

'Over here,' said a voice from behind a camp stretcher. 'Just doing a few push-ups.'

Arthur appeared at the entrance to the cave, rubbing his eyes, and stumbling as he approached.

'What's all the fuss about,' he mumbled. 'Why is everyone up so early?'

Gareth chuckled. 'None of us are the same, Arthur. My Auntie Dinnie used to say that all of us operate to different time clocks. Some of us are early morning larks and some of us are night-owls. You're probably a night-owl!' They all gathered around the camp fire for breakfast and, when they had finished, Willie said, 'I think our guiding thought today should be the Six Ps.' Turning to Porridge, Jimmy and Arthur, he explained, 'The Six Ps stand for a little saying we have, "Prior Preparation Prevents Pathetically Poor Performance".' The three chuckled and nodded their heads approvingly. Willie continued giving instructions for the day's activities.

'Gareth and I will concentrate on getting the Percival plane combat ready, and loaded with the Dreambombs. Penelope, will you get the Dreamshells, Laserlances and first aid kits ready to take down to the BRAFF troops in the village? Jimmy and Arthur, will you help Penelope, make sure that the tomotram is ready for a fast departure if required? Porridge, could you get the BRAFF soldiers to clear the ground of stones, so that there is a smooth take-off and landing strip for the plane?'

Everyone murmured their assent and immediately set to work. It was mid-afternoon by the time Willie and Gareth had assembled the Percival aircraft on the field outside the cave. The wings had been firmly bolted onto the mainly bamboo fuselage. The tiny but sturdy engine had been secured into the frame, and the fuselage bolted onto the tripod under-carriage sitting on its three bicycle wheels. Gareth had also been working by himself on the aircraft, while Willie had been questioning Porridge and the BRAFF soldiers about the local weather conditions that could be expected around the Ngaio Gorge.

'I've made some adjustments to the engine to give it greater power,' Gareth told him when he returned. 'I've also added some coolant, and a couple of gallons of more fuel to give you a longer range. If you just take it easy, and don't do any aerobatics, I reckon you'll get a good 20-25 minutes of flying.'

'That sounds great,' replied Willie, grinning. 'I don't expect to get into any dogfights!'

Gareth continued, 'I've also stitched on a couple of canvas sheets under the wing struts, which will give you better lifting power, and inserted a new canvas aileron towards the end of each wing. These should give you better manoeuvrability and stability in wind gusts. I've bolted a couple of old tin tea cases on each side of the pilot's seat which will serve as bomb bays. You should be able to carry about twenty Dreambombs, which should be enough to deal with 400 to 500 Teutonian troops.'

Penelope joined them, looked admiringly at the aircraft, and said laughingly, 'That looks like a real plane now instead of just a tangle of bamboo, wires and bike wheels you started with. But we need to paint our insignia on the wings. What signs do you think would look good?'

Gareth clicked his tongue and lifted his eyes skywards in exasperation. 'What signs do you think would look good?' he repeated. 'Is that all you girls ever think of? How to look good? This aircraft is flying into battle tomorrow. It doesn't matter how it looks, just so long as it does its job efficiently and dependably.'

'Hang on a sec though,' said Willie thoughtfully. 'Penelope has got a good point. We should paint it up, but not with insignia. What was it that "J" told us in his briefing about the Teutonians' gods?'

'Was it about Zeust, their God of all Gods?' suggested Penelope helpfully. 'The God that appears in the form of a flying dragon?'

'That's the one,' agreed Willie enthusiastically. 'Why don't we stitch a little bit more canvas onto the aircraft and paint a fiery red and yellow dragon on it?'

'Excellent idea,' said Penelope, clapping her hands excitedly.

'Hmmm, I'm not so sure,' cautioned Gareth. 'It will cause extra drag and that could reduce our flying time. On the other hand,' he said, brightening, 'It could cause real panic within the Teutons' ranks.'

Porridge's face was wreathed in smiles as he nodded his agreement. 'It will give them one hell of a fright,' he said, laughing delightedly.

'Right, that's what we'll do this evening,' decided Willie. 'Meantime, we'd better give this engine a bit of a whirl. Gareth and I will take old Zeust here on a trial run up the strip. Porridge, would you ask the soldiers to hold onto the fuselage behind the pilot's seat until the engine gets up a bit of speed, and then give me a push.' Willie climbed onto the pilot's seat behind the engine while Gareth swung the propeller. The soldiers held the aircraft firmly in place. After two or three attempts, the engine clattered noisily, and spluttered clouds of black smoke from its exhaust. Then it stopped.

'Give it more fuel,' directed Gareth. 'Push the accelerator forward as far as you can, and ease it back once we've got it started.'

'OK. OK,' said Willie, waving his hand in acknowledgement.

Gareth swung the propeller again. The engine coughed once or twice and suddenly roared smoothly to life. It created an enormous din. Willie could feel the aircraft vibrating about him, and the power of the engine wanting to pull the aircraft along. He eased the accelerator back, as Gareth came around the wings to his side, and made some adjustments to the engine with a screwdriver. Gareth's face was flushed with triumph and success. He gave a 'thumbs up' and motioned to him to switch off. The engine came to a halt as its clatter echoed and re-echoed around the nearby jungle-covered slopes.

'That seems to be running pretty well, don't you think?' Gareth asked.

'Sounds good to me,' replied Willie, adding, 'I reckon the great God, Zeust, would be proud to have such a mean machine named after him!' He jumped down off the pilot's seat.

'I think we should push it back into the cave now, where it is sheltered for the night, and we can continue to work on it quietly.' They had just completed pushing the aircraft into the cave, when there was a call of alarm from Porridge.

'Look over there,' he said urgently, pointing to a low hill in the jungle about two miles away. 'See that flashing light?' They all looked. Sure enough, a white light could be seen flickering in the distance high up in the jungle trees.

'That's the sunlight reflecting off something,' said Penelope.

'You're right,' agreed Willie grimly, 'and I hope it's not what I think it is.'

He went quickly to the cave and emerged a few seconds later with his field binoculars. He focused them on the far line of dark green hills and then onto the flickering light.

'Damn, damn,' he cursed softly. After a few moments he announced, 'It's what I thought it might be. It's a Teuton reconnaissance patrol all right. Probably heard the noise of the engine and climbed up a tree to investigate. They would probably be no more than three or four soldiers, so I don't think they would attack us. But if they get word back to Colonel Goroka about us before tomorrow we'll lose our element of surprise.'

He pondered for a moment.

'However, I don't think that they would have seen enough to cause them to hurry back to report, and anyway, there's only a couple of hours of daylight left before dark. They'll have to wait until daylight tomorrow before reporting back to their unit, by which time most of the action could be over.'

He looked at the others and smiled.

'I don't think we should be too worried. Time is on our side. But anyway, we'll try not to attract any more attention. I think we should move everything back into the cave for the night and keep a low profile. Our BRAFF escort can maintain their defensive positions outside the cave to deter that Teuton patrol from getting a closer look at us.'

They all nodded in agreement, and quickly moved their camp equipment and packs back into the cave. Jimmy and Arthur fetched some paraffin lamps from the tomotram to give brighter light and placed the camp stretchers in the tomotram itself. They then created a fireplace from some volcanic rocks and soon had a cheery fire glowing towards the back of the cave. The swiftlets remained in their nests in the dark vault of the cave's roof, seemingly confident that the intruders below meant them no harm. Gareth and Penelope stitched some additional canvas panels on 'Zeust, Mark 1' as Pearce's plane was now known, and then painted a bright red, fiery dragon on the whole aircraft. It looked impressive and realistic, with its mouth breathing fire around the engine, its talons over the bicycle wheels, and its tail coiled up behind the pilot's seat. When they had finished they all sat back in satisfaction, chuckling to themselves as to the devastating effect it might have on the Teuton troops.

'Corned beef patties, baked beans, onions, camp bread and Irish tea are on the menu for tonight,' announced Jimmy, grinning broadly. 'I call it the Borneo Delight.'

'It sounds delicious, Jimmy,' said Gareth. 'I could eat a horse, I'm that famished.'

'Me too,' said Porridge and Penelope.

'Well, we've all worked hard and well today,' said Willie. 'We should turn in early tonight, as we will need to get up at the crack of dawn tomorrow.' It was dark outside when they had finished dinner, so they all retired to the tomotram and settled down for the night.

All except Willie, that is.

He remained awake, his mind a clutter of thoughts. Finally, after much tossing and turning, he quietly slid out of his camp stretcher and moved silently out of the tomotram, across the cave floor to the entrance. One of the BRAFF soldiers was there on guard, his presence only betrayed by the tiny red glow of his cigarette.

Willie looked out into the blackness of the night. His thoughts roamed over the day's events and then focused clearly on the slave mine, the appalling conditions of the Ibans, and the menacing figure of Colonel Goroka. For some inexplicable reason, his mind flashed back to Lucifer-Mortlock. In his mind's eye he saw the Lag as the swaggering, bullying and cruel Colonel Goroka: a brute of a man who used his position to make himself increasingly wealthier and grander; a ruthless and savage slave-master who would stop at nothing to make himself more powerful. Yes, he was sure that would be a description of the Lag, as well as having been already proven to be a liar, a cheat and a fraudster. He remembered the quarrel between his father and Lucifer-Mortlock, and he suddenly felt that if he could beat Goroka and his forces he somehow had struck a blow for his father against the Lag.

He looked out into the inky blackness of the jungle. It was as if he was in a gigantic theatre, seated in the highest seat in the circle, and staring down at the black stage still swathed in its curtains. The actors, still to come on stage, were in their faraway dressing rooms, preparing for their performances and entrances at the appointed times. He, himself, was destined to play a principal role, together with his supporting props and actors. Above him stretched the immensity of the night sky, pierced by a myriad of twinkling stars. He felt so small, so tiny. A mere speck of human dust floating in the infinity of the universe. What could one so tiny and inconsequential as he hope to achieve within this vast arena?

He did believe that the cause of the Ibans was just, and he disliked the Teutons in Sarawak intensely. He and his group had the tools to make a huge difference for the Ibans. He was so fortunate to have such a good team around him, who looked to him for leadership. Together they would give the Teutons the hiding of their lives and the course of history for Sarawak would change for the better.

'Is everything all right?' whispered Gareth from his camp bed.

'Are you OK?' asked Penelope.

'Everything is absolutely fine,' reassured Willie with great conviction. 'I'm A OK. I'm really looking forward to tomorrow. We'll give those Teutons something to write home about.'

And with that he slipped into his camp bed, tucked his mosquito net under his blankets and was soon fast asleep.

17

THE BATTLE OF NGAIO GORGE

Colonel Goroka was feeling very pleased with himself as he sat at his desk at the Teuton Army headquarters in the Schloss. His plans for the final destruction of the BRAFF forces and complete subjugation of the Ibans seemed to be progressing well. His Emperor would be pleased, and when the job was done, he himself would be well rewarded with several thousands of acres of rich, arable land around the foothills of Gunong Nuyit. Not to mention the hundreds of Iban slaves he would have to serve his every wish.

He studied the battle maps on his office wall on which the attack plan had been marked. The plan for 'Operation Clean-up' was quite simple. He would use one infantry company and one artillery battery to create a firm base on the eastern edge of Ngaio Gorge. Once that was accomplished, he would then launch a two-company infantry assault across the gorge to establish a bridgehead. Then he would follow up with his fourth infantry company, supported by his second artillery battery, to fan out from the bridgehead, to destroy the remaining BRAFF forces.

His reconnaissance patrols had reported little of consequence. The Ibans seemed to have no inkling of his impending attack. Most activity seemed to be within the Iban villages, where the noise of chanting and dancing could be heard. Very few of the BRAFF forces had been seen, and even then they were only small defensive patrols. There had been rumours that the BRAFF had artillery, but the reconnaissance patrols had not seen any guns. The Colonel leaned back in his chair and took a large swig of local vodka schnapps, and raised his glass to a painting of the Emperor Wilhelm IV which hung on the wall beside the French doors.

'Well, my good Emperor,' he mused, speaking out loud, 'you'd better be very, very grateful to little Goroka here after he's crushed the BRAFF, and give him lots and lots of land. Otherwise, you might find yourself losing a diamond mine and possibly even the Sarawak Colony. You might even find yourself dealing with a new Emperor – Emperor Goroka the First of Sarawak!' He chuckled to himself as the notion of titles, castles and a heavily jewelled Emperor's crown flashed across his mind. He walked across the room to the French doors, pushed them open, and stood on the outside balcony. It was just after dawn, and already he could see his troops moving towards the Ngaio Gorge.

***

By dawn, the inside of the cave on Gunong Nuyit was buzzing with activity, as Willie's group made their final preparations. Porridge and Penelope had prepared packs of Dreamshells, Laserlances and first aid kits to be taken down to the BRAFF village by themselves and their escorting soldiers. Willie and Gareth were to launch the 'Zeust, Mark 1', now resplendent in its dragon regalia, and its bomb bays full of Dreambombs, as soon as a runner from the village informed them that the Teutons had reached the Ngaio Gorge. Jimmy, Arthur and Gareth were to provide a firm base for the group and prepare the tomotram for a fast exit from the cave should that be required. After a hearty breakfast of scrambled eggs, toast, marmalade and mugs of hot, sweet tea, everyone was ready. The dawn was just breaking as Penelope's team loaded up and started to move out in single file to the village.

'Good luck, you two,' said Willie to Penelope and Porridge. 'See you back here no later than mid-afternoon.'

'Thanks, we will,' replied the two from under their huge packs. 'But just don't go dropping any of those Dreambombs on us!' They gave a farewell wave and moved out of the cave, across the field and into the jungle. Willie and Gareth stood quietly at the cave entrance for a few minutes watching them disappear from view and into a light morning mist swirling around the high trees.

'She will be all right, won't she?' whispered Gareth.

'I'm sure she'll be fine,' assured Willie softly. 'They'll be at the village in about 30 minutes, and besides, she's got the BRAFF escort if there's any hint of trouble.'

His voice changed and became businesslike. 'Come on, we'd better get old Zeust Mark 1 out onto the tarmac and ready to fly.' They pushed the aircraft out of the cave and pointed the nose down the sloping field and into the light morning breeze. As Gareth made some small adjustments to the engine, and Willie checked the fuselage, they heard the first explosions of the Teuton artillery softening up the BRAFF positions overlooking the Ngaio Gorge.

Crump ... crump ... crump. The force of the explosions seemed to reverberate through the air. *Wheeeee ... thumppp.* They could hear the whistling of the shells before they landed, like banshees shrilling out a warning of death. Then came the crackling of rifle fire, as the attackers sought to disable the defenders.

'Sounds as if things are warming up a little,' said Gareth.

'Hmm, you're right. And probably a little quicker than we thought.'

In his mind's eye Willie pictured the Teuton infantry already sliding down the precipitous slope of the gorge, sprinting across the open rocky bottom to the opposite slope, and scrambling up the slippery, shingle scree. They would be taking advantage of the covering small-arms fire and the supporting artillery barrage. He pictured the confusion in the BRAFF defenders' ranks in the face of this relentless fire. The destruction of their defensive positions on top of the gorge and the terror of their women and children as shells exploded in their villages, showering their unprotected bodies with shards of hot molten steel splinters.

'Come on, Gareth,' he suddenly urged. 'We've got to go now, otherwise we'll be too late.' He climbed quickly into the pilot's seat of the Zeust Mark 1, while Gareth dashed to the front and grasped the propeller.

'Go,' shouted Willie and Gareth swung the propeller hard. The engine spluttered, coughed and stopped.

'Go again,' Willie ordered, and again Gareth swung the propeller. Again the engine spluttered, coughed and fell silent. Oh no, thought Willie, don't give up on me now.

'The accelerator,' shouted Gareth. 'Push the accelerator forward as hard as you can.' He did as Gareth instructed, and as Gareth swung the propeller for the third time, the engine roared into life.

'*Yes*!' Willie gunned the motor. He exchanged 'thumbs up' with Gareth, and the aircraft started to move forward down the slope.

Gathering speed, it lumbered down the field, its wheels bouncing off the odd rock that had been missed by the BRAFF soldiers and finally, reluctantly, it took to the air.

'Yeahah,' yelled Gareth, waving his arms in delight. 'You do look like a flying dragon!'

Willie guided the aircraft towards the Gorge, and managed to gain sufficient height to fly well clear of the jungle canopy. At 600 feet, and as he neared the gorge, he could see the Iban villages below and the explosions of the Teuton artillery shells slamming into houses and destroying some of the Iban defensive positions. He flew over the gorge and, looking down, he could see swarms of Teuton infantry in its depths. Some soldiers appeared to straighten up and point to the aircraft in great agitation.

Willie took the aircraft up a little higher to about 1000 feet and turned to position it at the head of the gorge. The air currents, warmed by the morning sun, made flying more difficult, and he was thankful for the extra ailerons that Gareth had fitted into the wings. He started his bombing run along the length of the gorge and directly above the Teuton infantry. Quickly, he threw out six Dreambombs, each of which exploded about 100 yards apart in the midst of the troops. He finished his first run and banked to the right as sharply as he dared to commence his second run.

Looking ahead and down into the gorge, he could see the first Dreambombs were already starting to have some effect. Teuton troops were running aimlessly around, some pointing up to the aircraft, others lying on the ground on their backs, their hands around their ears and their legs pumping the air as if they were having a tantrum.

He continued his second run up the gorge, throwing out another six Dreambombs, and then banked to the right again so that he was flying over the Teuton concentrations on the high ground. He commenced his third and last run, flying low over the trees and dropping his remaining Dreambombs on the clusters of Teuton troops scattering below. He was particularly pleased to drop one of his Dreambombs in the centre of the Teutons' battery of field guns, and to see the ensuing bedlam as the gunners left their posts and breathed in the hallucinating vapours that the exploding bomb released. With his bomb bays empty, he turned his aircraft back towards the safety of the cave and the landing field.

Below him he could see that the Teutons were in great confusion and chaos. Their command structure disintegrated as the officers also fell victim to the hallucinating gases. Each Teuton soldier seemed to be experiencing his own horrible fantasy or delirium. Some were clearly seeing huge worms and snakes swallowing their legs and arms, or felt them slithering out and hissing from their ears and nostrils. Others argued vehemently with a non-existent being, slashing at them with their bayonets. Some fought off an imaginary horde of scorpions intent on stinging them, while others felt themselves being choked to death by the roots of live trees. Others obviously imagined themselves in the presence of Zeust, the Greatest of All Gods, and fell into a transcendental trance, humming and smiling to themselves while sitting cross-legged on the ground.

It was then that the BRAFF gunners commenced their counter-battery fire using the Dreamshells given to them by Penelope. Hidden away in the safety of bunkers in the Iban village houses, the field guns were now wheeled out and put to work. Their guns reached out to the roads behind the Teuton soldiers, catching those that were retreating, causing even wider panic and hysteria. They pounded the Teuton infantry in the gorge, and the Teuton artillery further back which had caused them so much devastation earlier.

Meantime, the BRAFF infantry, some of whom were wearing gas masks given to them by Penelope, lined the top of the gorge and looked down on the helpless Teuton soldiers below. When the gases had cleared sufficiently, they would go down into the Gorge, pick up the Teutons' discarded weapons, and shackle them together as prisoners. No longer were the Teutons the conquerors of Sarawak. No longer were they the harsh subjugators of the Ibans. The tables had been turned, and it was they who would be led off as prisoners of the Ibans.

***

From the safety of the Schloss, Colonel Goroka watched in dismay and utter disbelief as he saw the destruction of his forces. He had seen the strange machine flying over his troops, looking like the Great God, Zuest, but he had recognised it for what it was. Simply a flying machine painted to look like the Great God. Colonel Goroka was not religious, preferring to deal in the realities of Life. However, he was smart enough to know that many of his troops were deeply religious and that the sight of the fiery dragon would have terrified them. He had no idea of the nature of the Dreambombs, but could see from his vantage point that what had been dropped from the flying machine had effectively disabled his troops. As he pondered his next move, there was a knock on his office door and an aide brought in a soldier who had been on a reconnaissance patrol the previous night.

He had seen something very unusual on the higher slopes of Gunong Nuyit. They had noticed a cave at the back of the mountain with some BRAFF soldiers outside it. But there was also something that looked and sounded like a motor, but had sails attached to it. After it had been running a while, the motor with its sails had been pushed back into the cave. Unfortunately, darkness fell and they could see nothing more. They had hurried back to the Schloss to make their report. Instantly, Colonel Goroka knew what the 'motor with attached sails' actually was, and instantly he knew what his next move would be.

He called together all his staff in the Schloss, and together they hurried off in the direction of the diamond mine at Batu Lintang.

18

COUNTERATTACK

Willie was ecstatic and flushed with triumph. He had successfully carried out his part in the destruction of the Teutons, and with a bit of luck the Ibans would now be able to finish the job.

At this moment, however, his very real problem was to land safely on the field outside the cave. He knew he had only a little fuel left and he would only have one chance to bring the plane down safely. He flew the aircraft low over the Iban villages and the jungle canopy, so as to approach the field for a low-angle landing. He concentrated his attention and looked down at the field now rushing up to meet him. He could see Gareth, Jimmy and Arthur outside the cave waving to him. Suddenly, the engine coughed, spluttered, stopped momentarily, and then, as if by divine intervention, reluctantly restarted to run smoothly again.

'Fuel problems,' thought Willie. 'Must be running out.'

He brought the aircraft down a little more so it was just skimming the treetops, making adjustments in response to some warm updrafts. He was over the tree-line now with the open field in front of him. He was in the last critical stage of his approach when the engine ran out of fuel and stopped. Automatically, Willie braced himself for a hard landing, pushing his legs down stiffly on the control pedals to meet the expected impact, and shutting his eyes tightly. As he did so, he also lifted the nose up, so that the bicycle wheels would be the first to meet the ground. Then there came a bone-shaking jolt, and a series of bumps as the bicycle wheels bounced, and the aircraft came to a halt just short of the cave entrance. There was a moment's silence, as if the world stood still. Willie opened his eyes.

'You did it!' shouted Gareth as Jimmy, Arthur and he ran towards the aircraft. The three of them were shouting gleefully as they reached Willie and thumped him on his back.

"Great work. Well flown, Willie,' applauded Gareth. 'I didn't think you were going to land safely. I thought you were going to hit those trees.'

'We thought you were going to crash,' said Jimmy, pumping Willie's hand.

'Yes, we thought you'd be splattered all over the field, Mr William,' nodded Arthur in agreement. 'Your guardian angel must have been working overtime!'

Willie grinned a mixture of triumph and relief.

'Yeah, I reckon I was blimmin' lucky all right. I just had enough fuel to clear the jungle. By the way, have we heard anything from Penelope or Porridge yet?'

'Yes,' replied Gareth. 'Penelope sent up a runner from the village to say that all was well and that she and Porridge would be returning in about an hour.' He added, 'We could certainly do with some cell phones here now!'

'That's great. It all sounds as if it's going as we planned,' said Willie. 'I think we should head back to the Consulate as soon as they come back and leave the battlefield mopping up to the Ibans. Let's get this aircraft dismantled now and packed into the tomotram, so we will be ready to move.'

They all set to, taking the aircraft apart in accordance with Gareth's instructions, and packing it carefully into its boxes in the tram. Because of the smoke particles from the camp fire, it was now quite easy to see the grey outline of the tomotram as the fine dust had settled over the Seethrough paint.

'We'll give the tram a thorough wash when we get back to the Consulate,' said Willie, 'and a touch-up with some more Seethrough paint. It would be much better if no-one sees us leaving.'

They had just finished packing the aircraft when there was a loud hail from the jungle edge, and Penelope, Porridge and Hassan emerged, escorted by a platoon of very tough-looking BRAFF troops. The three were all smiles and obviously delighted with the outcome of the battle. Hassan was overjoyed and rushed up to give Willie a huge hug of gratitude.

With tears in his eyes and his voice quavering, he said, in a hoarse whisper, 'Thank you, thank you all, for your special magic in helping my people gain their freedom. You were all so brave and put your own lives at risk. We Ibans will never forget you.'

Willie's face went as red as a beetroot. While he did feel a little embarrassment at Hassan's emotion, he also felt very proud of the accomplishments of Penelope and Gareth. He was also somewhat taken aback and suddenly short of words. Penelope came to his rescue.

'Thank you, Hassan,' she said brightly, 'for those kind words. But we have been delighted to be able to help you, and particularly so having seen your poor people working as slaves in the Teutons' diamond mine.'

'Ah, yes,' replied Hassan, 'that's right. My people in that hell-hole of a diamond mine. Could I ask a favour of you?'

'Yes, of course,' Willie answered. 'What would you want?'

'Well, as you can see, I've brought up a large escort party of BRAFF troops with us from the village. These troops are very special. Very tough and well armed. We have used them for operations to harry the Teuton Army. We would like to use them as a surprise raiding party to free our people in the diamond mine. Would it be possible for you to use the tomotram to transport them to a launch point close to the mine?'

'Yes, of course we can do that,' agreed Willie. 'I think we should be able to fit them all in with their equipment. They will have to perch where they can on our stores, as we've taken out all the seats. What do you think, Arthur?'

'Yes, Mr William,' said Arthur, nodding in agreement. 'I think we'll all be able to fit in all right. It'll be a bit cosy maybe. Just like a can of sardines.'

'OK, that's settled then,' decided Willie. 'Let's load up and get under way as quickly as we can.' He turned to Penelope.

'How did it go down in the village?'

'I think it went off pretty darned well,' replied Penelope. 'I gave the BRAFF gunners all the Dreamshells which they fired off. I gave most of the Laserlances to the troops defending the gorge. They simply blinded the Teuton infantry, who then had to lie down on the ground and wait to be taken prisoner. I've brought back all the Laserlances for possible future use. The first aid packs we took down were really good. I showed some of the Iban women how to clean and dress wounds and they quickly formed First Aid posts just behind the defensive positions.'

'Wow, you did so well,' said Gareth admiringly. 'That was a really serious effort, Penelope.'

'No doubt about that,' Willie agreed, nodding. 'Penelope, you're Number One!' It was Penelope's turn to feel a little embarrassed, and her cheeks reddened.

'Oh,' she said, making light of events and tossing her head slightly. 'It was nothing, really.' But the boys saw through her remarks, looked at each other and grinned.

It was about mid-afternoon when all the equipment and troops were packed into the tomotram and they were ready to leave. Hassan and a small escort of three soldiers stood outside the tram, as he was going to return back through the jungle to his village. He wished his BRAFF troops good luck for their operation to free the slaves in the diamond mine, and turned to the trio and Porridge.

'As soon as this business is all over, we will have a grand celebration,' he promised. 'Just take care of yourselves.' He smiled. 'I have some home-made Iban beer I'd like you to taste!'

Arthur and Porridge set the instruments on the tomotram for a position just short of the Teutons' diamond mine and started the motors. With a hum of increasing power, the tomotram left the cave and glided off into the blackness of the tunnels. The BRAFF troops, although alert to any danger, settled back, enjoying the comparative comfort of being transported, rather than having to march into battle. There was much laughing and joking, and some even started playing cards. Willie made himself comfortable in one of the driver's chairs beside Arthur. He wanted to be sure that they didn't inadvertently enter the cavern of the diamond mine, where the tomotram could be seen. The others settled themselves into their seats and chatted amongst themselves about their battle experiences. Suddenly, Arthur stiffened, peering ahead into the inky blackness of the tunnel.

'Quickly, Mr William, there are some headlights ahead of us,' he said urgently. Willie looked out of the driver's window.

'Is it another tomotram?'

But before Arthur could answer, there was a whoosh and a softly lit tomotram thundered past, its motors squealing at full throttle. It was full of Teuton troops, their helmets and bayonets glinting in the tram lights. Everyone scrambled to their feet, dazed and uncertain as to what was happening.

'What the heck was that?' Penelope shouted.

'Don't really know,' replied Willie. 'But it looked like a Teuton tomotram in a bit of a hurry.'

'Do you think they might be on their way to the cave on Gunong Nuyit?' suggested Gareth.

'Here comes another one,' interrupted Arthur, and a second tomotram squealed past at great speed, and disappeared into the blackness following the first Teuton trooper. It too was full of heavily armed soldiers.

'Wasn't Colonel Goroka in that one?' asked Porridge. 'I thought I saw him.'

'Well, I hope he didn't see you,' replied Penelope. She turned to the boys. 'We'll have to change our plans now, won't we?'

'Yes, you're probably right,' said Willie thoughtfully. 'We can't go ahead with the raid on the diamond mine now because we'll have the Teuton guards in the mine in front of us, and Goroka and his chums behind us after they find that we have left the cave on Gunong Nuyit. We can't risk returning to the Consulate in Kuching, in case Porridge was seen by Goroka, and he bottles us up there with his troops. Come to think of it, we can't really be sure that we've done our job properly until we've disposed of Goroka, or he's a prisoner of the Ibans.'

There was a few moments silence as they all pondered the meaning of Willie's words, and of the possible options open to them. It was Penelope who was first to speak. She turned to Porridge and Arthur.

'How many tunnel exits are there from Kuching?'

'Not many, not many at all,' replied Porridge. 'Just the main Far Eastern line running west to Singapore and east to Jesselton, and the Oceania line south to Australia and New Zealand. There are perhaps three or four local lines which are really culs-de-sac, like the line to the Gunong Nuyit cave.'

'Right, and Arthur, doesn't the Oceania line join the Far East line at Mulu?'

'Yes, that's right,' answered Arthur, nodding his head vigorously as he continued to drive the tomotram at a slower speed.

'And isn't the cavern of the spiders in the Mulu Caves?'

Arthur's eyes widened and his face went white as he remembered their previous visit to the Grotto and their lucky escape. 'Ye ... ye ... yes,' he stammered. 'But you're not going to go back there, are you?'

'Might have to,' said Penelope cheerfully. She turned back to the others.

'Why don't we try to get Goroka and his troops to follow us to the cavern of the spiders, give them the slip and let them take their chances, while we return to our business in the diamond mine?'

'That's not a bad idea, not bad at all,' mused Gareth, his grin broadening slowly as the idea blossomed in his mind.

'Yes, that's a pretty good plan,' agreed Willie. 'We can keep our interior lights on to make us easily seen and followed. Then that waterfall at the entrance to the cavern will wash all the dust off the Seethrough paint and we will be invisible. We could then park off to one side, let the Teutons enter the cavern, and then double-back here.' His voice hardened as he added grimly, 'we could even help them on their way with a little extra light.'

'Do you think Goroka will be silly enough to chase us all that way?' asked Gareth.

'Hmm … yes, it is a bit of a risk, I suppose,' agreed Penelope. "But I doubt that he's a happy boy now, and would dearly like to see us out of the way.'

'That's settled then. That's what we'll do,' decided Willie. 'Penelope, go and tell Jimmy, Porridge and the BRAFF troops of our plan. Gareth, you unpack the Laserlances ready for action. Arthur, you and I will reset the instruments for the Grotto of the Spiders.'

Colonel Goroka was *not* a happy boy. He was, in fact, an extremely unhappy and angry Teuton! He had glimpsed the Brittanican Consul, his visitors and the BRAFF soldiers as the tomotrams sped past one another, and had guessed that they were on their way to the diamond mine. It was starting to become clear to him now what had happened. Brittanica had intervened in his plans to overthrow the Ibans. They had brought in some strangers who were able to fly like birds and had used some powerful weapons to destroy his army. Not only had they demolished his troops, but they had robbed him of his rightful rewards for all the hard work he had put in to secure his future. The land, the slaves, the diamonds, even the possibility of being the first Emperor of Sarawak had all vanished because of them. A fierce hatred welled up inside him. He would *not* meekly accept defeat. He would *not* allow them to slip through his fingers. He would catch them and torture them horribly with fire and needles, before taking them to the Temple of Zeust, where he would kill them. He would chase them to the ends of the Earth to exact his revenge.

His troop transporters soon reached the cave on Gunong Nuyit, only to find it empty, as Goroka knew it would be. He quickly briefed his soldiers on his plan to follow and catch the Brittanic tomotram, offering each of them a reward of a house and land in Kuching if the occupants of the tomotram were all either killed or captured. The soldiers were delighted with this prospect, re-boarded their tomotrams and set off back down the tunnel. Colonel Goroka had climbed aboard the first tomotram so that he could direct the chase. Beside him he had two snipers, ready to shoot anyone in the Brittanic tram as soon as it came within range.

Behind him, his soldiers began sharpening their bayonets.

19

THE WEBS OF MULU

Arthur slowed the Brittanican tomotram down to a crawl while Porridge and Jimmy kept a sharp eye from the rear of the tram for the first glimmer of light from the Teutons' tomotrams. Everyone was tense and at the ready. Willie had instructed Arthur to keep the interior lights switched on and this made everyone feel very uncomfortable and exposed. He had also told Arthur to drive the tram from side to side in the tunnel as if the tram's steering equipment was faulty, and to give the appearance to the Teutons that their tram was damaged. It was probably the tram's side to side movement that saved Porridge's life.

Crack … crack … crack! Bullets pinged through the rear windows, shaved past Porridge's head and buried themselves in the tram's roof. Porridge dived for cover on the floor. The Teutons had switched off their tram lights and had been able to approach the Brittanican tomotram unobserved in the blackness of the tunnel!

'Full power, Arthur,' shouted Willie. 'For Heaven's sake, give it full power!'

But there was no need to urge Arthur. He slammed the accelerator down and the tomotram leapt forward like a sprinter out of his blocks. Its great motors quickly picked up speed and it hurtled down the tunnel on its way to the Mulu cavern. The Teutons' tomotrams followed closely and the two snipers in the front tram continued to fire at every opportunity.

Crack … crack …. zinnnng … zinnng. The bullets came thick and fast, smashing the windows and ricocheting off the steel sheathing.

Colonel Goroka smiled grimly to himself. He was pleased his troop tomotrams had been able to approach unobserved and get so close. Better still, it looked as if the Brittanican tomotram had been damaged. If he could get even closer his snipers might be able to hit the motors and force the Brittanican tomotram to a halt. Then his troops could attack at close quarters and use their bayonets. He felt success was near. Willie held his breath as the snipers' bullets peppered the rear of his tomotram. The Teutons were too near and the well-lit Brittanic tomotram was too easy a target.

'Switch off the inside lights, Arthur,' he shouted. 'We must look like a Christmas tree.'

Arthur did as he was instructed and suddenly all was black, except for the tram's external navigation lights. Immediately, everyone heaved a sigh of relief as the cloak of darkness gave them a sense of security. The snipers ceased firing as they were unable to see a suitable target.

'Are you OK?' whispered Gareth to Penelope, who was crouched down on the floor behind some sacks of potatoes.

'Yes, I'm fine. But keep your head down. Remember Rocky's advice. Cover from view does not mean cover from fire.'

'Yes, I know. I'm safe behind these barrels of flour,' replied Gareth. He was covered in flour and looked like a white ghost.

Just then the Teutons switched on their tomotram's headlamps. A ray of brilliant white light lit up the back of the Brittanican tomotram and the snipers began firing again. Immediately, Arthur took evasive action, moving the tomotram from side to side and up and down, within the tunnel.

Willie, crouching down behind the stout metal plate which formed the exterior skin of the tram, shouted to Porridge. 'Get some BRAFF snipers back here to knock out their lights!'

'They're on their way,' shouted Porridge, as four BRAFF soldiers moved quickly to Willie's side and started firing at the Teutons' trooper. Whenever the Teutons' headlamp lights could be seen, the four soldiers engaged it and the Teuton snipers with rapid fire. Their shooting was almost immediately effective. The leading Teuton trooper dropped back.

'We're coming up to the turn-off to the cavern shortly, Mr William,' Arthur called back.

'That's great, Arthur. The sooner the better. As soon as we get through the waterfall pull over to the left, stop and switch the motors into hover.'

'Right you are,' replied Arthur, privately thanking his lucky stars that he was not going to actually enter the cavern.

In the Teuton troop tomotram, Colonel Goroka was fuming with rage. His hatred for those in the Brittanic tomotram was growing by the minute. Despite his best efforts, his trooper had been unable to close with the enemy, and they were moving further away from Kuching.

Suddenly, his tram driver called back. 'Colonel, they've turned off the mainline down another tunnel. I think they've made a mistake and we might have them trapped!'

'Keep after them,' ordered Colonel Goroka. 'Don't let them out of your sight, or you'll pay for it with your life.'

The Teuton tomotram driver accelerated as hard as he dared, keeping a close watch on the navigation lights of the Brittanican tomotram, which were bobbing about from side to side and up and down in front of him, as they careered through the tunnel. Then, without warning, the Brittanican tomotram seemed to disappear through a wall at the end of the tunnel. The Teuton tram driver had a split second of indecision. Would he follow as he was ordered, or would he try to brake and stop before hitting the wall?

If he stopped, Colonel Goroka would exact a terrible punishment, and if he followed the Brittanican tomotram, surely they would go into the wall just like the Brittanican tomotram had done. He chose the latter, and heaved a great sigh of relief when he realised the wall was a sheet of water and not solid rock.

His trooper burst through the waterfall and emerged into the open. As the rivulets of water cleared from the windows, the driver saw a gigantic cavern before him. A cavern of stalactite columns, lit by the reflections of the sun's incandescent rays, and stretching as far as his eyes could see. Reaching up from the darkness of the cavern's floor were huge stalagmites. But the Brittanican tomotram was nowhere to be seen.

Colonel Goroka rushed up to stand beside the driver.

'Where are they?' he demanded, glaring out of the windows and shading his eyes from the bright light.

'I er ... I er ... I don't know, sir,' stammered the driver.

'Well, they must be just in front of us somewhere, so drive on,' ordered Colonel Goroka. 'Keep a sharp lookout. And be careful you don't crash into those bloody stone pillars. By Zeust, this light is so bright. It's unbearable. Take the tram down into the darker area so we can see what we're doing.'

The tram driver did as he was ordered, and began manoeuvring the tram around the stalagmites and looking up into the sunlit area above, searching for the Brittanican tomotram. In his rear-vision mirror he could see the second Teuton trooper closely following them. After a few minutes of searching, the tram driver suddenly realised that he'd lost his bearings. One stalagmite looked just like any other. There were no markers, and the further they proceeded, the brighter the sunlight became. The sunlight was so strong that it began to hurt his eyes, and he automatically took the tram lower to find the comfort of the darkness below. Colonel Goroka was also struggling to see in the bright light and, despite his determination to catch the Brittanican tomotram, knew that they would have to turn back to the safety of the dark tunnel beyond the waterfall.

'Damnation,' he cursed and barked to the driver. 'Turn around and go back to the waterfall. Get the sun to our backs, so we can see where we're going.'

Gratefully, the driver turned the trooper around and headed back to where he thought the waterfall might be. He drove the tomotram carefully around the stalagmites, which soared into the dazzling illumination above, like columns in a cathedral. There were row upon row of columns, all of which were alike, and all of which mirrored the others. They were trapped in a mirror maze. He frantically searched around to seek any clue as to their position, but could find none. They were lost, and his gnawing fear seeped through the trooper to his uneasy passengers.

'Get us out of here, driver!' snarled Colonel Goroka, 'and back to the waterfall.'

'Yes, sir,' replied the driver, 'but can anyone tell me which way to go?'

The Teuton troopers all looked out the tomotram windows, their eyes wide open, as they peered around trying to find some tell-tale mark or pointer. It was at this moment that Willie's team, who had been watching from their vantage point high up beside the waterfall, fired their Laserlances at the Teutons.

Zap ... zap ... zap.

For the Teuton soldiers, it was as if the world had exploded in front of their faces. In a millisecond the intense laser light had shocked the retinas at the back of their eyes, and they were temporarily blinded. Pandemonium broke out in their trams, as each soldier screamed and tried to shield his eyes from further agonising damage. They threw themselves to the floor, and buried their heads in their arms. The driver of the first trooper caught the full brilliance of the laser-light attack.

'I'm blind, I'm blind,' he screamed. He clutched his head in his hands and dived for cover under his instrument panel. As he did so, his body knocked a stabilising lever forward and the trooper fell out of control. It pitched forward slowly, crashing onto a stalagmite and smashing like matchwood as it fell and rolled over and over as if in slow motion. Troops and equipment churned around inside like marbles in a jar, before it split open as it came to rest with a mighty crash onto the spider webs and trees at the base of the column. The Teuton troops and their equipment were catapulted out into the mesh of spider shrouds on its impact. The second Teuton trooper, also blinded by the Laserlances, crashed into a stalagmite, and it too, plummeted into the blanket of spider webs, spilling screaming troops out as it fell.

Willie's team switched their Laserlances to white light and continued to aim them onto the devastation below. They were like theatre lights illuminating the last tragic death scene on a theatre's stage. Some soldiers were inextricably entangled in the spider shrouds, blinded and immobilised in the glutinous strands of the web and crying piteously for help. Others had staggered to their feet, cursing, their arms outstretched as they sought to free themselves from the clinging strands which they could not see, and could not break.

Agghhh ...help! ... help! They too called for help from any of their comrades who could see. But there were none. Outside the pools of Laserlight tiny pin pricks of greenish reflections could be seen from the myriad of spider eyes converging towards the Teutons, as the armies of Stretch spiders hurried to encase their prey in cocoons of fresh strands of sticky web.

'Look,' exclaimed Porridge, pointing down to the wreckage of the first tram. 'Isn't that Colonel Goroka?'

In the midst of the carnage stood the Colonel, shielding his eyes with one arm and shaking his fist towards them with the other. He was waist deep in the web tangle and screaming in murderous rage.

So intent was he in his cursing and swearing that he was unaware of the approach of the Stretch spider armies until they surged up his body and swarmed over his head and shoulders. He tried to escape and move his legs, but they were firmly caught in the web tangle. He threw his arms around his body and head in a desperate attempt to brush off the spiders, but there were too many of them.

Aggghhh ... aggghhh ... Noooo ... Noooo! He screamed in terror as the spiders commenced their cocoon. They started to spin their web of death on his head first, using his hair as anchors for fresh strands wound around his eyes, nose and mouth. As his breathing became more difficult, his screams became fainter. His defending arms started to tire to finally hang uselessly by his side. The spiders were quick to immobilise them with fresh webs. Goroka made a final desperate effort to free himself, his arteries in his neck bulging with effort, his final shrill scream echoing hauntingly through the cavern. But the spiders had him securely now, firmly woven into their blanket as a food reserve, ready to be sucked dry at their leisure.

'Oh, my God, that was horrible,' said Penelope, closing her eyes and shivering.

Below them the carnage continued as the vast armies of spiders fell upon the helpless soldiers. Their screaming continued unabated, as, one by one, the victims were immobilised, overcome with fresh web strands, and woven into the spider blanket. After half an hour there was silence. Only the wreckage of the Teutons' tomotrams and the scattering of grotesque new cocoons could now be seen. Everyone in the Brittanic tomotram was hushed, each struggling to come to terms with the horrific scene they had just witnessed.

Willie looked around and sensed the others were still in shock and needed to be comforted, and brought back to the task at hand.

'Well,' he said slowly. 'I think we've done our job here. Our plan worked brilliantly and we'd better start heading back to Kuching.' Then his voice became urgent and commanding.

'Come on you lot, let's get going. Douse the Laserlights. Start up the motors, Arthur, and set the instruments for the diamond mine. We've got to drop off the BRAFF troops yet. Get 'em as close as we can to the diamond mine. Rummage through the stores, Gareth, and see what we've got to eat and drink. Would you pack the Laserlances back into their cases, Penelope?'

Everyone jerked back to their senses in response to his

instructions and immediately busied themselves. Arthur had the motors running in seconds, set the instruments with the help of Porridge, and headed the tram back through the waterfall and the tunnels to Kuching. Gareth found enough tins of corned beef, bottles of pickles and sufficient bottles of Kentish Ale for everyone, including the BRAFF troops. The refreshments were doubly welcome. Firstly, as an escape from the horrors of the day and, secondly, as much needed nourishment as they had not had anything to eat since their breakfast before dawn.

Arthur drove the tomotram through the tunnels, right up to the entrance to the Teutons' diamond mine. In the far distance, and through the cavern's blackness, they could see the flickering fire-torches and some cooking camp fires. In soft whispers they all wished the BRAFF soldiers good luck for their daring attack on the Teuton guards. With scarcely a sound, the BRAFF raiding party slipped out of the tram, and climbed down the rock face to the floor of the cave. After the BRAFF soldiers had successfully deployed, Arthur moved the tomotram back from the entrance, and reset their course for the Consulate at Kuching.

***

Mrs Porridge was waiting for them when they arrived. She welcomed them with great delight and was very relieved to see that her husband was fit and well.

'Oh my, oh my,' she then scolded. 'Just look at the mess your clothes are in. It'll take me forever to mend and clean just to make them look respectable again.'

The all looked around at each other, and burst out laughing. Their shirts and trousers were torn and marked with grease and dirt from the tomotram floor. Their faces and hands were streaked with rifle oil and dirt from the cave on Gunong Nuyit. They smelled as bad as rubbish bins, with a potent mixture of gunpowder, bird guano and perspiration. Penelope's hair was in a tangle of jungle twigs and grease. Gareth was covered in flour from head to toe.

'Right,' said Mrs Porridge firmly, 'all of you are to be bathed, showered and in clean, fresh clothes before we have dinner, which will be ready in one hour. Now, upstairs you go, and that includes you, Jimmy and Arthur. I've put some clean clothes on your beds.'

They all trooped rather sheepishly upstairs and into their rooms as Mrs Porridge had ordered. It felt rather strange, after their adventures of the last few days, to have fought a war and freed a nation from slavery, only to return home and to be told to clean themselves up before dinner! An hour later, they assembled downstairs, scrubbed up and spotless in crisp new clothes, to be greeted by Mrs Porridge.

'Ah, that's much better!' she exclaimed. 'Now, take your seats and tuck in. You all look famished. There's a lovely roast chicken dinner waiting for you on the table with peas, baked potatoes and carrots. There are some bottles of best white wine. And there's an apple and rhubarb pie to follow for dessert!'

They all took their seats around the table, with Porridge at the head, flanked by his wife on one side and Willie on the other. Without further ado, they each filled their plates and set to, chatting among themselves, thanking Mrs Porridge for the feast, and complimenting her on her cooking. They had just completed the apple and rhubarb pie when Porridge suddenly rapped his knuckles on the table. He rose to his feet.

'A toast. Please charge your glasses.' He waited until everyone had a full glass of wine, and then he said, as he raised his glass, 'To Brittanica and a free Sarawak!'

'To Brittanica and a free Sarawak!' responded the others, smiling and raising their glasses. They all had a sip from their glasses, and, except for Porridge, resumed their seats. Porridge placed his glass on the table. He straightened himself and looked at the others around the table, who were now hushed and watching him expectantly.

'I just wanted to take this opportunity to thank you all for your part in making the vision of a free Sarawak a reality. Before you came, we were at our wit's end about the terrible situation here. Things were just going from bad to worse, and we really feared for our safety. The Teutons had us in a death grip and we had little hope. But our prayers were answered when you came, and we thank you from the bottom of our hearts. My wife and I toast you all, and wish you every success in the future.' He sat down, reached out and shook Willie's hand, as the others clapped in appreciation of his remarks.

Willie got to his feet to respond.

'Porridge,' he said. 'We're the ones who should be thanking you and Mrs Porridge! Without your help we could never have done what we did.'

'Hear, hear,' chorused everyone, rising to their feet, and applauding the brave couple. With that, Willie moved across to Mrs Porridge and kissed her lightly on her cheek. Mrs Porridge blushed, and she giggled.

'It's a great pleasure to know every one of you.'

It was almost midnight by the time they had finished dinner and finally made their way up the stairs to their rooms, yawning and thinking longingly of sleep. It had been a long, long day. Arthur and Jimmy went downstairs to sleep in the tomotram to ensure its security, and to do an early maintenance check the next morning.

Willie made his way to his room and sat on the side of his bed. He felt exhausted, triumphant, and yet somehow troubled. He felt that something was missing, like a piece of a jigsaw that was still needed to complete the puzzle.

He slid into bed and tucked the mosquito net under the mattress.

As he settled down to sleep, it suddenly occurred to him that the war against the Teutons in Sarawak was not yet over. Although all the Teuton forces that were presently in Sarawak had been destroyed or made prisoner, the long-term outcome now rested in the hands of the Teuton Emperor. William smiled to himself as he imagined the rage of Emperor Wilhelm on being told that his military forces in Sarawak had been vanquished.

The diamonds from Sarawak were important to him for the modernisation of his industries. He would be tempted now to send a bigger military force to re-conquer the Ibans and secure the diamond mines. It would require a large, well-armed Sarawak Army or, better still, an already trained, and well equipped, protective force from some allies to stop him.

Time was against a large-scale expansion of the BRAFF forces, so allied forces had to be found from elsewhere. Perhaps even some forces from Brittanica would do the trick. Yes. That was probably the best course of action to take next. Tomorrow he would have to become a diplomat and a negotiator. Otherwise, if he wasn't careful, BRAFF would have won the battle but lost the war against the Teutons. He decided that he would try to consolidate the BRAFF position with careful diplomacy while keeping well in the background. He felt much happier now that he could see a positive way ahead. He would talk to Porridge and Hassan tomorrow, and see what could be done about the longer-term security for Sarawak.

He smiled to himself, closed his eyes and was soon fast asleep.

20

DIPLOMACY

He awoke the following morning to the delicious aroma of fresh coffee, and bacon and eggs. He had slept in. It was already mid-morning, the sun was shining from a cloudless sky, and he could hear busy movements outside the Consulate and downstairs. He dressed quickly, did some exercises and went downstairs to the dining room to find everyone lolling about in deckchairs in the sun, having finished their breakfast.

'Morning all,' Willie said brightly.

'Morning,' Penelope and Gareth responded sleepily, not bothering to look up from their deckchairs, or move the hats shading their eyes.

'Good morning, Willie,' replied Porridge, smiling, and lifting his head up from the *Brittanican Financial Times* newspaper he was reading. 'I see there's an article here in *The Times* about Sarawak. This edition was published just a few days ago and Jimmy brought it down in the mail when you came down.' He passed the paper across to Willie for him to read. Willie helped himself to some coffee from the large silver urn, standing on the mahogany sideboard, and settled himself at the breakfast table, to read the article which Porridge had ringed in ink.

<u>DIAMONDS MORE THAN A GIRL'S BEST FRIEND</u>
Amsterdam. 15 June
Sarawak's national diamond production company, Natdis (National Diamonds of Sarawak) has announced that it expects to treble its production capacity next year. The current capacity of Natdis is about 100,000 carats of diamonds per year. If Natdis plans are

realised, Sarawak's annual diamond production may reach 500,000 carats annually, worth an estimated $300 million. Sarawak will surpass South Africa and become the Far East's third largest diamond producer after Burma and Thailand.

Natdis is largely owned by TeutonInvest, the investment arm of His Majesty Emperor Wilhelm IV of Teutonia. Diamond production from Sarawak is mostly industrial grade and centred on mines located near the capital, Kuching.

However, Sarawak's diamond industry is not without its troubles, having acquired a bad reputation of being based on slavery, although this allegation is hotly denied by Natdis.

Diamond Industry Reporter.

'Well, well, well,' said Willie, when he had finished reading. 'What do you make of that, Porridge, now the circumstances here have changed so much?'

'It's very interesting, isn't it?' replied Porridge reflectively. 'I had no idea that the diamond mining in Sarawak was so valuable and important. I wonder if Whitehall knew about this before the newspaper announcement.'

'Hmmm … They probably didn't know much more than you at the time,' Willie replied. 'But now that they do know, what do you reckon Woody and the Foreign Office might be thinking?'

Porridge laughed out loud. 'They'll be thinking what an idle Consul-General they have in Sarawak!' he chuckled. 'Three days have gone by since you and your team arrived, and they haven't heard a squeak from me. I'd better get cracking and write a report for you to take back. When do you think you will return to Brittanica?'

'I think we should make a move later today. Certainly by tonight,' responded Willie. 'By the way, will you be making any recommendations to Whitehall about future actions they might consider taking?'

Porridge suddenly became very serious. He looked carefully at Willie before nodding and saying, 'Well, yes, I was going to suggest one or two things for them to think about. But have you something you would like me to include?'

'Well, I was just imagining old Emperor Wilhelm's reaction when he hears what has happened to his forces down here, and he realises that he might lose his supply of diamonds. He's likely to go berserk, don't you think? He will have a right royal tantrum. Slobber at the mouth in rage, and all that sort of thing. Then he'll probably order his generals to send an even bigger military force to Sarawak to secure the diamond mines at any cost. I wouldn't care much for the Iban's chances – or anyone else's for that matter – if that happened. Mind you, the Teutons would think again if there was a well-prepared military force already here, don't you think?' He paused. He could see that Porridge was thinking hard and following his every word. He continued.

'What if, say, there were a couple of battalion groups already stationed here. The flow of diamonds would be choked off for the Teutons, and their war industries would be set back for many years, wouldn't they?'

'Well, yes, that's probably true,' agreed Porridge, nodding his head slowly. He grinned. 'It would certainly change the balance of power down here! Perhaps some army troops from Brittanica and, possibly, our allies would do the trick,' he suggested enthusiastically. But then his face suddenly clouded and he sucked in his breath. 'Couldn't do anything like that without the agreement of the Ibans, though.'

His brow knitted briefly and then he brightened. 'I'll have a chat to Hassan, and see if he and his Council would agree to invite Brittanica to provide them with military protection.'

'That's a great idea of yours,' said Willie. 'I think that would be very much in Brittanica's interests. Porridge, you have such an excellent grasp of the bigger picture. You'd better be careful or you'll be posted back to Whitehall, in charge of the Strategic Affairs!' Porridge's face reddened with pleasure at the very flattering remarks.

Just then there was a knock at the Consulate's front door which was answered by Mrs Porridge. On the front steps were a couple of smiling BRAFF messengers, one of whom held out a white envelope. It was addressed to

Hon. Spring-Rice (Porridge)
Consul-General of Brittanica,
Brittanica House,
Kuching,
Sarawak.

It was an invitation from Hassan, Chief of the Ibans, for them all to attend a Victory and Freedom celebration that evening at the Schloss, the Teutons' previous Military Headquarters. Porridge thanked the messengers and gave them his acceptance.

Everyone was delighted with the prospect of a party, although Jimmy and Arthur had to toss a coin to see which of them would remain on guard in the tomotram. Penelope and Mrs Porridge disappeared upstairs to try out some clothes and jewellery. Gareth went down to the tomotram station with Jimmy and Arthur to complete some after-action maintenance checks, while Willie settled down to read some old Brittanican papers and magazines. Porridge went upstairs to his office to write his report to Whitehall.

It was the sound of beating drums from the Schloss later in the afternoon that announced the coming celebration. Their deep, authoritative beat reverberated around the hills, and was answered by other high, sharper drumbeats from the distant villages.

'Hmm, sounds as if it's going to be a rather large party,' exclaimed Porridge, as he came down the stairs.

'It certainly does,' said Gareth, entering the room with Jimmy and Arthur. 'We could hear those really deep drumbeats down in the tomotram station.'

'Sounds as if we should be making a move to the Schloss, dear,' said Mrs Porridge to her husband as she, too, came downstairs with Penelope. She turned to the boys and gracefully gestured towards Penelope.

'Do you think the necklace suits her?'

'Absolutely, it looks terrific on her,' gasped Gareth.

"It sure does,' enthused Willie approvingly. 'They *do* look very good on you, Penelope.'

Penelope blushed. 'Mrs Porridge is loaning them to me for the party.' She put her hand up under the necklace, and turned it so that it reflected in the light. It was a gorgeous 18 carat gold, diamond, sapphire and ruby Cleopatra necklace that sparkled as if it was on fire.

'Well, the stones are not actually a *terrific* size,' said Mrs Porridge a little apologetically, misunderstanding Gareth's earlier comment. The trio immediately all spoke at once, reassuring her of their meaning of 'terrific', and they laughed together at the way language had evolved over time, so that the same words had come to mean different things.

'While we're all here,' said Willie, changing the subject, 'I just thought that I'd suggest that it might be a good idea if we all went early to the celebration, and left early, to get a good start on our return journey to Brittanica.'

'Yes. We also don't want to get involved in any publicity,' responded Porridge. 'Otherwise it might give the good Emperor Wilhelm and his cronies an excuse to take military action. Sorry about the party, girls, but this is one time we will have to miss.' Although Mrs Porridge and Penelope did look disappointed, they readily understood the wisdom of Willie's suggestion.

'Not to worry, dear,' said Mrs Porridge to Penelope. 'You keep the necklace until you have had an opportunity to wear it at a really grand occasion, and return it when next we meet.' Penelope was overcome with gratitude at this kind gesture.

'Thank you so very much indeed, Mrs Porridge. They are just so beautiful, and I will take great care of them.'

They set off from Brittanica House to the Schloss, which was just a short distance away, and soon arrived at its front door. The Schloss was an enormous, three-storied stone castle, with turreted towers, huge windows and magnificent French doors which opened onto wide, balustraded balconies. It was approached by a sweeping driveway, which rose up from an imposing forecourt of grass and gardens. Wide stone steps connected the driveway to a massive, panelled, double oaken door, set in a marble archway, and fitted with heavy brass door handles and locks. Centrally placed on each door was an immense bronze elephant's head, with extended ears and coiled trunk, which served as a door knocker.

The doors were opened upon their knock, and they were ushered in to an opulent reception hall. Hassan and Major Mamood both came to welcome them with outstretched arms and smiling broadly.

'How nice it is that you were able to come,' said Hassan. 'I was worried that you might have had to return to Brittanica already without hearing the good news. Our raiding party on the diamond mine was very successful and all the Teuton guards were taken prisoner.' He gestured towards two side-tables, one of which held a silver tray of fluted, crystal glasses full of bubbling champagne, while the other held a carved wooden tray with long beer glasses full of cold beer.

'Please help yourself,' he invited. 'The beer is my own "Kuching Homebrew" which I brewed up from an old Kentish recipe from Brittanica.' They all helped themselves to a drink, with Willie, Gareth, Jimmy (who had won the toss to attend the celebration) and Porridge, of course, choosing the Kuching Homebrew.

'I give you a toast,' said Hassan, raising his glass. 'To a free Sarawak and Brittanica!'

'To a free Sarawak and Brittanica!' they all toasted, and then, with impeccable timing, a brass band started up in the distance outside the Schloss.

'That sounds like a Brittanican brass band,' exclaimed Willie in astonishment.

'Well it is and it isn't,' said Hassan in explanation. 'I know it sounds rather odd to hear the brass band music which came from Brittanica, but the bandsmen themselves are BRAFF soldiers. We call it the BRAFF Battalion Brass Band. It is modelled on the 4th Ashford Rifle Volunteers Band from Kent. I don't know if Porridge has mentioned to you that Mamood and myself are brothers. Many years ago our father, Chief Emberly, sent both of us overseas to broaden our education. We travelled to Brittanica, where Mamood attended the Military Academy. I attended the Institute of Strategic Studies located close to Whitehall. We really loved the three years we were there and greatly admired Brittanican life.'

The brass band came closer and the rhythm of marching soldiers could be heard as they sang a marching song in their native Ibanese.

'What are they singing?' asked Willie.

'It's a centuries old Iban marching song, which we have updated. Roughly translated, it goes like this:

> "BRAFF Battalion fight for victory,
> BRAFF Battalion loyal and true,
> BRAFF Battalion fight for glory,
> And take the pride of the people with you,
> And we'll march, march, march to the enemy
> And we'll battle to the end.
> For peace, for Chief, and for freedom,
> Oh Yes,
> Victory will be ours".'

Willie responded, 'Well, they should be proud of themselves too. Their loyalty and bravery won the day.' He turned to face both

Hassan and the Major. 'By the way, do you happen to know General Clarendon, Brittanica's Chief of Army General Staff?' he asked. Hassan looked at his brother for a few moments and grinned.

'You're very sharp, William. Yes, we do. As it happens, the good General was in the same class at the Military Academy in Brittanica with Mamood, and Cecil Wodehouse, now *Sir* Cecil Wodehouse, attended the Institute of Strategic Studies at the same time as me. As I remember, Cecil, or Woody as we called him, was rather partial to homebrew.' He smiled understandingly.

'You may not have been as fully aware of the close and long connection we have had with Brittanica, and for that I apologise. But we had never met you before, and we were uncertain how much we could trust you. However, now that we have not only met you, but worked with you all, we are most impressed, and decided to take you into our confidence. We look forward to a close and continuing association with every one of you.'

'Oh, we understand,' replied Willie cheerfully, 'We had rather guessed that there was a broader plan. So I take it then that your long and close association with Brittanica will continue? Could, perhaps, include some joint military and trade arrangements?'

Hassan and his brother chuckled. 'Yes, of course. That is very likely, very likely indeed,' Hassan replied softly, nodding his head. 'We certainly hope so.' Then his voice became much more cheerful and matter-of-fact.

'But, coming back to our present business and our victory over the Teutons, we'd like to mark the occasion with some little gifts for each of you.' He walked back to the end of the room where a beautifully carved and inlaid table stood. On the table was a row of small, traditional, Iban goatskin-hide bags. He picked them up and presented a bag to each of them.

'It is with the gratitude of the Iban people, my brother and myself, that I would ask you to accept these small tokens of our esteem.'

Willie replied for them all. 'Thank you both for these gifts, and telling us your future plans for Sarawak. We'll have to leave now. But we look forward to the opportunity of working with you in the future. Next time down we'll remember to bring fresh supplies of homebrew!'

They all laughed and shook hands. As they left, the Victory and Freedom Party was starting to get underway with a huge gathering of Ibans dancing and laughing on the forecourt.

As soon as Willie and his party had returned to Brittanica House, they said their goodbyes to the Porridges, set their instrument panel for Whitehall, settled comfortably in their seats, and glided out into the blackness of the tomo-tunnels. They sat quietly in the soft glow of the tram lights for some time, each full of their own thoughts and reflecting on the day's events. It was Penelope who spoke first, or rather shouted first, as she held out her hand so the others could see.

'Look what was in the leather bag that Hassan gave me! Diamonds! A bag full of diamonds!' she shouted excitedly. The gems in her hand sparkled and glowed, with almost a life of their own.

'Crikey, you're right,' said Gareth, and he reached into his pack for the leather bag given to him. He fumbled as he opened the drawstrings of his gift. 'I've got diamonds as well,' he announced.

'And so have I,' said Willie in great excitement. Arthur and Jimmy opened their leather bags. They'd been given a big bag of diamonds as well. Everyone was dumb-founded at the generosity of the brothers. Each suddenly found themselves thinking about the good things that the diamonds might bring to their lives.

After a short silence, Penelope said, 'I don't know what's the best thing to do with these gems. When I think of all the horror that the Ibans suffered to produce these, I shudder. I think I'll just put them in our storeroom cupboard at Whitehall until I've got a better idea of what to do.'

'Yup,' agreed Willie, looking at his diamonds glittering in the goatskin pouch in his hand. 'You're right. I won't ever forget that terrible mine either. Perhaps we can sell them in Brittanica and send the Ibans something useful – like … um …'

'Some medical kits,' suggested Penelope.

'Or some cars and aircraft,' chimed in Gareth.

'Yes, that's right,' agreed Willie enthusiastically.

'Or bicycles … or electricity,' continued Gareth, warming to the subject.

'Books and libraries,' said Penelope.

'Even a museum,' said Willie, grinning.

They all laughed.

'But only if it's got a wormhole to the future,' said Gareth.

21

LEGACIES AND EXPECTATIONS

The trio returned through the green door and the Time Thread tunnel to emerge once more in the Curators' Storeroom. All was quiet as almost all the School's staff and the cadets had taken leave over the long weekend. They were able to slip back into their rooms unnoticed and complete some study for the forthcoming school examinations scheduled over the following two weeks. It was on the next day, however, that the three of them were asked by Reggie the Relic to report to the Museum for further familiarisation training. They found him in the Curators' Workroom having a cup of tea and reading a copy of the *Financial Times*.

'Ah, there you are,' he said, looking up from the paper with a broad grin. 'Please make yourself a cup of tea and take a seat. Did you all have an enjoyable weekend leave?'

'Yes, thank you, sir,' they replied.

'I know it was probably too short for you to return home, but there are always useful things you can turn your hands and minds to in the Museum, you know.' He looked keenly at each of them, smiling knowingly. 'Anyway, I thought that this might be a suitable time for me to show you some rather special exhibition galleries in the Museum, and, in particular, the gallery we're constructing for Professor Zharkov, and the Weapons Advanced Research Technologies Establishment. I generally refer to that gallery as the WARTE Gallery. The full name's such a mouthful.' He chuckled, and regarded the trio warmly.

'We've been planning to complete the gallery for ages but WARTE keeps coming up with new gadgets and inventions, which we feel should be included. Actually, it was your parents, Willie, that were helping me plan and arrange the exhibition. Perhaps the three of you might like to consider continuing to assist me in that role?' Willie returned Reggie's warmth with a smile and looked at Penelope and Gareth.

'Of course, sir. We'd be delighted.' The other two nodded their agreement.

'Oh, well, that's fine then,' responded Reggie. 'I understand that Professor Zharkov left some items for the WARTE Gallery after his recent presentation. I suppose you put them in the Curators Storeroom?' Willie gulped inwardly and his mind was suddenly in a whirl. He should have foreseen this situation coming.

'Yes, you're right, sir,' responded Willie, looking Reggie directly in the eye. 'He didn't really leave a great deal, and we did one or two little experiments of our own with them. Should we take what's left into the WARTE gallery?'

Reggie continued to smile. 'Yes, we should do that. How did your experiments go? Were they successful?'

'They were, sir.' He was relieved at Reggie's acceptance of his explanation. 'We achieved what we set out to do.'

They picked up the few remaining WARTE items and followed Reggie out of the Curators' Workroom and a side gallery leading off the main exhibition hall. Their way into the side gallery was blocked by a massive double door fitted with a combination computer and card locking system.

'Can't be too careful these days,' commented Reggie cheerfully as he swiped his card and punched in a six-digit combination. The door swung open to reveal a large room about 20 yards long and 20 yards wide with no windows, brilliantly lit, and packed with boxes of equipment of all sizes.

'I'm really not too sure what these boxes contain,' said Reggie, rather reluctantly, and not wishing to appear inadequate or lazy to the trio. He suddenly brightened up as if he had just had a good idea.

'Actually, Willie, your parents used this room much more than me, so I'm not at all familiar with how they had arranged things, or even if they had an inventory.'

He paused for a moment.

'It'd be very useful if you three Assistant Curators took over the tidying up of this room, as a longer-term project. Sort of look on it as a legacy from Willie's parents. What do you think of that idea?'

'It sounds like a very interesting project, sir,' said Willie, speaking up for all three. Reggie looked considerably relieved.

'All right then, that's agreed. I'll give you your own access cards now. The combination is 747678. I think you'll find it easy to remember. You can start the project as soon as you like.'

They left the Museum and returned to their Company Common Room, excited at the prospect of delving into the collected treasures of Professor Zharkov and the WARTE gallery.

'I bet we'll find some really terrific things,' speculated Gareth. 'Like cars with ejector seats, or tanks that can float on water or exploding ballpoint pens ...'

Both Penelope and Willie burst out laughing.

'Those things are pretty much "old hat" now,' said Penelope. 'I reckon we'll find some really advanced items.'

'I hope you're right,' agreed Willie. 'But it's all going to have to wait for the next few weeks, until we get our exams "done and dusted".'

The end of the school year was scheduled for the middle week in July. It was normal practice at Surrenden for the School Prizegiving and Formal Dinner to be held the night before when the examination results were announced and trophies awarded. Willie felt that he hadn't done well in the exams. He felt unable to concentrate and nobody seemed to provide much help.

'Just buckle down to do some good hard swot,' they advised. 'Go over previous examination papers from earlier years.'

What with his parents missing, the unresolved questions on their fate and his adventures in Brittanica he felt uncomfortable and unsettled. Perhaps the only settling things in his life at this time, he felt, were the military routines at Surrenden, his growing friendships with Penelope and Gareth, and the sure knowledge that there was always the back-stop of Auntie Gwen and Uncle Peter.

But he was also starting to become aware of others' expectations of him. He was unsure if he should accept, or refuse to accept them. Or even if it was worth all the effort to try. There seemed to be a big gap between the standards he felt people expected him to reach and his acknowledgement of their importance.

It was with considerable indifference that he attended the School's Prizegiving and Formal Dinner in the great Mess Hall, along with Penelope and Gareth, and the other cadets forming Alamein Company. Penelope, on the other hand, was eagerly looking forward to the event.

'Who cares who gets the prizes?' she said to Willie and Gareth. 'We've had a terrific term, and the Formal Dinner is just a great chance to dress up!'

Gareth was equally eager. 'It's the best opportunity we'll get all year to have a real blow-out. I don't care who wins prizes, just so long as the dinner is up to scratch!'

It was normal practice for the Prizegiving and Formal Dinner, for the Headmaster, staff officers, and invited guests, to be seated at a raised top table, with the cadets seated on benches at long tables in the body of the great Mess Hall. The school's band, conducted by Captain Nottles, was set out on a raised stage off to one side of the Mess Hall. The kitchens were on the other side of the Mess Hall, behind several long serveries. The dinner was usually served before the Headmaster's speech and Prizegiving, and for the band to play accompanying music during the dinner. Gareth's eyes gleamed as he read the dinner menu.

'This is going to be a REAL feast,' he declared. 'Just take a look at this menu. It's a mid-summer Christmas feast. Who would have thought to have turkey in July?'

It was indeed a sumptuous meal. The coffee was just being served when Professor Rutherford rose to speak. He was a very tall and imposing man. Dressed in his black academic robes, he was a commanding figure. His authority seemed to be enhanced by his habit of looking severely over the glasses perched on the end of his nose.

'Ladies and gentlemen, visitors, School staff, and cadets of Surrenden Military School,' he began, rather formally, 'it gives me great pleasure to preside over this year's Annual Prizegiving, and to formally welcome our visiting guests, and, in particular, a distinguished former student of the School, Sir Hannibal Lucifer-Mortlock. This year has been notable for its successes, both academically and on the sports field. Records have been broken and many scholarships achieved. We have quite a long list of prizes to be awarded tonight, and, without further ado, I will ask Sir Hannibal to make the presentations, assisted by our Deputy Headmaster Colonel Dane and Deputy Headmistress Professor Lusty. I should take this opportunity to introduce Sir Hannibal to those of you who are unaware of his outstanding background and achievements. Sir Hannibal graduated from Surrenden some thirty years ago, won a scholarship to the Royal Military Academy

Sandhurst, and was commissioned into the Corps of Engineers. After several postings overseas on active service, Sir Hannibal left the Army and commenced his mining career working for Global Metals International. He rose to be Chairman of that company, which has mining interests spanning the world. He was knighted two years ago for services to the mining industry. Ladies and gentlemen, Sir Hannibal Lucifer-Mortlock.'

There was polite clapping as Sir Hannibal rose from his chair and acknowledged the Headmaster's introduction with a wave of his arm. The disfigurement of the red scar from his mouth was accentuated in the light. It gave his face a rather sinister, lop-sided appearance. He was tall and balding. His black dinner jacket and slouching shoulders made him look like a vulture. He limped to the side of the top table where there was another large table on which the trophies, cups and book prizes had been placed. As the applause in the great Mess Hall subsided, everyone strained their ears to hear what Professor Rutherford had to say as he commenced the Prizegiving.

'To the senior cadet who has achieved the highest aggregate score in the final graduating year, in both the academic and military curricula, the Surrenden Sword of Honour. This year this highest award goes to Senior Under Officer Giles Hanbury of Alamein Company.'

There was tumultuous applause and drumming of feet on the floor as Giles rose to his feet, received the Sword of Honour from Sir Hannibal, and returned to his seat, flushed with triumph, and his face beaming with happiness. There followed a long line of prizes for the Senior and Middle year cadets, principally for academic and sporting achievements. As their names were called out by the Headmaster, the lucky recipients rose from their place in the great Mess Hall, received their prize and words of congratulations from Sir Hannibal, shook his hand, and returned to their seat.

'To the best junior cadet in their first year, the Lucifer-Mortlock Cup,' intoned the Headmaster. 'This year this very significant award goes to Cadet William McBride of Alamein Company.'

Willie could scarcely believe his ears! He had never won anything in his life before, and here he was about to receive the School's highest award for the whole of the Junior Cadet intake. His fellow cadets in Alamein Company rose to their feet and clapped in thunderous applause as Willie stood. This was, indeed, a vintage year for Alamein Company. Not only had their Senior Under Officer won the Sword of Honour, but one of their junior cadets had won the Lucifer-Mortlock Cup, a feat which had eluded the Company for thirty years. Willie made his way through the great Mess Hall and applauding cadets, to stand in front of Sir Hannibal.

Sir Hannibal the old Lag. Here was the man who had quarrelled with his father and who may have borne a grudge over those many years. Here was the bully, liar, cheat, extortionist and fraudster, who was even a possible suspect for having had a hand in his parents' death. Here was the man he had likened to Colonel Goroka, whom he had destroyed. With considerable effort, Willie controlled his emotions. He looked at the Lag and smiled thinly.

'Congratulations, Cadet McBride,' said Sir Hannibal, as he handed over the huge, gleaming silver cup. Although he was smiling outwardly there was grittiness in his voice, which lacked warmth, and he seemed reluctant to shake Willie's hand.

'Thank you, Sir Hannibal,' replied Willie, looking him straight in the eye and sensing Sir Hannibal's coldness and unease.

'Sorry to hear of your parents' untimely deaths in Labuan,' said Sir Hannibal, again without genuine warmth or concern.

'Yes, it was a great shock,' responded Willie, again maintaining direct eye contact with Sir Hannibal, searching for meaning behind the words.

'I do hope that nothing like that happens to you,' said Sir Hannibal flatly, and without emotion, still smiling coldly.

'I shall do my best to make sure it doesn't, Sir Hannibal,' stated Willie firmly, and with an underlying sense of challenge.

They both smiled icily and fleetingly at each other, knowing that, in their brief verbal exchange, they had touched on an area of common interest, and neither cared for the other. Willie returned to his seat amid thunderous applause, and back-slapping from Penelope and Gareth. The School's band suddenly struck up with the Post Horn Gallop, with the trumpeter playing the solo part with a rifle instead of a trumpet as his instrument. Its stirring, galloping notes echoed, and re-echoed among the roof beams of the great Mess Hall, lifting everyone's spirits with the promise of cheerful, carefree times ahead. It had been an unforgettable Prizegiving and Formal Dinner, and, as the cadets returned to their rooms, Willie's head was spinning from the shock of his good fortune. He slipped the menu into his Reference Folder.

The next day was the final School day for the year, and everyone was busy packing to return home for the holidays. Gareth was returning by train to his grandparents' house in Llanelli. Penelope was flying home to Jersey from Lydd, and Auntie Gwen and Uncle Peter were driving down to Surrenden from Oxford to pick up Willie. When they arrived, he introduced them to Gareth and Penelope as his two closest friends. They all got on extremely well, chatting about things in general and Wales in particular, as Auntie Gwen had close relatives living in Cardiff and in a village in the hills.

'The village has a simply unpronounceable name,' she said lightly. 'Too many "L"s and consonants for my tongue to get around, but it's a beautiful language to listen to. Anyway, as Willie's friends you must come and stay with us in Oxford when you can. Perhaps later on during one of the school holidays?'

Both Gareth and Penelope said they would be delighted to accept the invitation, and would be in touch with Willie at a later date. Auntie Gwen insisted on being shown around the School and inspecting its facilities, including Willie's room.

'It's so tiny, it's like a box!' she commented, shaking her head in disbelief. 'How on earth do you manage to fit into such a small space?'

'With considerable difficulty, I suppose,' chuckled Uncle Peter.

They packed Willie's suitcases into the car and drove back to Oxford, stopping at a roadside café for morning coffee and a toasted sandwich. They arrived back at Oxford in the early afternoon. To Willie, Squitchey Lane never looked so welcoming. The house looked cosy and inviting. The flower gardens were full of blossoms and the huge oak trees and fruit trees in the back garden offered shade and shelter from the heat of the sun.

'You're in your old room, of course,' called out Auntie Gwen from the kitchen, where she was making a pot of tea. 'When you unpack, just give me your washing for the laundry.' They had tea and Uncle Peter updated Willie on his parents' affairs.

'We've sold your mother and father's place in Woodstock Road, and the proceeds from the sale have been put in trust for you until you reach the age of 21,' said Uncle Peter. 'There's also some money from insurances, which have also been put in trust for you. So when you're of age you should have quite a large sum available to give you a good start.'

That night, it felt so good to be in his old bed. Willie curled up blissfully as he listened to the night noises through the open bedroom window. Provoked by his earlier conversation with Uncle Peter about his parents' house in Woodstock Road being sold and the setting up of a trust for him, his thoughts started to focus on his parents, and the mining accident at Labuan Island. Something was nagging at the back of his mind.

It was the deep-seated feelings of unease and distrust he had felt when he had received the Devil's Cup from Sir Hannibal. And the words used by Sir Hannibal. 'Sorry to hear of your parents' untimely death in Labuan.'

He was up early the next day as dawn was breaking, and went for a run around Summertown and down to Oxford station. He loved the clean, fresh air and the faintest chill of early morning. Auntie Gwen, Uncle Peter and he were going to go to the Ashmolean Museum later that day, and he wondered, with an inward chuckle, whether he would find the same magic in the Ashmolean Museum as he had found in the Surrenden Military Museum. It was later that morning that there was a polite knock on the front door.

'Willie,' called out Uncle Peter, 'you have a visitor. Sir Eyre from the Foreign Office is here to see you.'

Willie came hurrying downstairs from his room. Why would Sir Eyre come to visit him? Perhaps, he thought, he had some further news about his parents?

'Good morning, Sir Eyre,' greeted Willie with a smile as Uncle Peter left the room.

'Good morning, William,' replied Sir Eyre, and then adding, as if he could read Willie's mind, 'No, I haven't got any further information about your parents.'

'Oh,' said Willie dejectedly. He sat down on the settee.

'Well, while I don't have any further information which would shed some light on the incident involving your parents, I do want to talk to you about them, and their connection with the Foreign Office.' Sir Eyre seated himself opposite and looked at him directly.

'You see, Willie,' started Sir Eyre, 'your parents were not only working for the Foreign Office, they were working for the whole United Kingdom. They were, in effect, secret agents for our nation. Only one or two of us at the Foreign Office were aware of your parents' remarkable ability to relocate to the twin world of Brittanica. We now understand that yourself, and your two friends, Gareth Jones and Penelope Pendragon, also have this ability. In fact, if our information is correct, the three of you have already made three journeys to Brittanica. Am I right?'

Willie was dumbfounded by Sir Eyre's frankness. Then he quickly recovered his composure and returned his gaze.

'Yes, that's right.'

Sir Eyre continued. 'We were also aware of the extraordinary similarity of the two worlds, even though Brittanica is about a century in time behind our Earth world. Of course, we are vitally interested in this extraordinary situation of the existence of a twin world. However, pragmatically, we wish to keep the knowledge to ourselves, and to use it in our nation's best interest. We are particularly interested in the tomo-tunnels and the Sardin Scrolls. The tomo-tunnels give underground access to mineral deposits. We have noted that the location of rich mineral deposits in the Brittanican world are similarly located here on Earth. The Sardin Scrolls, as we understand it, provide a detailed map of the tomo-tunnel system in the Brittanican world, and may, therefore, provide us with the locations of similar tomo-tunnels and rich mineral deposits on Earth.'

Sir Eyre paused. He could see that Willie was following his every word and that it made perfect sense to him.

'Your parents have been exploring the tomo-tunnel system in the twin world, finding the richest mineral deposits, and bringing this information back to us. In turn, we have been able to use this information to guide us in our diplomatic strategy and mineral exploration abroad.'

Sir Eyre lowered his voice and leaned forward.

'Without the vital information your parents were giving us, our Foreign Office is somewhat blind and reactive to events abroad. We desperately need to maintain the linkages with Brittanica, and continue with the tomo-tunnel explorations.' Sir Eyre stopped, and leant back in his chair, waiting to see what sort of reaction he would get from Willie.

'I get it,' responded Willie. 'Am I right in thinking you'd like me to continue with what my parents were doing?'

'Yes, exactly. You would report to me personally, and I would ensure that you would receive whatever support you required.'

Willie nodded thoughtfully.

'Where do Lieutenant Shrewdfellow and Professor Zharkov fit in?'

'Reggie Shrewdfellow would be your operations support officer. His job is to provide you with a firm base for your journeys to Brittanica. Professor Golka Zharkov is your scientific support officer. He would provide you with whatever special equipment you may need.'

Willie continued to nod his understanding. 'Who else knew of my parents' activities?' he enquired.

Sir Eyre looked a little uncomfortable and shifted in his seat.

'Only the Minister of Foreign Affairs, the Minister of Defence and the Director of Science in the Ministry of Defence.'

Willie looked at Sir Eyre very closely and said softly, 'You don't think that my parents died in an accident, do you?'

Sir Eyre's face reddened slightly. He seemed unsure of what to say for a moment, and then appeared to make up his mind.

'I don't know, Willie. I just don't know. It is entirely possible that someone else knew of your parents' activities, and decided to do away with them. It could have been someone in commercial competition with us. It could have been an old personal enemy, or an operative from a foreign country. We've done our best to keep your parents' activities secret, but in this day and age,' he shrugged his shoulders. 'I just can't be absolutely sure that we've been successful.'

Willie looked at Sir Eyre and said with great deliberation, 'OK, Sir Eyre. I'll be an agent for the Foreign Office and continue the work my parents were doing. In fact, I have already taken the first step.' He paused. 'I don't think you were fully aware of the details of my parents' mission in Labuan Island, were you?'

Sir Eyre looked a little taken aback. 'Well … er … no. Not all the details. Your parents would normally just give me an outline of what they were doing. In this case, they just said that the Labuan Island mine could be of interest and that they would report on their return. Why?'

'Ah, I thought that might be the case,' said Willie. 'Because what my parents were following up when they were in that abandoned coal-mine was the very real possibility of there being an oil and gas field under Labuan Island. When visiting Labuan Island in our twin world earlier, they had found out about an oil and gas seepage at a crocodile farm nearby. They were checking to see if it existed in our world.'

'Oh, good heavens,' said Sir Eyre in astonishment and looking a little shell-shocked. 'Oh, my goodness me.'

He was visibly delighted and shook Willie's hand warmly. 'That's marvellous news. Not only to find out what your parents were actually doing on the island and about the oil and gas field, but also your decision to continue where your parents left off. Thank you very much, Willie. I know it's a courageous decision for you to make, what with the deaths of your parents, and the possible threats to your life you may attract. But at the end of the day you will be making an extraordinary contribution to the safety and well being of our nation.'

'Thanks,' said Willie with a grin. 'It's great to know that I'll be making a diff. I should also tell you about another discovery which we made. During our last trip to Brittanica we came across an industrial diamond mine in Batu Lintang near Kuching in western Borneo.'

'Industrial diamonds in Borneo, eh?' said Sir Eyre. 'Now that's an interesting find.' He looked at Willie with increased respect. 'You've really brought home the bacon with this trip. A possible oilfield *and* an industrial diamond mine. It could lead to some huge business for us.'

'What about Penelope and Gareth?' asked Willie, suddenly remembering his friends.

'Ah yes. Well, I've been giving some thought to their situation,' responded Sir Eyre. 'I was rather hopeful that the three of you could continue to operate as a team, and that you might persuade them to join you as two additional agents. You would make a really strong operational trio – a sort of Trinity of Surrenden.' He smiled broadly. 'What do you think?'

'We do work well together. But this request from the Foreign Office makes our operations in Brittanica much bigger. There's the possibility of them risking their lives. All we can do is put it to them and hope they'll agree.'

'Yes, I think you're right,' agreed Sir Eyre. He nodded, paused for a moment and pursed his lips reflectively.

'Why don't I arrange a field trip for the three of you at WARTE at Sedlescombe in, say, three weeks' time? That would give all of you an opportunity to see the size and scope of Professor Zharkov's activities. It would be a good place to approach both Penelope and Gareth about this Foreign Office request.'

'Yes,' said Willie, nodding his head in agreement. 'I think that'd be a terrific idea.'

'Right,' said Sir Eyre firmly. 'That's what I'll do. Meantime, we should maintain strictest security, even from your Uncle Peter and Auntie Gwen.' He pulled out a business card. 'Here are my contact numbers. You can reach me at any time, day or night.'

He called out his goodbyes to Uncle Peter and Auntie Gwen, and Willie let him out of the front door. As he left, he shook hands with Willie, looked him straight in the eye and said softly, with a warm and grateful smile, 'I know you have a Surrenden e-mail address so I shall be in touch by e-mail shortly.'

When he closed the door, Willie felt a wave of excitement surging through his body. He was now not only a secret agent for the British Foreign and Commonwealth Office with a legitimate purpose to go on missions to Brittanica, but he was also a secret agent for Brittanica.

Both tasks meant risks and dangers. But both were necessary to find out the truth about what happened to his parents.

The next step would be to see the secret research being conducted in WARTE.

22

WILLIE'S REFERENCE FOLDER

Item 1

SURRENDEN MILITARY SCHOOL
ORGANISATION

Headmaster
Professor A. S. Rutherford, PhD (Camberley)
Deputy Headmistress (Academic)
Professor W. A. Lusty, MA, PhD (Canberra)
Deputy Headmaster (Military)
Colonel M. H. Dane, JSSC, Wessex Guards
Head of Academic Wing
Associate Professor O. Haworth, MA (Malmo)
Head of Combat Wing
Major S. S. De Roche, MMilSt, Kelso Guards

Academic Wing
Head of English Department
Mrs P. Meikle, MA (Ironbridge)
Head of Languages Department
Dr T. Prezzio, MA, PhD (San Remo)
Head of Mathematics Department
Dr. M. Lazlov, MA, PhD (Kiev)
Head of Sciences Department
Mr G. P. Ohms, MSc (Silicon Valley)
Head of Business Studies
Mr J. P. Gardiner, MBusSc, LLB (Portsea)

Head of Information Sciences
Mrs C. Cheong, MInfSc (Canton)
Head of Arts
Miss P. Rankine, MA (Milford)

Combat Wing
Communications and Intelligence Centre
Battlefield Information Sciences
Captain P. F. Pronto, Communication Corps
Battlefield Surveillance
Lieutenant C. E. La Dolce, Intelligence Corps
Electronic Control Warfare
Captain M. L. Starlight, Electronic Engineers
Psychological Warfare
Captain J. M. Chimerical, Intelligence Corps
New College Matron
Mrs Gabrielle McPherson

Firepower and Mobility Centre
Missiles and Delivery Systems
Captain B. N. Sheldrake, Missile Corps
Strategy and Tactics
Captain J. L. Mitre, Wessex Guards
Armoured Warfare
Captain Lord L. Hardcastle, Cavalry Corps
Engineering Systems
Captain B. B. Bridger, Corps of Engineers
Old College Matron
Mrs Edna Higginbotham

Education Centre
Education Officer
Captain R. Mastermynd, MEd
Librarian
Sergeant C. C. Lumens, BEd
Military History Officer
Lieutenant R. A.Shrewdfellow, Ordnance Corps
Bandmaster
Captain S. Q. Nottles, Corps of Music

Victory College Matron
Mrs D. Warmingford

Ceremonial and Fitness
School Regimental Sergeant-Major
RSM L. L. Lord, Celtic Guards
Victory College Sergeant-Major
CSM L. Larkin, Kelso Guards
New College Sergeant-Major
CSM Z. Brain, Swansea Guards
Old College Sergeant-Major
CSM A. Truscott, Limerick Guards
Physical Training Instructor
Staff-Sergeant S. Hardman, Tasmanian Regt.

Administration
Chief Clerk
WO2 J. P. Hancox, Accountancy Corps
Quartermaster
Staff-Sergeant S. Squirrelle, Accountancy Corps
Security
WO2 M. P. Rangitira, Military Security Corps
Chaplain
Chaplain Class 2 M. O. Botherwell, MLitt
Hospital
Matron F. A. Sweetingham, Nursing Corps

Item 2

PRIZEGIVING AND FORMAL DINNER

Menu

Chilled Tomato Juice
Hors d'Oeuvres Varies
Consomme Mikado   Crème Brettone
Fillets of Halibut, Hollandaise
Rice Pilaw, Egyptienne
Pauiettes of Beef, Olives
Roast Leg of New Zealand Spring Lamb, Mint Sauce
Roast Tom Turkey, Chipolata, with Cranberry Sauce
Sweet Garden Peas au Beurre   Roast and Boiled Potatoes

Cold Buffet
Roast Beef   Ox Tongue   York Ham   Assorted Sausages
Salade de Saison   Mayonnaise and French Dressing

Sweet
Blackcurrant Gateau
Meringue Glace
Coffee and Cheese Board